WAGERSMART

WagerSmart

TOM FARRELL

WagerSmart©2023 Tom Farrell
ISBN paperback: 978-1-7365932-4-0
ISBN hardback: 978-1-7365932-5-7

Printed in the United States of America
Railbird Publishing LLC

Editing by Steve Parolini
Copy Editing by Susan Brooks
Cover Design by NovakIllustration.com
Typesetting by NovelNinjutsu.com

www.tomfarrellbooks.com

ALSO BY
TOM FARRELL

1

CHICAGO

FEBRUARY 2020

Uncle Mike and I stepped out of the elevator on the fourth floor of Thornton Racetrack and walked toward the executive offices. The hallway was empty and the office door closed.

I leaned over and whispered to Uncle Mike. "Where would we start?"

Arlene Adams, the track owner, wanted us to find out what had happened to her late husband, mob hitman Porter "the Pastor" Pearson. He'd disappeared in Jimmy Hoffa style years ago.

"I don't know," Uncle Mike said. "We find out where Porter was last seen and what he was doing."

"That was years ago. I have no idea where to look."

"Arlene called you," Uncle Mike said. "You should feel honored."

"She asked for you, too. You're the former homicide detective." I slowed to allow Uncle Mike to keep up.

"Burrascano sees us as a team," he said.

I'd told Arlene I wouldn't take the case. Then Uncle Mike called me into his office. Burrascano, the mob's gambling boss, had taken an interest. Arlene had applied some pressure and asked Burrascano to intervene on her behalf.

"What kind of deals do Burrascano and Arlene have?"

Uncle Mike shrugged his broad shoulders. "Who the hell knows? Maybe this track. Other properties. I don't know."

I looked around at the dated wood paneling that lined the walls. A section near the floor was warped and bellied out from the wall. The old track seemed to be slipping into history, and whenever I visited, I felt like I was slipping back in time with it. We passed a room stacked to the ceiling with old furniture, then walked up to the door of the executive offices and knocked.

A receptionist greeted us and led us to a small conference room with an old, creaky wood floor. The stuffy, sunbaked room reminded me of Uncle Mike's attic; a place with so many places for a kid to hide. I would use my flashlight to sift through trunks and boxes in search of secrets.

After we declined the offer of coffee and the receptionist closed the door behind her, Uncle Mike took a seat at the small round table. I took in the view. To the east,

I counted smokestacks of abandoned factories. To the west, a refinery chugged hydrocarbons into the February sky. Directly below, just beyond the track, blanketed by last night's snow, lay an arrangement of housing and barns along the backstretch. It was a beehive of activity. The harness races would soon give way to the spring thoroughbred meeting.

"I hope we can talk Arlene out of it," I said. "I hate to take anyone's money for a wild goose chase."

"Let's listen to what she says, okay?" Uncle Mike said. "Burrascano called. That means there's more to it, and I want to find out what. You should be jumping at the chance to sign up a new client. When was the last job for Eddie O'Connell Private Investigator?"

"Clients don't want a PI on crutches." If not for my job managing O'Connell's Tavern for my uncle, I'd be sleeping in my car.

"I know, I know. They think a PI has to chase bad guys down an alley." Uncle Mike swept a hand across his bald head. "But you're walking like your old self now, thank God."

"I threw those damn crutches into the dumpster." I pulled up a chair and sat down.

There was a brief knock on the closed door and Arlene Adams walked in, clutching several manila folders to her chest. She was alone, with no lawyer or assistants to monitor things or take notes. I almost didn't recognize her at first and hid my surprise as I stood to greet her.

"Eddie, Mike, thanks for coming." She took several quick breaths, dropped the files, and plopped into the chair.

Uncle Mike and I greeted her like royalty. She deserved respect. Although in her late seventies, she'd single-handedly kept horse racing alive in Chicago. According to reliable rumors, the owner of the north side track decided to sell to developers, which would leave Thornton Racetrack as the only game in town.

It had only been a couple of years since my previous meeting with Arlene Adams, but it was apparent the years had caught up with her. She was known for being chic, dressed to the hilt as if she'd just stepped out of one of her old movie roles as the cosmopolitan divorcee flirting with a new victim. At our last meeting, she'd worn a mink stole, her hair piled high by a beauty salon architect. Now she wore a baggy sweater and sweatpants. Her blonde hair had been allowed to turn gray and had been pulled back and tied into a makeshift ponytail. The bags beneath her eyes were visible, despite a quick swipe of makeup.

Arlene folded her arms and took a deep breath to signal the start of her agenda. "I tried to talk myself out of this. So many people have told me ..." She seemed to become lost in thought.

"Take your time," Uncle Mike said.

"You know what I thought of Porter." She stopped again and stared out the window. The clouds had begun to huddle up in the late afternoon wind chill. "I've got to do it. Three things have made it urgent."

There was another awkward pause.

"What three things?" Uncle Mike finally broke the silence.

4

She pulled at a stray lock of hair that had come loose. "It's silly, I know. First, I'm an old lady. That's right, I'm an old lady. There, I said it. And that's what makes it so urgent that I do something. Christ, the second thing is the dreams."

She leaned in and made eye contact with each of us. I wasn't sure how much of what she said was intended to persuade us or to satisfy her own lingering doubts. "They're constant now. In the dream, I'm standing by a window—the kitchen window or my office window. Porter appears outside. He's looking at me. At first, I freaked. Then it became a nightly rendezvous. Not Porter in flesh and blood, but Porter's ghost. He's talking to me. I can't hear what he's saying, but it's clear from his pain and anger he's trying to tell me something."

Uncle Mike cleared his throat. "Have you seen a specialist about this?"

She nodded. "I've given the psychiatrists lots to chew on. They're worthless. In the dream, I pound on the window, straining to hear what Porter is saying. You've got to remember he was the love of my life. He disappeared—"

Tears welled. She pulled a lace handkerchief from her sleeve and dabbed at her eyes. We gave her a minute.

Her lips grew taut. "The thing is…I know exactly what he's saying. 'Why aren't you looking for me, Arlene? Don't you care what happened to me?' I'm a strong woman. I'm not usually like this."

"What's the third thing?" Uncle Mike said in his soft and steady cop voice. "You said three things made it urgent."

She hunted in the pile of dog-eared folders that appeared to be packed with newspaper clippings, faded typewritten pages held together by binder clips, and handwritten notes. She pulled out a scrap of paper and grabbed the reading glasses that hung from a chain around her neck. "I've been able to make contact with a certain party who——how shall I say it—a certain party who I strongly suspect knows what happened to Porter. I do know for a fact and this is confidential…"

"What you say is held in the strictest confidence," I said. "You're my client."

"That's right," Uncle Mike confirmed.

"Thank you, gentlemen. You see, you two have certain indispensable resources that others in your line of work do not. You both have the necessary contacts in the–" She hesitated in search of the word. "Both of you are able to bridge the gap to certain people."

She meant Burrascano and the mob.

"Who is this 'party' you've made contact with?" Uncle Mike asked.

I filed away for future use the way Uncle Mike dispensed with the sensitive subject of our involvement in the underworld.

"Well," Arlene said, focusing on a wrinkled page from the folder. "I thought he was dead. He used to work with Porter. You know what that means—"

"Contract work," Uncle Mike said.

"Yes, exactly. Porter's contract work." Arlene's voice trailed off.

Then she seemed to find a reservoir of energy. "I knew Porter was involved in some rough stuff, but not murder." Her voice quickened as she spread the pile of folders across the table like the middle cards in a game of Texas Hold'em. "These folders were put together by several investigators I hired after Porter disappeared. One of the investigators used to work for the FBI."

She needed to reconcile the discovery of Porter as a hitman with her love for him, and perhaps the dreams were a guilt-ridden product of those emotions. But that was a psychiatrist's territory, not mine.

I wanted to return to the information on the wrinkled page. "You were contacted by a man who worked with Porter?"

"Worked with Porter? You're talking about the Deacon?" Uncle Mike's shoulders straightened, and he scooted to the edge of the chair. "I haven't heard about him for years."

I'd heard the stories, too. The Deacon and Porter "the Pastor" Pearson had probably gone a little overboard with the religious overtones of their contract killings, but that was the idea. They'd amp up the fear level to compel people to surrender to the demands of the mob without the need for murder.

"Yes, I'm talking about the Deacon," Arlene said. "I know what I'm asking is dangerous. The degree of risk talking to someone who—"

"Where did you find him?" Uncle Mike asked. "Did he contact you? Has he found Jesus or something? What the hell, Arlene?"

I found myself on the edge of my seat as well. Arlene wanted us to meet with a legendary hitman.

"He called me. That means something. He probably heard how distraught I've been."

"He called you out of the blue? My God, I've got cold cases the Deacon could help me with—"

"Now wait, Mike," she said.

Uncle Mike had cold cases that had haunted him. I grew up living with my aunt and uncle, and he was often shuffling through those damn files in the middle of the night.

"Porter comes first. The Deacon wants to meet this Saturday." She looked at Uncle Mike first, then at me. "In Vegas."

"Super Bowl weekend?" I asked. An overflow crowd could be expected at O'Connell's for the big game. I had employee schedules to juggle, food and beverage inventory to manage, and a million last-minute items.

"Maybe the Deacon isn't happy with you asking the wrong people questions," Uncle Mike said. "You've stirred up a hornet's nest."

"Vegas will be packed," I said.

"I know," Arlene said. "And I also know that a man like the Deacon wants the cover of big crowds. I'm not stupid, gentlemen. But this may be my one chance to get answers for Porter."

"Jeesus," Uncle Mike said. "What do you think of Vegas, Eddie?"

I'd need to get things done ahead of time at O'Connell's. Maybe the Deacon yearned to bare his soul before he died. If anyone could get him to divulge his secrets, it would be Uncle Mike.

Then there were the poker tables, the suckers stupid with the adrenaline rush of the Big Game, and, of course, my old friend Nicole.

I shrugged. "There are worse places."

2

Whenever I came to Vegas, it seemed as if I'd stepped into a party midstream, and no matter how hard I tried, I'd never catch up.

Uncle Mike sat across from me at a table in Caesars Palace's main bar. The bar and its adjoining tables, bordered by a wood railing, were a few steps up from the walkway. To our right, we overlooked the concourse leading to the sports book, and, to our left, we could monitor the action at rows of table games.

A jam-packed craps table caught my attention. I tried not to squirm in my seat. "I still think the Deacon is out to con the old lady." Arlene was a woman of means. She'd invested her earnings wisely from her Hollywood career in California real estate and then struck it big with Porter after inheriting his interests in racetracks and casinos around the country.

The piped-in, classic rock music made it difficult to hold a conversation, but also made it impossible for anyone to overhear us. My uncle leaned toward me. "C'mon, Eddie, the Deacon decides to swindle her after all these years? He must be in his late seventies."

"Why not? Arlene told us about the torch she carried for Porter over a year ago. She's probably told others. For all we know, the guy who contacted Arlene wasn't the Deacon at all but some imposter."

Uncle Mike sipped from his bottle of Budweiser. "Nah, she'd recognize his voice. Porter and the Deacon were partners for a long time."

"After all these years?" I used Uncle Mike's argument against him. "You hear what you want to hear. Maybe it's wishful thinking on Arlene's part." As I saw it, the biggest part of our job would be to protect Arlene from herself. With age and loneliness, her unbridled love for Porter had most likely ballooned out of control. Porter would never live up to the legend of lost love she'd built up in her mind. She was chasing a dream.

Uncle Mike scratched the few gray hairs at his temple. "I'm willing to take a chance. All the Deacon wants so far is a meeting. He hasn't asked for money."

"Burrascano told you the Deacon lives in Chicago. Why does he want to meet in Vegas? Sure, the crowds provide cover, but there are plenty of crowded places in Chicago."

Uncle Mike's fingers drummed the tabletop as he craned his neck to check out the roulette wheel, then leaned back toward me. "He's probably got connections with illegal bookies out here. It's a big weekend."

On the way from O'Hare, Uncle Mike had been quiet. Maybe he had been lost in thought about those cold cases and how the Deacon could help solve them. Or maybe my uncle had been thinking about something else.

"The guy who calls himself the Deacon is pulling our chain," I said. "Why hasn't he returned your calls? Thank God Burrascano was able to snag us a couple of rooms."

"Take it easy. The Deacon texted me, didn't he? Did you expect him to pick us up at the airport? Carry our bags to the room?" Uncle Mike belched. "Have a beer and relax."

I sipped from my iced tea. Every night in Vegas was a long night. Relaxation wasn't in the cards. Fans would be placing their bets early.

One of the partygoers screamed out the ritual cheer I'd heard a dozen times already. "Suu-per Bowl!" It was followed by competing cheers for the Chiefs and 49ers. I should be checking for a move in the point spread.

Uncle Mike's cell buzzed. "Dammit, the Deacon changed the time to nine-thirty."

It was 8:55. "He's playing us."

"No, he's watching us."

I scanned the surroundings. "Would you still recognize him?" Uncle Mike and his past partner in homicide, Liz, had questioned the Deacon about a case many years ago.

"Depends. The Deacon's crafty as hell. Always uses a different alias. Probably has some right-hand man scouting us out. How do you think he stayed alive all these years?"

I didn't like being the guy in the fishbowl and I especially didn't like to think about unknown third parties with guns. The crowd at the blackjack table cheered on a flashy player with dreadlocks. Only one guy stood quietly. He seemed to look away as I glanced in his direction.

"What about Nicole?" Uncle Mike asked. "Were you able to get in touch with her?"

"She's playing in a cash game at the Bellagio." My uncle's attempt to distract me wouldn't work, but I'd play along.

Uncle Mike grunted. "Your old girlfriend is quite the celebrity, isn't she?"

"She gets lots of press, but I don't know if that translates to big money. She wants to meet up later." Nicole had gone from being a fixture on the pro poker circuit to a familiar face for the newest rage—sports betting.

"Nicole is going to drag you back into the scene." Uncle Mike pointed a finger. "Mark my words. I won't be able to get you out of Vegas. I should start looking for a new bar manager."

I laughed. "I've changed. Don't worry."

"I've heard that before."

"What about you? When does that card game start?" A group of Uncle Mike's poker buddies had retired to Vegas.

"Whenever I get there. Why? I don't want you showing up."

"I'm not invited?"

"It's okay if you want to say hello, but I don't want you to sit in."

"Why not?"

"Dammit, Eddie, these guys are on a fixed income. They don't need a card shark at the table."

Behind us, near the entrance to the baccarat room, a man with his arms folded looked down at something on the floor. The more I checked out the crowd, the more suspicious people I found.

Arlene's files held a crop of ripe cold cases, low-hanging fruit for an investigator if and when the Deacon surfaced. The files made me realize the attraction for Uncle Mike. They were a scrapbook of murders. One file reported on the murder of a witness in Detroit who'd been killed the week before a criminal trial involving union officials. A news clipping detailed the discovery of several bodies found at the bottom of a pond on the west side of Chicago. A murder in Florida of a dog racing promoter also made for interesting reading.

The investigators Arlene had hired after Porter's disappearance were able to accumulate a staggering array of evidence. Handling her files made me feel as if I were holding a bottle of nitro. The incriminating collection might point back to the person who'd ordered the killings, which might account for Burrascano's interest in the Deacon. The more my imagination worked the variables, the more tentacles led from the Deacon to others.

There was a lot of shit in those files. Damn Porter's ghost.

"You see anyone suspicious?" I asked, surveying the crowd, which passed by the railing bordering our el primo seats.

"Forty people at least." He winked. "Maybe they just want our table."

I ignored the joke. "You said you met the Deacon in early two-thousand?"

"Yeah. It was a brief meeting. He used some bullshit alias. We had to let him go and then when the investigation circled back to the guy, we couldn't find him."

Uncle Mike's hazy description didn't sync with my uncle's steel trap memory. I'd been unable to find anything in the clippings about the Deacon's real name.

"How about before that meeting?" Porter had gone missing in Vegas in 2002. "You ever bump into him in the eighties or nineties?"

"Before?" Uncle Mike smiled, then shook his head.

"There's stuff in Arlene's files. Stuff about you. About Mexico."

My uncle's face froze. "Goddamnit. You're getting to be too fucking smart."

"I wondered why you were so interested in Arlene's job."

"Son of a bitch. You better have those files in a safe place." Uncle Mike pointed his finger again.

"I've got them stashed, don't worry. You taught me well." I waited. I knew where this was going.

Uncle Mike took a long pull on the bottle of beer, then wiped his mouth with the back of his hand. "It was Mexico."

I tamped down a rush of emotion. "Dammit, Uncle Mike. You should've told me."

When I was a baby, my mom had been pushing me in a stroller through a park when she'd been taken. A rapist and murderer by the name of Childress confessed. He'd thrown her body in a culvert as if she was garbage. Childress had relatives with pull in the downstate Illinois county and the judge set him free on a bullshit technicality. Uncle Mike and Burrascano's right-hand man, Joey L, had gone after him.

Uncle Mike had told me little about the encounter. I'd assumed it was something he chose not to relive, and I'd been happy with the ending—Childress caught and then dragged behind a shrimp trawler in the dead of night along the coast of Mexico—but I'd never gotten the full story.

"I want the full play-by-play," I said. "What did the Deacon have to do with Mexico?"

3

I WANTED TO KNOW, BUT I DIDN'T WANT TO KNOW. THE FULL play-by-play might threaten the foundation I'd constructed in my mind. Imagining the killer's screams swallowed up by the ocean waves of an ink-black Mexico night offset my anger.

Being the kid with the backstory was hard. Living in my aunt and uncle's house like a juvenile out on probation, I was a burden. They had three daughters of their own to provide for and I didn't come with monthly child support. My father went missing long before my mother died.

Maybe this was why I'd escaped into gambling and boxing. Or maybe I used it as a convenient excuse. All I knew was that I dealt with a vicious cycle of conflicting emotions I couldn't hope to control.

"I knew I'd have to tell you about the Deacon when we took this job for Arlene," Uncle Mike said. "I've been dreading it. But I wanted to wait until the last possible moment. I don't want you dwelling on the incident."

Even the word "incident" pissed me off. Why didn't he call it a rape and murder? "Don't worry. I'll shut up and listen for a change."

"Don't get bent out of shape," he said. "It's tough for me, too. If the Deacon dogged us and didn't show up, we'd both have gone through all kinds of hell for nothing."

It would be a similar type of hell for my uncle. He and Mom had a whole other history before I came along. Those pictures of Mom I found inside a box in Uncle Mike's attic—a young lady standing in front of a VW bug, wearing bellbottoms and a Dark Side of the Moon T-shirt. Another snapshot of her outside in the snow, a scarf around her neck, one of her laughing outside a school. Her wide-set eyes, thin lips, and brown hair, a reflection of my own features, smiled at me. Mom was forever a mystery to me, but Uncle Mike knew exactly what I'd missed.

I nodded. "You're right. It would be hell."

Uncle Mike sipped from his beer while the crowd around us jockeyed for openings at the table games. He set his bottle gently back on the table. "The Deacon was with me and Joey L. I can't remember every goddamn detail, but I remember what's important. When we chased Childress down to Mexico, there was still a good chance the decision would be overturned on appeal. The ruling that freed Childress was complete bullshit. My younger sister had been raped and murdered. The smirk on the bastard's face sent me into a tailspin. I didn't know what I was doing. I planned to drag his ass back when we got the decision."

Why did I demand to hear all this? I felt like a kid in trouble sitting in my aunt and uncle's kitchen, waiting to be punished.

"Childress had a head start. He was no dope. He had friends and money and was running for his life. I knew Joey L, at least who he was. I thought the Deacon worked for him because Joey L seemed to be the guy in charge. He'd peel C-notes off a bankroll the size of a softball. But I was wrong. The Deacon ran things. He and his guys had people star-struck. Bartenders. Guys who ran the local poker game. The goddamn Deacon was a legend. They refused cash. They all wanted to meet him. Shake his hand. The phantom come to life."

I'd heard the old timers talking about the old days of the outfit. The Deacon and his longtime partner, Porter, tracked down people for the mob.

"The Deacon had four guys posted around El Paso. Two at a train station and bus depot, one scouring the truck stop cafes, and another trolling the bars." Uncle Mike rubbed his chin. "My job was to check in with the local cops. The bastard Childress liked to talk up the young women on his way through town. Before he skipped one small town, he assaulted a woman who worked in a drugstore. I showed her a picture of the slimeball. She identified him."

Childress was a serial predator even while he was running for his life.

"Come to find out, instead of heading straight across the border, he'd taken a side trip through New Mexico and Arizona. It's like the fucker had a sixth sense. We finally caught up to him in a bar in Mazatlán and the Deacon went apeshit. He threw a bar stool. The rapist ducked, then fought like hell.

And dirty. Kicked guys in the crotch. Tried to gouge their eyes out. Bit like a rabid dog. I've apprehended a lot of badass characters in my time, but damn."

Uncle Mike would've been a young cop. A guy trying to make detective, make a name for himself in Chicago.

"Should've just shot him and been done with it," I said.

"The Deacon wasn't about to let Childress off that easy. We hogtied and gagged him, dragged his carcass back to our hotel, and then bribed the local cops and the bar owner to keep quiet. I knew what the Deacon planned to do next, and I told him no. Joey L backed me up, of course."

Uncle Mike chewed his bottom lip. "Childress looked at me, expecting some kind of salvation. I was police. You know how that feels? To be the one with true hate—the bastard killed my sister—and I'm the guy he's banking on to save his ass. It was fucked up."

Anguish was written all over my uncle's face. Justice meant everything to him.

"I thought I had the Deacon, and the others chilled out. But Joey L and I let our guard down, and they were gone. I didn't think any of them would go against Joey L, but the Deacon had more pull than I realized. Or maybe these guys were just pissed about Childress kicking and biting in the bar. We knew where they planned to take him. It wasn't like they hadn't talked about what they wanted to do. We hustled down to the boat dock."

The Super Bowl crowd roared around us. When they quieted, Uncle Mike continued, "We didn't make it in time." He stared at his hands. As if there was blood on them. "I never heard any man, woman or child scream the way he was screaming."

The wrong kind of justice. I wanted the shark fantasy back.

"Why I ever took Joey L up on his offer to grab Childress shows how fucked up I was."

His cell buzzed. Uncle Mike read the text. "Dammit. The Deacon wants us to meet him at Walt's Collectibles. You know where that is?"

"Yeah. It's a sports shop down in the mall."

4

THE INDOOR MALL CONSISTED OF ONE LONG MAIN CORRIDOR
bisected by several shorter, narrower hallways, each leading to
additional shops. The main corridor was filled with people
using it to avoid the sobering brisk wind outside on the Strip.
The side passageways were one-way halls leading to a magnet
store and attracted less traffic. Years ago, I'd gotten an
autograph from Pete Rose at Walt's Collectibles located at the
end of the hall.

When we got to the turnoff from the main corridor, Uncle
Mike stopped. "Hold on, Eddie."

I knew what my uncle was going to say. He'd read my
reaction at the table and during our walk through the casino
and into the mall.

I'd gotten what I wanted—the full story or as close to it
as I could get. It was the next best thing to being in the boat,

yet the play-by-play had rocked my understanding of the events in Mexico.

I'd always felt rewarded by the story's ending. Childress dragged behind the trawler, ripped apart by sharks.

Now I'd learned that Uncle Mike only wanted to hold Childress and await the results of an appeal. Justice for Childress was the last thing I cared about. Revenge was the building block of my Mexico story. And it was my story. Mine and my mom's. It was all we had, and I wanted to hang onto it the way I originally knew it.

The one part of Uncle Mike's story I inwardly cheered was the part about the screams—"I never heard a man scream that way." Yes. Righteous revenge was what I needed.

Did Childress deserve justice? According to Uncle Mike, he did. But I wanted what the Deacon had delivered. Screw the appeal of the judge's bullshit order that allowed Childress to walk.

The Deacon was my fucking hero.

Uncle Mike glanced at his watch. "Don't bring up Mexico when we meet the Deacon. You know how these guys are— he might deny the whole thing."

"Even with you, a witness, right there?"

"C'mon, Eddie. The Deacon was a hitman for the mob. He won't admit shit. Ever. Unless he brings it up himself. Besides, we've got Arlene to think about—your client, remember? We're supposed to get information for her."

"So why tell me about Mexico at all?"

"Because I've got to depend on you, too. I'm the ex-cop, Eddie, talking to a sworn criminal, a killer. The Deacon starts talking about Childress, you just–"

"Keep my fucking mouth shut? I don't believe this."

"Jeez." Uncle Mike shook his head. "Let's go then."

The hallway leading to Walt's was lined with other shops. The lack of people down the side hallway at this time of night wasn't surprising. "Why don't I go first and you cover me?"

Uncle Mike focused on the narrow hall and rubbed his chin. "Lots of nooks and crannies. You smell a trap?"

"You were the one who said the Deacon is unpredictable." When my uncle and I had done past investigations, I was the one who did the physical stuff—chasing guys down fire escapes or getting into fights. I'd recovered from my prior gunshot wounds and wanted to prove it.

Uncle Mike smiled. "I knew I brought you along for a reason. Okay, how do you want to work it?"

I told him my plan.

I waited until a group of shoppers turned down the passageway to Walt's and followed them closely. At the Gucci store, I stopped near the entrance, protected by the bay windows that jutted out on either side. Uncle Mike had taken an outpost at the intersection of the main corridor and the side hallway. He nodded in my direction to let me know things looked good, no one suspicious tracking me. When another group of shoppers strolled past, I followed them to the next stopping off point. We repeated the routine until I neared Walt's.

Up ahead, an opening marked "Employees Only, No Exit, No Access," drew my interest. I stood with my back to the wall and, without being too obvious, side-stepped toward it and peeked around the corner. A janitor stood behind a cart loaded with cleaning supplies, a mop, and broom handles sticking up. He was about five feet back from the entrance. It was too perfect.

"Is the men's room down this hall?" I called from around the corner, allowing him to see my face.

The janitor wore one of those masks janitors used when they cleaned toilets. It covered the bottom half of his face and nose. His hat was pulled down low and a stack of toilet paper and plastic containers made it difficult to see his hands. Towels hung off to the side and brushes occupied the underside of the cart.

He ignored me, so I called out again. This time, he looked up.

"No, the goddamn men's room is across the hall."

I knew it was across the hall, but dumb questions can be expected from partiers in Vegas.

"You're sure?"

He took a closer look at my face. "Yeah, I'm sure. Hi, Eddie."

I took one step toward the cart, still partially shielded by the wall, one hand on my gun. I nodded. "It's me."

He wore overalls with a nametag of "Joe." He kept his hands hidden behind the tray of cleaning supplies, but around his wrists, beneath the cuff of the sleeve, I could see the edges of black gloves. No tattoos or other identifying characteristics were visible, except for flashes of a silver chain around his neck. He was not quite six-feet tall and well-built for a man in his mid-seventies. The mask garbled his speech. I wouldn't be able to identify his voice if we met later.

A door at the end of the short walkway behind the Deacon would provide a safe exit for the former mob hitman. Did he have a partner in the main hall or one outside that door behind us? Maybe both.

"Let me see your hands," I said, my hand still behind my back on the butt of my gun.

He slowly brought up his hands, the black gloves now fully visible. No gun. I did another quick three-sixty sweep of the surroundings as I crossed the entrance and signaled to Uncle Mike. It would allow me to watch Uncle Mike's progress down the hallway toward us, while I kept the opposite wall to my back. "You're the Deacon?"

"Call me Joe for now," he said, laughing. "You guys plan things out. I like that." He touched an earpiece. "Your uncle is on the way. I've heard a lot about you, Eddie. They say you can walk on water."

Flattery—a typical way to get someone to let their guard down. I smiled. "The Deacon is a legend."

"Okay if I lower my hands?"

"Wait for my uncle. Then we can all get cozy. Maybe clean toilets together."

The Deacon once tracked people for the mob. Outside Walt's Collectibles, I should've asked for his autograph, but my antennae made me keep one hand on the gun at the small of my back.

Uncle Mike hustled up to us. He stopped short when he saw the man with the mask and overalls.

"Hey, Mike. It's been a while," the Deacon said.

"It's been a long time," Uncle Mike said, catching his breath. "You had some work done around the eyes?"

"Not only the eyes, but my entire ugly face," the Deacon said. "I'm handsome now. Sometimes I look in the mirror and don't recognize myself. Like you're shaving a stranger."

"Let me have a better look," Uncle Mike said.

The Deacon/Joe the Janitor laughed. "No way."

"You've been watching us?" Uncle Mike asked.

"Sorry. It's a habit. I have people I trust who handle it. Whenever I reconnect with the Deacon, I have to take precautions." He looked at me and smiled. "Okay to lower my hands?"

"Sure," I said. I didn't like the way he talked about the Deacon as if it was a role he reenacted for dinner theaters. Some star athletes talked about themselves in the third person as well and I always thought they were egomaniacs. I didn't want my new hero to be one of those. "You know why we're here. To find out about—"

"Before we get into that. And before we talk about my old partner, I need to talk about something else. I heard Arlene has this scrapbook. What the fuck?"

"How did you hear about that?" I asked.

"That's not important. Tell you the truth, I think the wonderful old lady spread it around just to get my attention, you know. Well, tell her she's got the Deacon's attention. I'd like to live out my last few years nice and quiet, instead of the way Whitey got it."

"Bulger? You know him?" Uncle Mike asked.

"Sure, we got a club," the Deacon said.

Even Uncle Mike laughed at that one. I kept my eyes on the shifting crowd coming in and out of Walt's behind me and the restrooms across the hall. I watched the Deacon, too. Just because he was my hero didn't mean I trusted him.

"The FBI has been dancing around the Deacon for years. I'd like to keep it that way. The Deacon worries about two things—the law and the virus," the Deacon said. "It's a fucked-up world."

"The government says the virus is nothing to worry about," Uncle Mike said.

"Bullshit," the Deacon said. "People are globetrotting all over."

I needed to make progress for my haunted, heartsick client, not discuss current affairs. "Arlene deserves answers."

"Look, it's bad enough I have to talk with you and Mike about all this. The Deacon is really a good guy if you get to know him," the Deacon said. "Mike, I hear you're retired."

"You going to hide behind that cart all night? Don't tell me retired homicide detectives make you uncomfortable?" Uncle Mike asked.

"Even retired homicide dicks don't make the Deacon feel like spilling his guts." He pulled his hat down lower over his eyes and touched an ear piece.

Each movement by the Deacon was slow and deliberate. What kind of weapon did he have within easy reach on that cart?

"I've got questions," Uncle Mike said.

"Cases to close?" He nodded. "The Deacon might be willing. He doesn't have time right now."

"We came all the way out to Vegas—"

"I know, Eddie, I know. And I appreciate it. You're here. That tells me a lot. My story must be worth a lot to Arlene."

"No one said anything about payment," I said. "It's about what's owed."

"C'mon," Uncle Mike said. "You're going to dip into an old lady's pocketbook?"

"The Deacon feels more comfortable when both sides have skin in the game, know what I mean? You had to come to Vegas. So what? It's the Super Bowl. What are you, a couple of commies? It's America's game." His eyes flashed. "We'll need to work out a time and place. The payment can be handled with crypto. No sweat."

"Payment for what?" I intended to protect Arlene from any hint of a scam.

Uncle Mike folded his arms. "I can't fucking believe this—"

"Take it easy, Mike. You too Eddie. The story is worth it, believe me. You could make a movie. The Deacon deserves to go out with top billing."

"Go find a scumbag movie producer," I said.

"From what I hear about Arlene's money, my modest demands won't break the bank."

"That woman is depending on me. And I'm not going to listen to your bullshit about turning it into a payday," I said.

"Mike, you did good with this kid. He's not taking shit. Don't worry, this is just step one. But I know what you mean.

You want something to show Arlene we mean business. Show that the Deacon knows what happened to Porter and why. Tell her this—tell her 'Rosario and Roberta at the Flamingo.' She'll know what it means."

I wanted to get Arlene on the phone. Get something worked out on the spot. I was worried the Deacon might go underground again and there'd be no way for us to get back in touch with him.

But the Deacon's delay was part of the process. People like the Deacon—killers, criminals—required special handling. Almost like breaking a wild horse. Because deep down at their core, these individuals lacked any trust whatsoever.

"I'll pass along the message, but you can forget about any money," I said.

"We'll see, Eddie." The Deacon stiffened. His hand moved behind the cleaning supplies. My hand went to my gun. Then voices filled the hall behind us, a crowd of people walking past toward Walt's.

The Deacon slowly withdrew his hand, his eyes never leaving me. The way his hand had moved seemed an instinctive response to my refusal to talk about payment, as if he was a man who was accustomed to getting his way. His "look" clearly conveyed a threat, something that seemed to be second nature to him.

Then the Deacon turned toward Uncle Mike. "You're not still pissed, are you, Mike?" His voice had transformed back to the casual and playful voice of before.

"No," Uncle Mike said. I could tell my uncle was lying.

"Eddie," the Deacon said, directing his attention back to me. His head shifted to the side as if he evaluated me from another angle. "I did you a favor once. You owe me."

The wrinkles around his surgically repaired eyes crinkled with amusement. I should be shaking his hand and buying him drinks instead of shooting him a poker face. "I don't owe you shit. You're the one on the hot seat. Think about Whitey."

The Deacon laughed and shook his head. "We'll talk some more. Everyone needs skin in the game." He stepped back from the cart. "Now, if you don't mind walking back down the hall and into Caesars? My guys are watching. We can meet tomorrow during the Super Bowl. Get things settled."

"Let's go," Uncle Mike said.

"Tomorrow." I walked past the Deacon and joined my uncle.

5

IT HAD BEEN SEVERAL YEARS SINCE I WAS A POKER AND sports book regular, but walking down the Strip from Caesars made it seem like yesterday. Lots of gamblers attempt to conquer Vegas and I'd tried to join their ranks. When I finally escaped Vegas, it left me with a bitter taste, but now I could see it was for the best.

Uncle Mike had left to join his retired buddies at their poker game after we called Arlene. She was enthusiastic, but frustrated about our report on the meeting with the Deacon.

"What do I care about money at this point?" Arlene had said. "I'd wonder what the hell was wrong with him if he didn't talk about money."

I told Arlene the Deacon might be running a scam.

Uncle Mike explained to her that a small, token payment might, in the Deacon's way of thinking, be considered a way for him to gain trust. "If people are paying for info, then we're guilty of something. It gives people like the Deacon a certain comfort level."

"Yes, a small, token payment," I said. "Not a large sum."

We told Arlene the Deacon hadn't discussed an amount. He wanted to meet up tomorrow before the Super Bowl.

"So, I have to be patient for one more night? Fine."

"One more thing, Arlene," I said. "The Deacon mentioned something as a show of good faith. He said to tell you, 'Rosario and Roberta at the Flamingo.'"

Uncle Mike and I waited for Arlene to respond.

Finally, she spoke up. "Interesting." Her voice was soft with an undercurrent of amusement, as if memories were being unlocked.

I asked her if she could tell us more, but she brushed us off.

I stopped outside to watch the fountains, then walked into the Bellagio. I found the small, dark café lodged between a closed coffee shop and an open gift shop. A chain was draped across the entrance to the café with a sign out front informing the tourist crowd it was closed. Guests were redirected to one of the high-end steak and seafood restaurants for dinner, instead of offering them a chance to order a cheeseburger with fries.

I walked up to a twenty-something guard with a bright smile and heavy eyeliner, who sat outside the gift shop.

"I'm meeting Nicole Nicoletti," I said.

"You Eddie?"

I nodded.

She undid the chain. "Help yourself to coffee."

"Thanks."

I walked back to several tables shielded by a divider from guests' prying eyes.

I grabbed a paper cup and filled it with black coffee from one of the stainless-steel tanks and then sat facing other employees at the tables. No familiar faces.

Nicole and I had been lovers during the time I lived in Vegas. We still kept in touch and called each other every other month or so. Our calls were a lifeline of sorts, a way to keep a tenuous connection going.

When I called Nicole last night to tell her I'd arranged a last-minute trip to Vegas, she seemed to hesitate at first, then became almost ecstatic. She couldn't wait to meet, but had so much going on. I didn't ask for details. Maybe she had a new man in her life. My most recent relationship broke off when my woman friend was reassigned by her employer to Washington. Things happen and people move on.

Nicole swept around the divider that separated the makeshift break area from the tide of tourists and walked toward me. I got up to meet her. A smile lit up her face. It was a smile she showcased only for me. This was the woman I knew. Her dark eyes, long wavy black hair and slim figure brought back a flood of memories.

I took her up in my arms in a bear hug. We hugged longer than acceptable for friends and tighter than family. It surprised the hell out of me. Her kiss came quick and short like an exclamation point, meaningful if done once, meaningless if done too often.

"It's been too long," she said, stepping back. "Missed you."

I wished I'd come to Vegas just to see her, not because of a job. "I've missed you, too."

We were both out of breath, exchanging dumb smiles, glowing as we headed to the table.

Nicole Nicoletti had grown up around the horses. In Chicago. Her father, Sal, still trained a small string of horses on the Chicago circuit. She had learned the importance of the odds, applied it to poker, and then used it to pave her way into sports betting.

"Want coffee?" I asked.

"I'd love some, but I don't have much time."

"A good game?" I didn't ask if she was winning. If she was, she'd tell me. If she wasn't, we'd ignore it.

"Yes. Having fun." She pulled off her light jacket and sat down.

I stepped over to the coffee setup and got her a cup with a little cream the way she liked it. When I looked up, I noticed Nicole had drawn the attention of the employees. They waved and smiled her way, then the workers turned to scrutinize me.

I walked back and placed the hot coffee on the table.

"Thanks," she said. "I confess I'd made a wager. I bet myself that you'd call tonight and tell me you couldn't meet me because you were held up at a blackjack table or craps table."

I laughed. "Okay. Pay up."

She sipped the coffee. "I guess I wanted to hedge a little in case you didn't show." She reached across the table and touched my hand. "It's wonderful to see you again, even if you're here on a job."

"I hope we can spend some time together." I returned her touch. "Everybody here seems to know you. You're a celebrity."

"It's the cable show."

"You'll have to tell me all about it."

"It's great. I'm one of several women who actually gives out picks and offers analysis. I don't just ask the male experts prepared questions and then sit there and smile at the camera."

"That's great." I was proud of her.

"People watch my show religiously and follow my picks. They actually thank me. They tell me how they love my insight, especially what I have to say about the players. The other night, a lady from Boston told me how much she appreciated the nice things I had to say about Tom Brady as if Tom Brady was her adopted son." She laughed, throwing her head back and pulling her hair back from her face. "I swear, Eddie, the show is a whole new life for me."

Her broadcasts were a way out of the poker room, just as poker had been a way for her to escape her father's way of life. She seemed to always be searching for the next thing, or trying to escape the previous one. Which led me to wonder, where did that leave me, the old boyfriend?

I knew the ways of the gambler. I'd been a horse player, a sports bettor, and a poker player, in no particular order. Now I was officially a PI. Maybe I was always looking for change, too. Maybe you find your one true passion and maybe you don't, but at least you keep on trying.

"You know what my fans really want, Eddie? They want to play poker with me. Before I know it, we rush over to the poker room."

"Unless they watch the reruns of your days on the poker tour, they haven't seen you play on television."

She nodded. "My poker past is a big deal on The Sports Betting Insiders. I cringe every time the announcer opens with, 'Nicole Nicoletti brings her poker skills to sports betting.' Like I'm a guru of percentages and numbers. Some sort of human-computer come to life."

"Aren't you?"

"I don't need the pressure. No one is right all the time picking football. Guys fumble or have a rotten game." She shrugged. "Hopefully, my fans don't bet too much on the games I get wrong. But God bless them, we sit down at the poker table like we're in their living room on Saturday night."

"Do you clean up?"

"I know they're only a bunch of fish. I try not to revert to killer mode, you know, try to ease off, gear down. I don't muscle them off hands with a re-raise. Let them have their fun. When I see them shaking and shivering like a puppy in a cold wind, I'll fold." We laughed together. "Let them bluff me. We'll be friends forever."

"That's what counts."

"They're fish, but they're my fish, so I don't want you sitting down with us. I know you. You can't help yourself. You'd be in attack mode."

"You're right. I'm not sure I've got your self-control." It was the second time today I'd been warned not to join a poker game. I guess I had to work on my social skills. "The life of a celebrity. Perfect for the glitz and glamor of Vegas," I said.

"Yeah. But not so good when I'm handicapping the races or sitting at a serious cash game. The fans gawk and try to strike up conversations while I'm trying to concentrate. It used to be I couldn't wait to sit down with the pros in the twenty-five-thousand-dollar buy-in game. It was a proving ground, but also my comfort zone. Compared to poker with the pros, picking football games is a piece of cake. Which reminds me, I've got a new challenge on my hands. After the Super Bowl tomorrow, everyone will be focused on college hoops and I've got to get up to speed fast or I'll be yesterday's trivia question."

Nicole knew I'd won at college hoops in the past. At O'Connell's, college basketball was not simply a matter of the Final Four, but a full-time pastime.

"I'm your guy on hoops." I wasn't sure if I could go from sports fan to prognosticator or if I'd even have enough time considering the demands of the Deacon and Arlene's case, but I was game.

"I knew I could count on you." Her smile faded, and she looked down at her coffee.

She checked her watch again. "I have to get back. There's so much more we need to talk about—"

"That's right."

She shifted to the edge of her seat. "I have to attend my sponsor's pre-Super Bowl party tomorrow afternoon. Can you join me?"

"Sure. It's a date."

She stood up. "Are you free later, too?"

"Yes."

"I know you're here on a job and I don't want to ask what it's about because it's confidential and you probably have a full day tomorrow."

"No, I have time."

She put on her coat. "I feel like celebrating. I don't have to go back."

"I thought your fans were expecting—"

"Hedging."

We laughed.

———

I asked her if I could see her house. On one of our phone calls, Nicole had told me that she'd taken the big step to home ownership. She'd called it a major milestone.

Nicole pulled up to a large four-bedroom house in a new development west of the Strip. She drove into the garage.

"I've been looking forward to showing you around," she said. Instead of walking into the house from the attached garage, she led me around to the front of the house. The well-lit area in front had xeriscaping that included a variety of desert plants.

"It's terrific, Nicole."

"There's construction going on, but I don't care. As one of the first buyers, I got a good deal from the builder."

I used every superlative I could think of as we made our way into the house for the grand tour. There was a winding staircase leading up to the second floor. The entryway had white tile beneath an ornate light fixture. To the right of the entryway was a large dining room.

Through a short hall, we entered a large room at the back of the house. The room included a kitchen with all the amenities and a family room with a large flat screen TV on one wall. She hit a switch that drew back the window treatments to reveal the night sky through the windows. From the outside deck, we had an unobstructed view of the Strip four or five miles away.

"I kept telling myself that I had to put my poker winnings to use," she said. "Of course, poker isn't exactly the type of steady income that gets you a mortgage at the bank. When I got the job on the sports betting show, I was able to swing it."

We went back inside, where she opened a bottle of chilled white wine. We toasted to her success.

"My Dad said it was too much house for a single woman," she said.

I shook my head. "Times have changed."

"Yeah. Maybe I bought it as proof to my dad that I'm making all the right moves. He wants me to come home. The house is a big responsibility, but I work harder because of it." She sipped her wine. "When you and I were together, it was..."

"A different time and place," I said.

"That's right. We were trying to make it at poker."

"Some of us made it and some of us didn't." I was the one who didn't.

"And some nights when we won big, we were on full tilt," she said.

"A good way to lose your winnings," I said.

She reached out and touched my hand. "That's why we should take things slow, don't you think?"

"If we've learned anything, we've learned that much."

"Now, how about some cake? This is a celebration. I bought your favorite."

"Chocolate?"

"You bet."

6

THE NEXT MORNING, I CARRIED A TRAY OF COFFEE AND breakfast sandwiches through the glass front doors of Caesars main entrance to the sidewalk outside. Uncle Mike had taken up a post at the smoker's station on a patch of fake grass a few respectful yards back from the crowded walkway. Although smoking was allowed in the casino, Uncle Mike had a habit of standing outside with his stogie in the morning and I knew better than to get into an argument about it.

The steady stream of people hustled past, probably in hopes of getting one of those cushy seats in the sports book for the Super Bowl festivities. Maybe if they'd camped out overnight, they'd have half a chance. The sports book was already packed to the rafters.

"Good morning, sunshine," I said to Uncle Mike.

He moaned in pain and reached for the coffee with a shaky hand. "Thank God."

"How late?"

"When you're the big winner, it's not polite to leave a poker game early."

"How much?"

"I made a killing. Almost a hundred bucks."

I squelched a laugh. "What do you guys play for, nickels? Any text from the Deacon?"

"Nothing." He sipped his coffee. "How is Nicole?"

"She's doing well. She was entertaining fans at the poker table, but we met up later. I saw her house. It's really something."

"No shit. You stay the night?"

"No, we're taking it slow. This afternoon, her sponsor is giving a pre-Super Bowl party."

"That should be interesting."

I stared down the long-curved drive that led from the busy portico to Las Vegas Boulevard and into a bright desert sun. To my left, a line of taxis and limos and other vehicles picked up and dropped off guests to and from the airport. The valets dragged suitcases back and forth.

Sports fans paraded past, holding cups of beer, some in Native American headdresses and some in superhero costumes. Like a typical NFL game, lots of fans felt the need to dress up. A woman in a sleek black Catwoman costume caught my eye. What team was she rooting for?

"I don't want another situation like yesterday," I said.

"Give me one of those sandwiches." Uncle Mike crouched down and placed his coffee cup near the outside ashtray. I handed him the egg and cheese bagel sandwich. We were alone at the smoker's station. "What situation?"

"A meeting in a near-empty mall with a guy in a mask," I said.

He tore the wrapper off the sandwich and bit into it. "Not bad. What did they put in this bagel, cranberry?"

"I want to see the Deacon's face." I wanted more than that. I wanted to know the Deacon, what made him tick, and why he decided to do what he'd done to Childress.

"A million guys before you have tried to get to know a guy like the Deacon." Uncle Mike blew a cloud of cigar smoke toward one of several Roman statues tucked into an arched, recessed portion of the wall. "I'm telling you; you can't do it. Guys like that are in constant conflict with the world. They think the world owes them. It makes them suspicious of everything and everyone."

"How am I supposed to know if the Deacon is telling us the truth about Porter?"

"We have Arlene's scrapbook. That's our hole card."

A man in a gorilla mask walked past.

"The way the Deacon mentioned Whitey Bulger yesterday didn't make me think we had any leverage," I said. The Boston mobster had been captured by the FBI and then beaten to death by prison inmates. No wonder the Deacon was so careful.

"What are you saying?"

"You saw it. The way the Deacon seemed to grab for a gun before that crowd of people walked past."

"And you want to get close to him?"

This morning, standing in line for coffee and sandwiches, I thought through everything the Deacon had said and done, trying to determine what he wanted. I came to one conclusion.

"Maybe the Deacon doesn't care about the scrapbook. Maybe he doesn't care about Arlene paying money."

Uncle Mike stopped chewing and smoking. He squatted down and picked up the coffee. "What does he want?"

"He wants one thing. When he steps into the role of the Deacon, he's vulnerable. He's forced to hide. I think he wants to leave the Deacon behind and you're the one he's worried about."

"Me? Why? Because of Childress?"

"No. There's something else. Some other murder investigation you might have been involved in. You were a homicide detective in Chicago for years. I think the Deacon is worried about one thing—his past. Right now, he's golden. He has a new life. In his mind, the Deacon is history. No one can trace him. Arlene isn't a worry. You heard her over the phone last night when we told her what the Deacon had said, 'Rosario and Roberta at the Flamingo.' Arlene swooned like a schoolgirl. She's living in a dream world. She'd never turn that scrapbook over to the cops to catch the Deacon. That would be like ratting on Porter."

"You think we're being set up?"

"I hope not, but think about it. You're still working those cold cases. If you were to get murdered in Vegas, nobody would make the connection to Chicago. Burrascano is the one who called you. Why did he get involved? Arlene is a beloved figure and I don't doubt her story. She's just being used."

"Jeesus, you're a cynic." Uncle Mike picked up the sandwich. "Gives me a headache."

I sipped my coffee and watched the parade. A woman in a wedding dress and a man in a tux wearing football helmets, one with a 49ers's helmet and one with the Chiefs, walked past arm in arm. Why not get married in Vegas during the Super Bowl?

A taxi drove off with a family headed for the airport. I'd watched them load up the luggage. It was close to noon and the Super Bowl wouldn't start until 3:30 p.m. Pacific Time. People left Vegas at all hours to save a few bucks on air fare, yet dropped a chunk of their paycheck into the slots.

"The Deacon could be standing nearby and we wouldn't even know it," I said.

"Okay, Mr. Paranoia, what do you propose we do?"

"We need more backup. The Deacon watched us, right? He's got some partner out there. If we show we've got more guys behind us, he'll be forced to change his plans."

Uncle Mike coughed. "I like it. Keep the Deacon off balance. Makes sense."

"It's a chess game. The Deacon made a move yesterday, watching us, so we make a move. We need more than a scrapbook as insurance." A diesel pickup truck roared out from beneath the portico past a taxi, hip hop blaring out of the speakers.

"I've got my poker buddies. Hell, I was sitting across from a Vegas homicide detective last night. Everybody is working security for the casinos to put a little extra spending money in their pockets. You remember Vogel from the precinct? He's over there by the valet stand at work for casino security."

I looked over. A crowd with stacks of suitcases waited their turn for a taxi. It was checkout time. "I don't see him. He's a short guy, isn't he?"

"He may be short, but he knows how to handle himself. I could get four or five guys. Is it in the budget?"

"Arlene gave me the okay on reasonable expenses."

"I like the idea. The Deacon won't respect us unless we show up with reinforcements."

"And I'd like to pull the Deacon's chain. When he texts you, let's set a later time. Maybe during the game."

Uncle Mike chuckled. "You're an asshole. I like it."

"It's my specialty."

Another truck revved up, its speakers blaring, and edged away from the swarm of taxis and vehicles beneath the portico. Its chrome reflected the sun, and then I spotted another reflection from inside—the barrel of a gun.

"Get down!"

I grabbed Uncle Mike, and we ducked down behind one of the waist-high stone walls that bordered the sidewalk as shots rang out. People on the sidewalk ducked down behind the walls.

"Get down," someone shouted from the valet stand.

The shooter opened up on the statues, firing away.

If only I'd had time to grab my gun. But shooting back would make us, and those around us, a target.

7

TIME SLOWED.

"Don't be stupid, people. Stay down," the shooter screamed out again between each barrage. Chaos reigned in the direction of the boulevard where the crowd had the opportunity to make a run for it.

The thought of the 2017 Vegas shooter firing down on a concert crowd from the thirty-second floor of a nearby casino came to mind. His only goal had been to kill as many people as possible. Folks were forced to run for their lives. This seemed different, more organized.

Around me, no one was running. We were huddled up behind the wall that bordered the sidewalk. Glass shattered and more statues on the other side of the main doors were defiled. Stay down.

People at the valet stand and scattered beneath the portico were lying face down. Interminable seconds passed. "No one gets hurt." I heard the shooter laughing. Faux marble sculptures disintegrated into a cloud of faux marble dust. The truck edged closer to us and away from the portico. What the hell was he doing?

The engine revved and whined. "Let's go," someone shouted. The smell of exhaust hit me. Tires screeched. I dared to look over the wall.

The truck with the shooter swerved down the drive toward the boulevard.

I stood upright, unsteady on my feet. I'd been knocked out in the ring before, so I put some of my training to use. Deep breathing, focus on a fixed point.

People began cussing, screaming, and shouting.

"What the fuck?" Uncle Mike groaned.

"You okay?" The shock began to wear off.

"Yeah. Except for the coffee on my shirt. And my elbow hurts like hell. Next time you toss me around, give me a heads-up." He struggled to his feet. "Where's my cigar?"

Even Uncle Mike, who'd seen it all, grappled with confusion.

Others also began to stand one by one.

A flood of security staff and emergency personnel stormed out of the casino.

We heard the rumors—someone was shot. We could have been too. If it had been a few minutes later, those on the sidewalk would've been in the line of fire.

Near the crowded portico, people crouched behind a taxi or other vehicles. Valets, men, woman and children lying down between stacks of suitcases and handcarts, and others under vehicles, emerged slowly from their hiding places. Many were crying uncontrollably.

A valet blew his whistle and waved his arms. A security guard spoke into a cell phone.

An ambulance and other emergency vehicles sped down the boulevard and whipped into the drive of Caesars. My heart was already beating fast and sped up with the arrival of the emergency vehicles and the chorus of screaming sirens.

People stood on their toes for a better look. Others around me started to ask what happened.

"Found it." Uncle Mike clamped his jaw on the stogie and stood. "I guess the Deacon gave us his answer."

"I don't think it was the Deacon. Those guys weren't shooting at us."

"You could've fooled me. Look at those statues."

"Over by the valet stand. Some people were shot."

"Damnit. Where's my lighter?" He checked his pockets. "Shit, what about Vogel? He was over there."

Anger welled up in me. "I don't see him." There were too many people around the valet stand to see much.

"Get back, get back," the staff yelled into the crowd.

Uncle Mike and I ran over and pushed past others who were stepping back like zombies. The casino entrance had been blocked off for authorized personnel only.

Blood and shards of glass were everywhere. A guy was lying on his back, paramedics working on him. Others had been shot as well. More emergency people streamed out through surrounding vehicles—paramedics, firemen, and police.

Vogel sat about five yards from the man everyone was working on. He had his right arm clutched tight. Blood seeped through his fingers. He was staring straight ahead, probably in shock.

"Hey, Vogel, it's me, Mike O'Connell." Uncle Mike tore apart his shirt. He wrapped it around Vogel's arm. "You shot anywhere else?"

"Huh?" Vogel said.

I got down on one knee and applied pressure to stop the bleeding.

"Eddie, keep talking to him. I'll get a paramedic over here."

"How you doing?" I asked Vogel. "What's your name?"

Vogel looked in my direction. A good start. His eyes were glassy and his face pale. His breathing labored.

"Your first name and then your last name," I said. "C'mon."

Vogel grinned up at me, then bared his teeth and hissed, "Goddamnit, what is this grade school?"

"Welcome back, Vogel."

8

I MET NICOLE OUTSIDE A SMALL BALLROOM IN THE BELLAGIO that had been reserved for the pre-Super Bowl party. We hugged.

"Eddie, thank God you and Mike are okay," she said, looking up at me with tears in her eyes. "I can't believe you were in the shooting. Do they know who it was?"

"Not yet. Uncle Mike knows a police detective and a guy working security. They'll tell us."

She shook her head. "These shootings don't even make the national news anymore. It's business as usual here at Bellagio. You'd never know there was a shooting next door." She paused. "It could have been you."

I held her in my arms just like the old days. Her voice held a parlay of love and anger that made me regret our time apart. I wanted to block out this morning's shooting and move on, but the voice of the shooter and the feeling of helplessness continued to haunt me. "Thank God, Uncle Mike and I were lucky." From what I'd seen and heard, several people were wounded, but only one person had been killed. "C'mon, you've got a job to do."

The room had a view of the fountains and had been reserved for the private shindig by the host, WagerEasy, a Euro sports betting conglomerate worth billions, let loose on an unwary American public ready to dump their dollars.

A buffet had been set up, consisting of a carving station of prime rib and turkey in one corner, complemented by a layout of shrimp, crab claws, and oysters on the half shell at the opposite corner of the room. In between, two long tables were piled high with cheese and crackers and every other munchie I could think of. The lucky invitees grazed from table to table. Two temporary bars at either end were busy serving a thirsty crowd.

Nicole wore a black cocktail dress and high heels. I had thrown on a sport coat. Nicole had given me a badge with a name tag. We surveyed the scene. Where to begin, the drink line or the food? Maybe we could mix in with the crowd and then find a quiet spot.

Nicole tugged on my arm. "Stay with me. Some of these fat cats get a few drinks in them and hit on me. It can be uncomfortable."

"Sure." If the Deacon did get in touch with us, I told Nicole I'd have to leave the party early.

A cocktail waitress appeared and greeted us with a smile. "What can I get you?"

Nicole ordered a glass of wine and I ordered a beer. I had to match wits with the Deacon at some point later today, and I couldn't afford to be off my game. Maybe I'd try to choke down a few shrimp, although I wasn't sure if my stomach had rebounded from this morning. Uncle Mike and I were one of the first in line to give our statement to the police, but we hadn't been able to add much.

"See that guy over there?" Nicole asked with a sideways glance toward a skinny guy in jeans wearing a backward baseball cap, talking to two tall blondes who could pass for fashion models. "He did pre-game podcasts at college games from around the country and developed a loyal following. It was just him and his buddies doing locker room jokes, talking up the point spread, and sitting in a local donut or pizza shop. They drove from game to game in a ten-year-old RV. One of the sports betting conglomerates bought the guy out for something like a billion dollars."

"Damn. Looks like the kind of guy who thinks his farts are hilarious."

She laughed and hit me on the shoulder. "Like some people I know."

"Hey, cool it. Who else do we have contributing to WagerEasy's bottom line?"

"To the left of that lucky podcast dude is another prized WagerEasy customer. He bought The Kremlin Casino. His name is Karmazin, another proud Russian billionaire, I heard. I also heard he laid off half his staff."

Karmazin was tall, about six-foot-seven, and overweight. He had a stack of shrimp and crab on his plate.

"The woman talking to the hotel manager near the carving station works for WagerEasy," Nicole said. "Her name is Carla Franzen. She's in a tough spot trying to keep home office happy back in London. She also has to schmooze the high rollers and sponsor our broadcast while raising her son as a single mom."

Franzen barked orders in one direction and then twisted around to smile and greet guests. She was in her late forties with unkempt brown hair. I could picture her working at a WagerEasy branch office.

I hadn't told Nicole about the time I had worked for WagerEasy in Chicago. Most of the employees I knew had left, but I recalled the pressure from home office to grab market share and the cutthroat corporate culture.

"None of these customers are like my fish who were sitting down with me at the poker table last night for a friendly game. I asked if I could invite them to the party and Franzen laughed in my face. But don't blame her, it's not her fault," Nicole added quickly. "She tries hard. These big parties are reserved only for the cream of the crop."

"Like me."

"Funny."

The server came by with our drinks. I sipped my beer and glanced out the window at the fountains.

"Did you make a bet?" Nicole asked.

"I went with KC. The moneyline had moved over at Caesars," I said. When you get a free pass at a drive-by shooting, luck must be smiling down, and a wager is in order.

"The moneyline moved? It must be the California money pouring in. They're betting hot and heavy on the 49ers." She nudged me. "I don't get the chance to talk about that angle on the show. I try to tell my fans to shop for odds, but—"

"You need to make a pick, right?"

"That's right," Nicole said. "I have to give them a definite opinion. Here comes Eliot Scullion. Our first test."

Before I could ask what she meant, Scullion had ambled up to us. He wore a dark blue suit and light blue shirt open at the collar. He was about forty pounds overweight, with gray hair. Sweat had broken out on his forehead. The bartender in me wagered that he'd had several drinks already.

Nicole introduced us and we shook hands.

Scullion then ignored me and smiled at Nicole. "I enjoyed your pre-game analysis. You picked the Chiefs, right?"

"Right," Nicole said.

"But that was a few days ago. You're probably having second thoughts."

"I haven't had any reason to have second thoughts."

"Really?" Scullion looked around with a smirk on his face. "I hear the money is pouring in on the 49ers."

Nicole shuffled her feet, a sign of her impatience. "Yes."

Another man walked up. Scullion turned to the man. "Landis, we're discussing the game. Get in on this. You like the 49ers."

Nicole introduced me. Landis Tanner was of medium height and build with sandy hair. He was in his early fifties and was drinking a bottle of water. He had a deep tan and looked like he worked out religiously. He was probably one of those I saw jogging this morning before the shooting.

Scullion took a sip of his drink, addressing the three of us. "I know KC is favored, but defense wins championships and San Francisco has the number one defense against the pass. They're number two in defense overall. The Patriots shut down the Rams in last year's Super Bowl with defense—thirteen to three, remember? Remember, Landy, we won big."

"The Chiefs haven't won a Super Bowl in fifty years," Tanner said.

Nicole smiled. "Well gentlemen, I appreciate your arguments, but KC is favored for a reason. I don't want to rehash everything I've said before on the show."

"What do you think, Landy?" Scullion asked. "Let's get some money down on San Fran. The usual bet." Everyone tried to convince a buddy to go along on a bet. If you lost, misery loved company, and if you won, you'd be able to celebrate together.

Tanner studied his bottle of water. "I can't."

"C'mon," Scullion said, jabbing him with an elbow. "That's not like you. I'll place the bet for you on my account. I have a good feeling about the 49ers. The WagerEasy odds are better than here in the casinos."

Scullion had done his homework. I assumed he'd identified the West Coast factor. The California 49ers fans had flooded Nevada to bet their team; WagerEasy had its main North America office in New Jersey.

Scullion waved to Franzen. "Carla," he called. The WagerEasy rep walked over. "What's the balance on my account? I have my person standing by to place my bet in New Jersey." Scullion had a wide smile as he turned back to us. "Best move I ever made was moving back to New Jersey. It's only a quick helicopter flight to my Manhattan office."

Franzen checked her iPad and then showed Scullion the screen.

He nodded. "Okay, fifteen million. We've got money to play with, Landy."

I didn't flinch when I heard the amount. Many people bet big in Vegas. After all, these high rollers kept the casino lights burning. But the sum did get my attention.

I tried to read Franzen's reaction. I assumed the whole idea of today's outing was to get wagers into the WagerEasy's coffers, but she bit her bottom lip and studied Tanner, her arms tense cradling the laptop.

Tanner glanced toward Franzen. "I don't like the game."

Scullion laughed. "Landy, your company is about to go public. You're about to be a billionaire. What's wrong with you?"

"It's the Super Bowl," I said. "The spread is only a point or two."

Nicole poked me as a signal to butt out.

Tanner looked around like a guy trying to find the exit.

"We'll bet the moneyline," Scullion said. "The 49ers are going to win, no problem. It's all about defense."

Tanner rubbed his chin. What was their usual bet? WagerEasy had come to Vegas to chip away at what was once the legal U.S. monopoly on sports betting held by the Nevada casinos. Those who didn't bet on the Super Bowl were like the kids who didn't get a present at Christmas.

What choice did Tanner have but to play? I could see the wheels churning in his mind. His defenses were breaking down.

"Okay, okay, I'll do it. The usual bet," Tanner said.

I knew he'd give in. I would've bet on it.

Scullion clapped him on the back. "I knew I could count on you." He grabbed his cell and texted, presumably to his New Jersey contact. At the same time, he said, "Nicole, why don't we have a side bet?"

Nicole placed her free hand on her hip. "What?"

Scullion sipped the last of his bourbon and water. A waiter magically appeared by his side and held out a tray with a fresh drink. Scullion set his empty on the tray and grabbed the next. "If San Francisco wins, then you agree to play me heads-up."

High rollers had begun challenging the pros to heads-up poker over the last several years. It all started with a banker from Texas or a Saudi prince. The pros viewed it as an opportunity to fatten their payroll, but Nicole's clenched jaw told me there must be other factors at play.

Some of these billionaires had been coached by experts. They didn't always lose.

"It's a bet," Nicole said as if she were ordering a ham and Swiss at the deli.

"I have a bottomless bankroll," Scullion said with a sly smile and a quick slurp of courage from his glass.

"And I appreciate the chance to get to the bottom of that bankroll," Nicole said.

Scullion hesitated. "I'm here all week."

"You know where to find me," Nicole responded, staring him down.

Scullion looked away first.

Tanner had set down his bottle and clapped. "This I have to see."

Once Tanner decided to wager, he was ready to join the party.

I stepped toward Scullion and twisted the knife. "Nicole accepted your wager. If the 49ers win, she'll play you heads-up. What if the 49ers lose?" I asked.

Scullion shot me a cold stare then shrugged.

"We can still play poker heads-up, but what do I get if the Chiefs win?" Nicole asked.

"Let's say a hundred grand?" Scullion asked. "And you will be free to decide if you want to play me heads-up or not. Okay?"

My cell buzzed. It was Uncle Mike.

Tanner stepped close to his buddy. "Hey Eliot, I know our usual bet is for one million, but I might want to make some other prop bets, too."

I knew what this was all about. The stakes had to be raised again and again to catch that "zing." A psychiatrist could explain the need for the familiar adrenaline rush that drove the need for more action, but I could tell you all about it from first-hand experience.

"Your credit is good," Scullion said.

I moved away from our group and answered the cell. "Yeah?"

"Eddie, there's a problem," Uncle Mike said. "Something's come up with the shooting."

"What?"

"I think you better get down here. I'm in the lobby."

9

I TOOK THE ELEVATOR TO THE LOBBY OF THE BELLAGIO. Uncle Mike practically ran to meet me.

"We're headed to the coroner's office," he said.

Leave it to Uncle Mike to get my attention. "What is it?"

Uncle Mike walked toward the door. "The homicide detective at last night's poker game. His name is Woodyard, Sam Woodyard. Hell of a nice guy. He invited us. They want to see if we can ID the guy."

"What guy?"

Uncle Mike stopped. "The guy killed during the drive-by shooting this morning. They don't know who the guy is. He didn't have any ID or cell phone. His face was shot up bad at close range."

"Damn. Are you thinking what I'm thinking?"

"Yeah. It would explain why we haven't received a text from the Deacon."

"Wait," I said. "How could the drive-by shooter get off such a perfect shot?"

"He didn't. They haven't done ballistics yet, but according to Woodyard, it seems the drive-by was a diversion. In the chaos, an accomplice got close enough to put a few in the victim's face at close range."

"You didn't tell Woodyard about the Deacon?"

"Hell, no. I just said how we were at the smoking station outside and saw some people walk past and that we wanted to help. I think he knew it was bullshit, but he gave me the invite."

We walked outside to get a cab.

———

Sam Woodyard was a few years younger than Uncle Mike, but his shoulders slumped like an older man. His eyes looked tired, and it took an effort for him to smile. I'd seen it before with detectives on the force in Chicago. The burden of what it took to actually deal with America's daily dose of violence had to land on someone.

Woodyard led us down an empty white hallway toward a doorway guarded by an officer. "It's not often we get a drive-by shooting on the Strip, but it happens. The casinos will hope we can play it down. The Super Bowl of all days."

"We're not here to make waves," Uncle Mike said.

What were we here for? I'd seen what a large caliber handgun could do to a man's face and skull. How could we possibly identify the Deacon, a man we'd met wearing a mask?

In an investigation, you go through the motions and sometimes there's a payoff and sometimes there isn't. I reminded myself of that again. Plus, we wanted to reinforce our new connection to Detective Woodyard. Uncle Mike always stressed the need for a pipeline to the local police. They could provide us with forensics and other information.

If the Deacon had been a victim, our investigation would only be beginning. I wasn't sure if Arlene would continue to pay our way, but I wasn't about to give up and go back to Chicago, and Uncle Mike was a bulldog who refused to allow murder to end an investigation.

Woodyard led us past the officer and into the room. A doctor, a forensic pathologist, and her assistant stood near the body. The room had all the characteristics of an operating room—bright lights, tables with scalpels, scientific monitors, and computers—but none of the urgency. The autopsy room reeked of disinfectant and death.

"We got here as fast as we could, Doc," Woodyard said.

The doctor smiled. "Plenty of time. Do you want us to stay?"

"No, just tell us what you got so far and then I'll let you know when we're done." Woodyard turned back to us. "Ready?"

The doctor pulled down the sheet. "One shot appeared to enter the left temporal lobe probably when the victim was lying face down."

"Jeesus." Uncle Mike took the unlit cigar from the corner of his mouth.

A wave of revulsion hit me. Could this be the Deacon? The man I dared to match wits with, the one who'd told me he'd done me a favor once.

It was as if the face of the man had been turned inside out, exposing the underside of the skin, blood vessels, and muscle, right down to the skeletal structure. Unreal eyeballs stared out at us.

"Damnit," Woodyard said. "The poor guy is lying face down while the drive-by sprays the place and then the guy gets it in the side of the noggin."

I was reminded of how helpless I felt when pinned down by the shooter.

The doctor droned on. She referred to notes on her laptop, but then looked up from the screen, giving us the layman's version. "The force of the initial gunshot probably twisted the head forty-five degrees to the right, exposing the opposite side of the face. The second shot ripped apart the cheek and jaw area. A third shot took off the rest."

The doctor picked up her laptop and stepped back. "That's only my initial exam. I'll have my final results later."

"Thanks, doc," Woodyard said. "Can you give us a minute?"

Before she walked out, I asked, "Any distinguishing characteristics, doctor?"

She seemed to notice my presence for the first time. "A birthmark near the knee, but it's faded over time. Not much help, I'm afraid."

"Thanks," I said, taking a look at the knee. I would've never noticed the small patch of slightly darker skin just above the right knee.

The doctor and her assistant left.

When they were gone, Woodyard turned to us. "Anything?"

Uncle Mike shook his head. "He's about the right age, weight, and size, but that's only a guess."

"Nothing," I said.

Woodyard breathed a sigh of relief. "If we've got a John Doe, the casinos will be happy. There won't be much publicity. Without any ID on him, the media will probably report the victim as a homeless person. My job and my case will hit a brick wall, depending upon additional information. The dental reports or DNA might give us a clue."

"What about surveillance?" I asked.

"A guy in a hoodie with a gorilla mask." Woodyard shrugged. "It's the Super Bowl."

"What about the drive-by guys?" Uncle Mike asked.

"Stolen vehicle. We found it a block away. They wore ski masks." Woodyard looked down at his shoes. "I don't suppose you guys can tell me anything about the shooters?"

Uncle Mike chewed on his cigar. "No, we ducked down behind the wall along the walkway."

"How about his personal effects?" I asked, thinking of the silver chain.

"Those are locked up. I'd need additional clearance from the DA." Woodyard cleared his throat. "You know how it is sometimes, Mike. A case like this with a John Doe—we get inquiries. People looking for their long-lost relative or somebody. And then sometimes we get inquiries we take seriously, but know they'll never tell us anything. We had such a guy in here earlier. He looked at the body. He couldn't help us or wouldn't help us, if you know what I mean."

The detective was talking around it, but we knew what he meant. Guys who couldn't help or wouldn't talk, but had the "pull" to take a look at a shooting victim, qualified as members of organized crime.

"Sure. I know what you mean," Uncle Mike said. "Want to tell us who?"

Woodyard rubbed the back of his neck. "I don't want to be forced to write a dozen reports, Mike. The Feds will crawl up my ass. He's outside. Wants to meet you. You and Eddie."

Uncle Mike turned toward me. "Looks like we're getting popular, Eddie. I hope I brought enough cigars."

10

A BIG MAN IN A DARK SPORTS COAT MET US OUTSIDE AND motioned for us to follow him. He walked several steps ahead of us around the corner to a limo idling in a parking spot marked "Emergency Vehicles Only."

The big man opened the passenger door of the limo.

Uncle Mike looked at me. "Want to risk it? It could be interesting."

"Let's go. We might find out if that was the Deacon on the table or not."

"Okay." Uncle Mike hunched down to look inside. "What the fuck?"

I looked in as Uncle Mike slipped inside. "What the fuck? Vic?"

It was our old "friend," Vic DiNatale. I took a seat opposite Uncle Mike. DiNatale, with his massive frame, took up most of the wide seat below the back window. Burrascano's handpicked successor had a habit of dropping in on our investigations.

Despite the fact DiNatale had risen in the ranks, he was still the mob's chief relief pitcher. He threw nothing but heat and was sent to the hot spots whenever mob interests were in jeopardy. If rival gangs tried to grab mob territory, DiNatale would put a quick end to the drama. When a mob informer decided to recant key testimony, rest assured DiNatale roamed the streets nearby.

"Hello, gents," DiNatale said with a big smile. His husky, garbled speech made him difficult to understand. I'd heard it was a broken windpipe from a fight in his youth. "We meet again."

"Fancy meeting you here," Uncle Mike said.

"We could use a ride back to our hotel, thanks." I didn't offer a smile.

"What's wrong, Eddie? Aren't you glad to see me? How about a ride down the Strip? We've got some things to talk over."

Most people wouldn't agree to "take a ride" with a mobster, but I'd ridden in DiNatale's limo before on past jobs for Burrascano.

"Mind if I smoke?" Uncle Mike asked.

"No problem. This limo has all the extras." DiNatale flipped a switch. An overhead fan beneath the sunroof started up. A dome light came on at the same time. He tried several switches to turn off the light, his face growing red. One switch lowered the glass partition between us and the driver. Finally, he found the right one and turned off the light. Then he resumed his phony Emily Post hospitality act. "Want a drink? It has a wet bar. Fully stocked."

"No thanks," I said. "We heard you viewed the body. What's your interest in the victim?"

"I'm just a concerned citizen looking out for my fellow man."

"And I'm President Trump," Uncle Mike said, lighting a cigar.

I was grateful for the cigar smoke. I wouldn't have to inhale DiNatale's cologne. I was also fed up with the gamesmanship. "Is that the Deacon in there?"

DiNatale gritted his teeth. Over the intercom, he told the driver to "drive us around." He looked at Uncle Mike, and then at me, his eyes becoming thin slits and his hands balled into fists. He nodded slowly. "Fuck."

"How do you know?" Uncle Mike said.

"We got ways," DiNatale growled.

DiNatale had a deep hatred and distrust for me and Uncle Mike and the investigative jobs we'd done for Burrascano. He didn't think outsiders were necessary.

I didn't want to let DiNatale off the hook. "Like what?"

"Yeah," Uncle Mike said. "What ways?"

"We'll get to that. Burrascano wants to let the Deacon go in peace. No cops. No FBI. Let the fuckers leave him on the Most Wanted List and keep chasing their tail."

"You expect us to tell the authorities about the Deacon?" I asked. "No fucking way."

"The guy's face is shot off. I haven't seen the Deacon in years. He wore a mask when we met him," Uncle Mike said.

"Good," DiNatale said. "Just so we're clear."

"You heard we met the Deacon?" I asked.

DiNatale nodded. "I heard. Arlene wants to know what happened to Porter."

"Can you tell us about Porter?" I asked.

Uncle Mike smiled in my direction. Seeing DiNatale on the hot seat answering and evading questions was better than the Super Bowl. The limo came to a stop in traffic. A few stragglers jogged past us to catch the big game. Everyone had settled into position to watch the Super Bowl, drink in hand. Everyone, that is, except the added police and security guarding the casino entrances in response to this morning's drive-by.

DiNatale shrugged. "If I knew, Burrascano would know."

It made sense. Burrascano had intervened on Arlene's behalf. The mob's gambling boss wouldn't want us talking to the Deacon for no reason. Unless, of course, we were being set up.

"Burrascano wants to know what happened to Porter?" The mob boss had talked to Uncle Mike yesterday, but I wanted to confirm it.

"Yeah," DiNatale said.

"Our only lead to find out what happened to Porter has been presumably shot and killed," Uncle Mike said. "Killed in what appears to be a sophisticated and well-planned hit. You got the shooter, the driver, the timing with the trigger man versus the Deacon walking into or out of the casino, all within a crowded perimeter. Almost impossible for a team to pull off, unless you're in the business."

"What do you mean 'presumably'?" DiNatale growled. "But you're right, Mike. We concluded the same thing. Burrascano wants the guy or guys who did it. Wants them bad. The Deacon was a goddamn legend. When I was coming up the ranks, I spent time working for him."

"What are you doing to find the killer?" I asked.

"Burrascano wants you guys to find the killer." DiNatale's jaw worked as if he'd swallowed something foul. "We got lots of guys out there trying to find out something. Nothing so far." He slouched in his seat.

"What's that? Burrascano wants what?" Uncle Mike said, cupping one ear. "I couldn't hear you."

"Burrascano wants to hire you guys," DiNatale shouted, sitting up straight. "Usual terms, usual fees."

"Fine," Uncle Mike said. "But I'll need to confirm it all with him."

DiNatale stared hard at Uncle Mike. Uncle Mike met his stare. I managed to shut up for a change.

DiNatale reached into his coat pocket. I made a move for my gun. DiNatale saw my movement, and a smile flickered on his face. He pulled out a cell, probably a burner phone. "Burrascano's standing by for your call."

Uncle Mike raised the palm of his hand. "First, I got a couple more questions."

"Ask Burrascano," DiNatale said.

"I'm asking you," Uncle Mike said. "How do you know it's the Deacon?"

"Burrascano is satisfied. That's good enough for me," DiNatale said.

"You want us to ask him?" Uncle Mike said.

DiNatale scratched his left eyebrow as if considering how much he should tell us. "The Deacon always calls Burrascano at a set time. He never fails to call, but today he didn't call in. We can't get in touch with him. Burrascano had me take a picture of the body."

I assumed that Burrascano knew about the birthmark. Another wave of anger rose inside me. Maybe I'd held out a slim hope that the victim wasn't the Deacon.

"Who do you think did it?" Uncle Mike asked.

DiNatale shifted around in his seat. "I know a Russian by the name of Karmazin. He owed the Deacon money."

"Karmazin," Uncle Mike repeated the name. "Oh yeah, the guy who runs that broken-down casino off the Strip?"

I'd seen Karmazin at the pre-Super Bowl party, but I knew better than to tell DiNatale. Uncle Mike and I would need to gather more information before I discussed matters openly with the mobster.

DiNatale swore under his breath. "They renamed it The Kremlin Casino."

"Cute," Uncle Mike said.

"We're going to need a whole lot more than that," I said. "We need to know what the Deacon was doing in Vegas. You want us to maintain silence about the Deacon—what can I tell my client, Arlene?"

"Tell her to fuck off," DiNatale said. "If you want my opinion, it's your bullshit meeting with the Deacon that tipped off the killer."

"C'mon, Vic," Uncle Mike said. "That doesn't make sense."

"No fucking way." I began to get up out of my seat.

"Easy," Uncle Mike said, his hand grabbing at my arm. "It's just Vic letting off steam. Right, Vic?"

DiNatale smiled. "Right."

I settled back into my seat, surprised at my anger.

"The Deacon wasn't killed because of our meeting," Uncle Mike said. "We met him just last night. The Deacon had someone watching us before we met. It's clear to me the Deacon was in the habit of using every precaution to remain in hiding. He was worried about ending up like Whitey Bolger. This morning's shooting was a sophisticated operation that would take time to plan."

DiNatale bit his bottom lip like he didn't agree with what Uncle Mike had said, but wouldn't continue to argue the point. "Burrascano said to give you guys room to maneuver. He said the usual fees and terms. And he told me to call."

11

OVER THE INTERCOM, DINATALE INSTRUCTED THE LIMO driver to take the interstate and then loop back toward the Strip. The mobster then made the call to Burrascano. He straightened his shoulders and pulled at his tie. He cleared his throat and mumbled, "Yes, sir, they're here." He listened, then nodded. "I understand. Yes, I told them what you want."

I got to see the reserved, respectful DiNatale as he talked to Burrascano. I kept a straight face, but I treasured the moment.

DiNatale set the phone down on the console between him and Uncle Mike, and then DiNatale pulled out a cigarette. I slid to the edge of the leather seat. While the 49ers and the Chiefs were taking the field, the limo took the ramp to the interstate. We cruised parallel to the Strip as the lights of Vegas came on one by one.

The speaker phone emitted static and then a raspy voice.

"It's a sad day, my friends," Burrascano said.

It was almost impossible to understand Burrascano's words. He had to catch his breath to utter a few frail words, then breathed deep again. The hum of machines at his bedside droned through the speakerphone.

Burrascano had been hospitalized two years ago. His illness, still unknown to us, seemed to rage for a while and then subside. It must've returned with a vengeance, but the man's will to survive knew no bounds.

"How are you, Rosario?" Uncle Mike said.

I knew my place. "Hello, Mr. Burrascano."

"Mike, are you smoking one of those cigars of yours?"

"You bet."

"Wish I could be there. Vegas is great. A great place." He gasped for breath. "Vic taking good care of you?"

DiNatale glanced at us as if to warn us not to complain.

"We're good," Uncle Mike said.

"Okay." Burrascano was silent for a long moment. "What I'm going to tell you, no one knows."

I sucked in a wave of cigarette and cigar smoke, but didn't care. When Burrascano said, "no one else knows," I assumed he meant those outside the mob, but DiNatale's reaction told me that the mob guys also did not know.

Burrascano struggled to find his voice. "I promised him I'd never tell nobody. He wanted a new life, a reincarnation." He laughed a brief laugh, then coughed. "He was done with all that shit before."

Uncle Mike glanced my way. I wasn't sure if it was a look of impatience or bewilderment. The Deacon, the mob's legendary hitman, wanted another life.

"What I say stays between us. Understood?"

"Of course," Uncle Mike said.

DiNatale and I muttered agreement.

"Unless it involves a crime," Uncle Mike said.

"No, no, nothing like that, Mike. It's the identity of the Deacon. He uses another name."

"An alias?" Uncle Mike said.

"Yeah, an alias. The Deacon used the name Tony Zino. I don't know why. He's been Tony Zino for a long time."

"Tony Zino?" Uncle Mike snapped his fingers. "I've heard of him. He runs Team Player, right?"

"Not day-to-day no more, but he's in charge."

Team Player was a collection agency that provided cover for the mob's bookies.

Burrascano attempted to clear his sandpaper throat. "It's important we keep the Deacon out of it. Promise me that. Team Player is a legit company, or at least most of it."

"Why was the Deacon in Vegas?" I asked.

DiNatale shot me a look. Uncle Mike shook his head. I needed to stay in my place.

"Eddie?" Burrascano uttered. "I'm glad you're on top of this investigation. Zino was here to attend a conference. It will provide cover for you guys."

Uncle Mike rubbed the back of his neck. "You want us to attend a conference?"

"Yeah. Like you guys do. Tell them Zino's got the flu or some bullshit. Vic has the name of the Russian bastard who owes money to the Deacon. You can also talk to the guy who runs Team Player day-to-day."

"The usual arrangement on our fee and turning over the killer to the authorities," Uncle Mike said.

"Right. I just want the Deacon's killer." The determination in Burrascano's voice made me believe Burrascano would use every last ounce of his strength to be certain we got him. "If the fucker gets turned over to the cops and confesses, I'll give him a pass. Just get him."

What if Burrascano couldn't win the battle over his illness? What would DiNatale do? I tried not to think about that.

"Fine." Uncle Mike glanced at me. I nodded. I was all-in. "We'll look into it."

––––––

Uncle Mike and I sat in Uncle Mike's suite at Caesars. I had a cup of coffee and Uncle Mike had a beer.

I was fired up about the job for Burrascano. I wanted the Deacon's killer more than anything, but I was skeptical. "How are we going to step into Zino's shoes? The first minute I open my mouth, I'll give myself away. What do I know about Zino's collection business?"

"Take it easy," Uncle Mike said. "I've been to a lot of police union conventions in Vegas. It's disorganized. There's an exhibit hall where people meet and drink. Then you head into the casino and gamble and drink. We can meet people on an informal basis, buy them drinks. It's perfect."

Informal discussions talking shop with other people well-versed in the business only increased my anxiety. "This is nuts."

"I never told you, but I worked at Team Player part-time for a few years."

"You did?"

"Don't look at me like that. I didn't take any bets. I didn't even know the place had any mob connections. I was trying to make a few bucks to make ends meet. I'm an honest cop, remember?"

"What did you do?"

"I worked the phones. I called to collect on past-due department store accounts placed with Team Player. I'd talk with folks who owed money on their washer and dryer or TV, and arrange payments. I was pretty good at it, too. It's a lot like talking to a perp. Instead of describing the charges and the amount of serious jail time to get the perp talking, you tell a debtor about how Team Player will seek a judgment and then garnish their wages. Then you listen. They all have a story. You treat their problem like it's your problem and tell them that we've got to work together to solve it. With the extra money, I was able to keep the bar afloat and pay a chunk of tuition for the kids."

"You're a jack of all trades," I said. "Did you ever meet Zino?"

"No, I worked on the collection floor. The executives hung out upstairs. My manager used to shit bricks every Monday for the performance meetings. I forget his name now. The guy was a chain smoker who'd been there for years and thought he'd be fired any minute. We were in competition with another agency across town for the department store placements. Team Player was paid a contingency on what was collected and, in turn, I got a small percentage on what I collected in addition to my hourly. The place was high stress, but compared to being a cop, it seemed like a walk in the park."

We'd been given the name of the guy who ran Team Player's daily operations. "How about O'Rourke? Ever meet him?"

"Nope. Like I said, I haven't worked at Team Player for a long time. They were just starting to use computers. We used a ledger card for each account and made hand-written notes on that."

"Back in the dark ages?"

"Yeah. File cabinets and witchcraft." Uncle Mike laughed. "Let's give O'Rourke a call. Maybe that will help give us an idea of what we can expect at the conference."

"No one at a collection agency conference will be involved with the Deacon and his murder," I said. "It's a dead end."

"You wanted to know more about the Deacon, right? Haven't I taught you anything all these years? You can't jump to conclusions."

He was right as usual, which pissed me off.

Uncle Mike pulled out the burner phone we'd received from DiNatale and dialed O'Rourke back in Chicago. Uncle Mike put it on speaker.

"O'Rourke," a man said, answering on the first ring.

"Mike O'Connell."

"Yes, I was told to expect your call." O'Rourke's voice was rigid, like a man coming to attention.

"We wanted to talk things over."

"Anything you need, Mr. O'Connell."

"Call me Mike. Eddie, my nephew, is here with me."

"I've heard of you guys."

"To start—"

"Mr. Zino has the flu, sir. I can confirm Mike O'Connell and Edward O'Connell are employed at Team Player, but that's all I can say. Have a good day." O'Rourke chuckled.

Uncle Mike laughed. "That's what you'll tell anyone who calls?"

"Yup. And rest assured any such call will be directed to me, just like any call to confirm employment. Look, Mr. O'Connell, you need to know where I stand." O'Rourke hesitated.

What was the extent of O'Rourke's involvement in Team Player's activities? Was he involved with the mob? What had Burrascano or DiNatale told him? He hadn't mentioned the murder of Zino.

Uncle Mike sipped from his bottle of Budweiser. "Go ahead."

"I'm an ex-con. Mr. Zino hired me when nobody, and I mean nobody, would give me a chance. I've worked for Team Player and Mr. Zino going on fifteen years—good years. There was never a question about my past when it came time to consider promotion. Mr. Zino never held my prison gig over my head. He always treated me like anyone else."

"I appreciate hearing that," Uncle Mike said.

"I did time for manslaughter. I'd been charged with murder, so I lucked out. It happened during the commission of a burglary, but I didn't kill the guy." O'Rourke's voice didn't waver.

"You understand why we're calling?" Uncle Mike asked, growing impatient.

"I do, but you also need to know what Mr. Zino means to me and others around here. What Team Player means to us. You might be counting on me, but we will be counting on you."

"Rest assured we'll keep the best interests of Team Player in mind at all times," Uncle Mike said.

"Thank you. Now, what do you need?"

It was what we wanted to hear.

12

LATER THAT NIGHT, I DROVE A RENTAL CAR DOWN THE STRIP following DiNatale's limo. Uncle Mike and I had discussed the risk. If I got caught following DiNatale, it might jeopardize our entire investigation. The mob's trust in us had been built over the years through numerous investigations, but that trust could crumble with one careless move. DiNatale would make it his job to retaliate to the fullest extent possible.

At the moment, we had what we wanted—the chance to find the Deacon's killer and get justice—and Burrascano would get what he wanted—the Deacon's killer. But we were forced to take chances. We were like those little fish swimming alongside the shark. Each respected the other, and each profited off the other, but it was the little fish who were taking all the chances and hoping like hell there were plenty of other fish to eat.

I slammed on the brakes. A late-night Super Bowl partier decided anytime was a good time to cross the boulevard, DiNatale's limo jetted ahead.

I cussed under my breath at the stumbling gambler, then accelerated.

Burrascano told us he needed to find the Deacon's killer before he could let anyone in the mob know the Deacon had been killed. The Deacon held that kind of exalted status.

The game was on. Uncle Mike and I had been given the Deacon's most well-guarded secret—his alias and why he was in Vegas.

I'd read through the websites about the conference and about Team Player and found out there was a whole lot more to the collection stuff than what Uncle Mike had described. O'Rourke had given us some information on certain clients we would need to schmooze on behalf of Team Player and other people we should avoid.

I had given Arlene a made-up story about the Deacon requesting a delay, which seemed believable enough. The Deacon might've requested a delay if he wasn't lying on a slab, his face scrambled by his killer into an abstract painting.

The casinos were packed. People cheered. It had been a long day of partying for the Super Bowl. The losers would need to wait another year.

KC fans were still celebrating. I'd called Nicole to congratulate her on the hundred grand she'd won. Would she play Scullion heads up? She was working on it, she'd said.

Nicole would need other pros to back her to take on Scullion's massive bankroll. In return for investing in Nicole's bankroll, each pro would receive a corresponding percentage of what she ultimately won. The pros liked the action—it was almost as good as playing the high roller themselves, and almost as profitable.

I had also won on KC and had considered a trip down to the sports book to parlay my winnings on whatever horse races might be running on a Sunday night or make my inaugural trip to the craps table. But then I reconsidered. I had all the action I needed with the investigation.

DiNatale's limo took a left toward The Kremlin Casino. Karmazin was out of bounds for DiNatale and his people, since the agreement with Burrascano required that Uncle Mike and I have room to maneuver.

The limo drove into the parking garage behind The Kremlin. A gate made me take a ticket, so I'd need to pay on the way out. A sign said to park at your own risk, followed by a block of fine print I couldn't read. I assumed it absolved the owner of "any and all liability." That meant no cameras, little lighting, and lots of trash in the stairwells and elevator.

My headlights led me through the shadows to the second floor. The limo had come to a stop on the floor above, so I hunted for a spot. I was lucky to find a parking place on the other side of an oversized pickup. I parked the car and got out.

I was going to head into the casino and wait for DiNatale and his entourage, but the limo continued to idle above me. I heard voices. I hiked halfway up the ramp and ducked down between some parked cars. Through the crossbeams of the structure, I could see the wheels of the limo twenty yards away and guys standing around. A couple of cars had entered the garage and searched for open slots, drowning out any conversation between DiNatale and his men.

I smelled their cigarettes. They were waiting for something. A meeting with Karmazin?

Earlier, I'd looked up Karmazin and some of his exploits on the internet. He'd been charged for various crimes, including drug dealing, illegal gambling, and murder, but never convicted. There was a picture of him smiling at the opening of The Kremlin, a joint that seemed to change owners every year.

I was about to head back to my vehicle when some people exited the parking lot elevator. Loud voices and swearing ensued. I held my ground. Burrascano had reiterated that it was imperative we keep the Deacon's murder a secret.

The feet within my field of vision shuffled around and they weren't waltzing. I slipped around a couple of cars for a better look. As I did, I heard DiNatale swearing and someone gasping. Punches were being thrown.

When I got to a better vantage point, I saw DiNatale's boys working some guy over.

"Never —" DiNatale yelled. I couldn't make out the rest. If DiNatale planned to accuse Karmazin of the murder, he'd have to disclose the fact that the Deacon had been murdered. DiNatale's breach of Burrascano's order could provide us with some much-needed leverage if DiNatale caused trouble for us.

The sucker whimpered and pleaded. "Stop. I'll do it."

The sucker's chin hung down. One of DiNatale's men had pinned the victim's arms back. They hit the victim again in the gut, but didn't follow through with an uppercut. It was a polite beating.

Then the sucker's face came into view—it was Landis Tanner, another person I'd met at the pre-Super Bowl party.

What the hell? I heard footsteps below. Someone was in the garage on the floor below me, watching me. I could sense it.

I had to get out of there.

As I moved to my car, noises echoed from below. A car door opened. My heart pounded. If it was one of DiNatale's guys, he'd call out. Nothing. Who could it be?

I got into my vehicle, turned around, and drove out of the garage. But I saw nothing suspicious.

13

THE NEXT MORNING, UNCLE MIKE AND I TOOK THE escalator up to the conference floor and stepped off to the side.

"First, we need to register," Uncle Mike said, "and then we need to find out where they keep the coffee and the Danish."

"I've been thinking," I said. "Buying and selling debt creeps me out. When my gambling debts were hanging over my head, I'd stay up nights wondering how I was going to pay them or if some mob guy would decide to break my arm just to hear the snap, crackle, pop."

"This is the Debt Exchange. All the debt gets funneled here to be shopped around, bought and sold. Debt is a business."

"It still sucks."

"Okay, Mr. Clean, what about the tobacco companies who say their research shows smoking doesn't cause cancer, the oil companies gouging us at the pumps, the health care companies forcing doctors to order tests to see how high they can run up your bill, drug companies jacking up the price of a lifesaving drug, the insurance companies denying coverage—"

"I get it."

"Debt is just another business. No one is looking out for the little guy. A government agency says they're looking out for us and that's all bullshit. The head of the government agency in charge of enforcement leaves so he can lobby on behalf of the companies he was supposed to regulate. The whole thing is a racket."

He had a point, but there was simmering anger beneath the surface of Uncle Mike's talk on behalf of the "little guy." "I hope you can get this out of your system before we go to the meetings," I said. "We need to keep a low profile."

"Maybe we do and maybe we don't. We won't learn anything if we don't stir the pot. But remember, the clients are the most important thing. When I worked at Team Player, we were always bending over backwards for that department store. According to O'Rourke, Team Player gets credit card debt directly from banks to collect."

"I know. We need to keep the welfare of Team Player in mind." We faced a balancing act at the conference. We had to stir things up, yet keep clients happy.

We got into a short line at the registration desk. Attendees had their cell phones out and appeared nervous and uptight. Based on the nametags I had glanced at, people were here from all over the country. According to the conference website, there would be hundreds of attendees. This was not the convention of party animals that Uncle Mike had described.

Uncle Mike and I reached the head of the line. "We're from Team Player Collection Agency," Uncle Mike told the registrar.

The woman looked up at us from her computer screen. "You are? Where is Mr. Zino?"

Uncle Mike looked at me.

"Mr. Zino won't be able to make it this year," I said.

"Oh, I hope nothing's wrong."

"A case of the flu," Uncle Mike said.

"Mr. Zino is so nice," the registrar gushed. "He's been coming to this conference for years. I hope he gets better soon. You know my dad got the flu and at his age it became serious. As a precautionary measure, he went into the hospital." She went on with the story and we listened respectfully. Her father had a three-day stay in the hospital and recovered.

When she finished, Uncle Mike said, "Mr. Zino is in the hospital as well. We had to fill in at the last minute."

We had taken the added precaution of asking Burrascano to take care of Zino's admission to a local hospital. DiNatale knew a Vegas doctor who could be trusted. One of DiNatale's boys would occupy the hospital room under the name of Zino with strict instructions not to talk or meet with anyone.

The registrar shook her head. "I hope Mr. Zino recovers soon." She turned toward me. "Mr. Jalbert, the president of the organization, asked me to let him know when Mr. Zino arrived." She pronounced Jalbert, "Jall-berr."

"What does Mr. Jalbert want?" Uncle Mike asked.

"I don't know."

We finished the registration process and obtained our ID badges and lanyard. As we stepped away with our bags of conference materials, a tall woman in a business suit who had been standing nearby during our registration process stopped us.

"Excuse me." She smiled and handed me a business card. "I understand you're from Team Player. I'm Shelly Urban from Seamless Dataminers."

I introduced myself and Uncle Mike.

She pulled a folder from her carryall bag and then placed her bag on the floor. "You said Tony Zino isn't here?"

I explained about the flu and that we were filling in for him.

"That's a shame." Her smile had been replaced by a sneer.

"Is anything wrong?"

She took out a stack of papers and thrust them at me. "Unpaid invoices. A large overdue balance owed to us. More than six months past due to Seamless Dataminers."

I took the stack of papers. "I'm afraid I'm not familiar with this."

Uncle Mike looked over my shoulder as I leafed through the stack. The total past due was twenty-one thousand dollars, accruing a fat eighteen percent per annum. Was Team Player one of those companies that stiffed their creditors?

"I'm a collection manager at Team Player so I don't know about it either," Uncle Mike said.

"I was afraid of that," she said. "Can you check with them? I'd like to get something worked out while we're at the conference, if possible."

"We'll certainly discuss it with them, Ms. Urban. Can I keep this copy of the invoices?" I asked.

"Yes, those are for you."

"We have a busy conference schedule," Uncle Mike said, "so we can't promise anything."

"Unfortunately, Mr. Zino doesn't return our calls. In fact, no one from Team Player has returned our calls. We've had a good working relationship for ten years. My company is concerned."

"I suspect there's a good reason why they're not calling you back," Uncle Mike said.

Some people had congregated around us and stopped and stared. It was the last thing Uncle Mike and I needed. Most of them seemed to know Ms. Urban.

"Seamless Dataminers provided skip tracing information in good faith," she said, loud enough for everyone around us to hear. "Just let me know what Team Player says."

"We'll look into it," I said.

"What's going on here?" A middle-aged man walked up. He wore a cream-colored sport coat, a red knit golf shirt and black pants. A nametag hung down from a lanyard around his neck. The nametag had several colored strips added to the bottom of the nametag, including a red strip that identified him as a "speaker." It was Jalbert, the Debt Exchange president.

Urban turned to him. "Mr. Jalbert, so nice to see you. I was just about to—"

"About to do what?" he demanded.

She grabbed her bag. "Later." She yanked the straps of the bag over her shoulder with a sigh of disgust and strutted off.

14

JALBERT WATCHED URBAN WALK AWAY AND THEN GAVE US
an engaging smile. His brown hair was dyed and styled to fluff
up the thin hair on top. He was a few inches shorter than me,
stocky, and despite the immaculate casual business attire and
confident expression, something struck me. There was a
flaw—a wide half-inch scar at the corner of his mouth. It was
the kind of scar you got from a fist to the mouth. It upended
his near perfect salesman smile. I wondered who hit him and
why.

I stuck out my hand. "Eddie O'Connell."

He shook it. "Stefan Jalbert."

Uncle Mike shook hands with Jalbert as well.

"I understand Mr. Zino isn't here? The registrar pointed
you out to me. I'm not happy with Ms. Urban. She's been
bugging people all morning with her list of receivables. I
assume Mr. Zino talked to you about the agenda and our

disagreement. Are you going to give Mr. Zino's speech?" Jalbert studied his fingernails and then looked up at me.

I didn't like the casual way Jalbert said "Mr. Zino isn't here," as if he knew Zino wouldn't be here. Was I going to give Zino's speech? Uncle Mike gave me a quick nod. If Zino had a disagreement and was going to give a speech about it, I'd play along. Uncle Mike and I were stepping into Zino's shoes. It was time to stir the pot.

"Yes, we're filling in for Mr. Zino. I'll be giving the speech."

"You're up to speed on the issues?" he asked with a tilt of his head as he bit at the tip of a fingernail.

We hadn't been here ten minutes and already we were confronted with "issues." Jalbert wasn't happy.

Uncle Mike cleared his throat. "We're in touch with Mr. Zino, but we'd be glad to hear your take on the issues."

"Why don't we step over to one of these empty tables where we can talk?" Jalbert led us to a table. We sat close to the entrance of the exhibit hall. People ran into the exhibit hall while others walked out with a cup of coffee. Many stood near the windows to make phone calls. We were in the middle of the conference rush hour.

Jalbert slipped into a chair with his back against the wall. Attendees tried to get a look at my nametag or Uncle Mike's nametag. We were new on the scene, but here we were sitting down with the Debt Exchange president.

"Let me tell you a little more about myself." Jalbert leaned in across the table, talking fast as if he was trying to sell us something. "I'm President of the Debt Exchange, but I also run my own collection agency in Michigan–Vortex Collections. We're based in Michigan and we're expanding into other states. You'll have to excuse me, Eddie, Mike. I'm not familiar with your positions at Team Player. I can't recall if Zino had mentioned either of you before."

"I'm not surprised," I said. "I'm a recent hire. Just got my MBA. I was in Operations and now I'm working in Client Development." I tried to sound upbeat. I was supposed to be the new Team Player recruit, anxious to learn more about the business.

"I'm surprised Mr. Zino hasn't mentioned me before," Uncle Mike said. "Those of us in the trenches never get the credit we've got coming. I've been on the floor for years, one of Team Player's collection managers."

I was almost convinced that Uncle Mike was a collection manager at Team Player. I hoped I'd been half as convincing when I explained my role. Thank God both of us were missing in action when it came to social media. There was no way Jalbert could check up on us.

According to O'Rourke, there was little chance that Jalbert would want to check up on us. "I attended a conference once with Mr. Zino. I was invisible," O'Rourke told us. Since Mr. Zino usually attended these conferences alone, he'd explained, a recent hire filling in at the last-minute makes sense. When we asked O'Rourke about a collection manager at the conference, he laughed. "In that crowd, a collection manager is the lowest life form, don't worry."

"We wouldn't get far in this business without collection managers," Jalbert said. He turned back toward me as if I was the one with the decision-making power. "It's not easy to move from Operations to Client Development, Eddie. They are two different parts of the company. At Vortex, in order to comply with government regulations and client audit requirements, almost a third of our staff is now dedicated to compliance."

"In grad school, I had classes in government regulations, but they didn't tell us about the cost." I enjoyed watching Jalbert sweat. I'd be a tough sell, in part, because I had no clue what was going on.

Jalbert smiled and nodded as if we'd bonded. "How do clients expect us to make money? Vortex is not a charitable organization. Clients went to a 'pay for performance' model. They cut our rates, explaining that the bonus based on performance would make up the difference. Then when we worked our asses off and hit the bonus, they raised the goals. When we hit those goals, they raised them again. When we finally hit those nearly impossible goals, they dropped the bonus program altogether, leaving us with the lower rates."

I nodded along like a guy who'd graduated at the top of his class. It sounded like he was getting screwed. The clients reduced the amount he was being paid, yet demanded more and more. This was MBA first year class 101.

That was the problem with these undercover jobs Uncle Mike and I did for Burrascano. I had to absorb a lot of information fast and fake my way through it at the same time.

Uncle Mike snorted. "Try getting your collectors motivated month after month to hit those bullshit goals. They want to spit in your face."

I was glad Uncle Mike commented, so I didn't have to.

"Right," Jalbert nodded. "That's why my deal with Globex Bank works for everyone. You see, we buy the debt from Globex Bank direct and work our own accounts."

The commercials for the Globex Bank credit card ran every five minutes on TV. Jalbert's deal must be huge.

Jalbert studied me and then explained it again to win me over. "All the small players come together and pool their money to buy the Globex delinquent accounts and each of us becomes our own boss. Instead of charged-off accounts being placed with us for collection by Globex, we own the accounts. We each cover our own geographic area. We're no longer subject to outrageous client demands. What's wrong with that?"

I couldn't find anything wrong with the Globex deal, but I assumed Zino was against it, and that was why the speech had drawn Jalbert's attention. "Tony makes a good argument as well," I said.

Uncle Mike hunched forward. "We're supposed to talk with people and get their opinions and then talk to Mr. Zino."

If everyone kept talking, we'd learn more, and that was our goal.

"Fair enough, gentlemen," Jalbert said, slapping his hands face down on the table to signal the end of the discussion. "That's an excellent idea. I'm giving a dinner tonight at Felipe's at seven and you're invited. Ingrid

Lundstrom from Globex will be there. I'm sure her input will be invaluable." He looked at his watch. We all stood up and shook hands.

"We'll be there tonight," Uncle Mike said. "At seven."

———

We went into the exhibit hall and found a coffee station. The exhibit hall was bigger than two full basketball courts lying side-by-side. Five or six rows of ten-by-ten-foot booths extended the length of the room. The booths were manned by companies offering everything from collection software to process services. Uncle Mike and I each got a cup and found a remote corner far removed from the flow of attendees.

"How about that?" Uncle Mike said. "Felipe's."

"Have you eaten there before?" I asked.

"Hell, no. I don't like to piss my money away."

"Let's hope Jalbert is buying. Did you see the way people were looking at us? The president of the whole thing sits down and wants to talk 'issues.'"

"You did good, Eddie. You told him you'd give the speech, and that Zino makes a good argument. I loved that. You made Jalbert sweat and got us an invite to dinner. Maybe we can find out what the hell is going on."

"Yeah, but now I'm committed to giving a speech I don't know anything about. Why didn't O'Rourke tell us about the speech?"

Uncle Mike sipped from his coffee. "Let's call O'Rourke later. Maybe he knows. Globex Bank is huge. How much do these agencies make buying debt for pennies and then collecting the full balance?"

Uncle Mike took another sip of coffee. "I must be working too hard. Who is our first meeting with?" He dug into his bag of conference stuff we'd received at registration.

I pulled out the business card handed to me by the woman with the unpaid invoices. "Let's watch for Ms. Urban. Here we are at a collection conference about debt and what's the first thing that happens? We get beat up over a past due debt."

"We'll have to ask O'Rourke about that, too." Uncle Mike had pulled out our agenda. "I didn't like what the registrar said about the flu. That going into the hospital is a 'precautionary measure.' We'll need to work on that."

"Yeah, we don't want people trying to contact Zino. I hate to think about our fake Zino posted at the hospital actually talking to somebody."

Uncle Mike nodded and then read from the agenda. "Hey, here is Zino's speech. It's on the schedule for Wednesday, right after the keynote speech."

"Damn."

"Hopefully, everyone will be too hungover by then to listen to your bullshit. Hey, you ever hear of this guy giving the keynote?"

I took the copy of the schedule from Uncle Mike. "Eliot Scullion is giving the keynote? That's the guy who wants to play Nicole heads-up."

"Never heard of him."

"I'm not surprised. He's way out of your league, he's got billions. He bet a million on the 49ers."

"Good."

I got a chuckle out of Uncle Mike's comment. "Scullion's buddy, Tanner, also bet a million on the 49ers."

Uncle Mike laughed. "That's the guy you saw last night, right?"

"Yeah."

"We could ask Vic why he was giving Tanner a beating."

"You know where that would get us," I said.

"Nowhere. They want us to solve their murders, but when it comes to mob business, they turn mute." Uncle Mike shook his head. "We've made a deal with the devil again. But what choice did we have?"

No choice. "The way Jalbert gave us his sales pitch about the Globex Bank deal makes me think there's a whole lot at stake."

"I got the same idea. Zino must've fouled up Jalbert's deal, and this speech must mean trouble for Jalbert."

"You think Zino's opposition to the deal could lead to murder?" I asked.

"People get killed for a lot less."

"Wouldn't that be something? The Deacon gets killed as Zino, his reincarnated self."

"Jeesus, that would be something. If so, we've got a lot more to worry about than your damn speech. The minute we tell our 'Zino has the flu' story, the killer will know we're lying."

"If the killer is Jalbert, we're already on his list. He may've invited us to dinner to see how much we know." I fully understood the dangerous game we played. If and when the killer came after us, the killer risked exposure, and we would be risking our lives. It was a high stakes game of cat and mouse and we had to stay a step ahead.

This was the way Uncle Mike and I worked. We had limited time to find the killer, and during every minute of that short span of time, we had to put as much pressure as possible on our suspects. We weren't the police, but we adhered to a code of our own. No, we didn't advise anyone of their rights and no, we didn't identify ourselves. But on the other hand, we couldn't ask questions as police detectives. We lacked the authority to intimidate simply by probing and asking questions or pointing out how the suspect's story had changed this time around. We played imposters, and we pushed the limits until the killer blinked.

Uncle Mike pointed towards the exits. "It looks like everyone is headed out for the meetings. Who's first on our list?"

15

FROM O'ROURKE, WE HAD RECEIVED A LIST OF THE
informal meetings set up by Zino with various companies at
the conference on behalf of Team Player. Our first such
meeting was with Jennifer Hadlow of Gusher Debt Brokerage.
We located her in one of the small meeting rooms off the main
floor. Before we walked down the hall and knocked on the
door, I pulled out my notes.

"According to O'Rourke, Team Player has done a lot of
business over the years with Gusher Debt Brokerage," I told
Uncle Mike in a low voice. "Zino bought debt from Gusher
and then collected on the accounts at Team Player. O'Rourke
says Team Player has a good relationship with Gusher."

"Sounds easy enough," Uncle Mike said. "Let's see what
Ms. Hadlow has for sale."

"Maybe she knows more about the issues Jalbert was
talking about."

"Right," Uncle Mike said.

The meeting with Gusher might sound easy, but we couldn't assume that any meeting would proceed smoothly. Not only did we need to watch for a killer's reaction to our "Zino has the flu" story, we had to think about the welfare of Team Player. Burrascano was concerned about Team Player, a legit company that provided cover for his illegal bookies. If we screwed up the interests of Team Player, Burrascano would hear about it, and he might pull the plug on our investigation before we started.

We knocked on the closed door.

"C'mon in," a voice called.

We walked into the room.

A woman stood when we entered and gave us a warm smile. "Team Player?" She glanced at our nametags. "Where is Tony?" She was a thin woman in a blue business suit with designer glasses. Her silver hair was pinned back in a fashionable wave and her glasses hung down from a chain around her neck. Other than her laptop and a stack of papers on the table surrounded by chairs, the room was white walls and a white ceiling with bright lights.

We explained how we were filling in for Zino and what our jobs were at Team Player. Uncle Mike and I slipped into our respective roles as we introduced ourselves to Jennifer Hadlow.

"You'll have to give me the name of the hospital. He'll be expecting my call," Hadlow said.

Uncle Mike didn't hesitate. "Sure, I'll get it for you, but I don't think he's allowed to take any calls."

"Of course. That's silly of me. Let me know when he's feeling better."

"Just between us," Uncle Mike said. "Mr. Zino has suffered complications from the flu. He has pneumonia."

Uncle Mike and I decided to make Zino's condition something worse than the flu to discourage people from checking up on our cover story. We would add that what we said about Zino was "just between us." That way, we'd convey the serious nature of Zino's illness and keep people from making inquiries.

"I'm so sorry," she said. "Tell him he's in my prayers."

She peered into her laptop and stopped to wipe away a tear. "Tony Zino and I have worked together for years, but I don't know what to tell you. Business has dried up. 2ndBetOnDebt has cornered the market on buying debt."

"How did they do that?" Uncle Mike asked.

"The Second Bet outfit buys the debt from the banks at unheard of high prices," she said.

O'Rourke had told us the majority of the debt being sold by the banks was charged off consumer credit card debt and sold for pennies on the dollar. He'd mentioned that Team Player was getting accounts from 2ndBetOnDebt to collect, but Team Player didn't own the accounts.

"How can Second Bet afford the high prices?" Uncle Mike asked.

"That's the secret everyone would like to know," Hadlow said.

"It sounds like an old-fashioned industry take over," Uncle Mike said.

"You hit the nail on the head," Hadlow said. "Then we've got one of the biggest banks, Globex, planning to sell all of their debt to Jalbert. Second Bet is not happy about that. They buy a lot from Globex. Plus, Second Bet only places their accounts with a few select agencies."

"If you're not part of Jalbert's group or one of these select agencies working with Second Bet, what have you got?" Uncle Mike asked.

"Not much. People come to me anxious to find something to buy," Hadlow said, putting on her glasses and checking her computer. "What can I tell them? I don't have a lot of good stuff left to sell. I had some sweet tertiary stuff from a bank in Omaha, but it went fast— small balance accounts that everyone wants."

I wasn't sure what Hadlow meant by "tertiary," but before I could ask, Uncle Mike asked something that seemed more important.

"Why would Globex sell to Jalbert and not to Second Bet?" Uncle Mike asked.

"That's the question everyone asks. Globex and Jalbert have shaken up the entire Debt Exchange membership. I'm not sure who's a member of Jalbert's group and who's not. You'd have to ask Tony. Every time I talk to somebody, the group changes. My debt pipeline has run dry. If I had half the inventory I used to have, I'd be able to retire." The tired debt broker took off her glasses and rubbed the bridge of her nose.

"You said that some people are part of Jalbert's group and then they aren't?" I asked. "Why is that?"

Hadlow shrugged. "I was talking to some of the guys, friends of mine, who are also Tony's friends. They run agencies in other parts of the country and were part of the Globex deal originally. They'd planned to go in with Jalbert, and everybody would receive a flow of accounts from Globex based on their territory."

"It seems like a sweet deal to me," Uncle Mike said. "We understand Zino is against the deal. What happened?"

She tapped her fingers on the table. "It's not like the old days where people worked together and everyone made money. These days, everyone tries to undercut everyone else. Jalbert is firing agencies and then sets up shop in their state. He has a bullshit explanation that their collection numbers aren't good enough and he's acting on behalf of the bank, but I'm not so sure. To top it off, Jalbert hires away their employees."

Hadlow clearly didn't approve of the new ways where everyone stabbed each other in the back. I liked her.

"So Jalbert is working to carve out his own empire," Uncle Mike said.

"Jalbert has Lundstrom, the Globex Bank rep, in his hip pocket," Hadlow said.

The Second Bet outfit was taking over the industry and Jalbert was fighting them. One monopoly was fighting another wannabe monopoly, with me and Uncle Mike in the middle. We could play one against the other.

Uncle Mike rubbed his forehead as if bank logic made no sense to him. "If Globex sells the accounts to Jalbert and his group, why would Globex care about the collection numbers of these other companies in the Jalbert group?"

"Lundstrom says it's about partnership between Globex and each agency. Not only will Globex sell exclusively to the agency in that territory, but the chosen agency will handle the bank's forward flow."

A low whistle escaped Uncle Mike's lips. "Forward flow—those are the fresh accounts that aren't charged off yet. Those are very lucrative for a collection agency."

"Globex demands that the same agency that handles their forward flow must also be a part of Jalbert's group. Otherwise, Globex has to send auditors to two places and they don't want to absorb that additional cost."

"It seems that Jalbert is in the catbird seat on his power play," Uncle Mike said.

"I wouldn't be surprised if Jalbert doesn't try to hire both of you and open in Chicago." Hadlow looked at each of us as if to measure our potential as traitors to Zino.

I liked the way Hadlow tried to judge our loyalty. She seemed to be on Zino and Team Player's side in all of this.

"A lot of people are counting on Zino. I assume one of you will give the speech? These people rely on the accounts placed by Globex Bank to drive collections."

"Eddie will give the speech," Uncle Mike said. "Don't worry."

There was no way I would be getting out of this damn speech.

"We're all worried," she sighed. "I'm not sure what Zino can say to stop Jalbert's Globex deal or Second Bet.

Tony is the type who could lead everyone down the right path. He could rally us."

"We'll do our best to make him proud," Uncle Mike said.

I liked Uncle Mike's optimism. I only wished I could share it. I imagined myself standing up in front of hundreds of attendees, their eyes locked on me. What was in that speech? How did Zino plan to rally the collection companies against Jalbert or the Second Bet outfit? Uncle Mike and I had to come up with something more definite.

"Dang it, it just won't be the same conference for me without Tony," she said. "We usually sit around the sports book. Tony has some good tips on horses that are running back in Chicago. I don't know where he gets his information, but we always seem to get a winner or two." She laughed.

I could imagine where Zino got his information on the horses, but I didn't say anything. The Deacon would have had plenty of ties to what was going on behind the scenes at Thornton Racetrack.

"I know Tony would want me to sub for him," Uncle Mike said. "Why don't we meet later and tip a few?"

Uncle Mike was at the top of his game. He realized that Hadlow provided good information on the ever-widening dispute between the two key power players. It was also clear that Zino had been right in the middle of this rift and there was a lot at stake for all of them. Hadlow's continued input would be critical for us.

"I'd like that. I'd like that fine," Hadlow said. "Like I said, I'm not as popular as I used to be. With Second Bet and Jalbert in the picture, no one takes me out to dinner. A lot of changes from the old days."

———

Uncle Mike and I decided to meet in his suite for lunch. We needed to talk things over with O'Rourke. I stood in line to order lunch while Uncle Mike went upstairs to call Aunt Maureen and check on things at O'Connell's. I needed to give Arlene my daily update on our ongoing negotiations with the Deacon. What could I tell her? I also needed to get in touch with Marini for some basketball picks. Nicole would be taping her show tomorrow afternoon.

I got back with the bag of food from the deli and Uncle Mike let me in.

"I'll spread the stuff out on the table," I said. "Everything good back in Chicago?"

"Just the usual fires. O'Connell's had a record day for the Super Bowl."

"Sorry I missed it." I tried not to think about all the fun I'd missed.

"What have you got?" Uncle Mike asked. "I'm starved. I thought they'd have a choice of pastries with the coffee downstairs, but they had nothing. At our conventions, they wouldn't dare run out."

"I bet they didn't. For your police conventions, they probably had semi-trucks loaded with pastries." I had an iced tea, and I'd gotten Uncle Mike a Diet Coke.

Uncle Mike sat down at the table. "What's this? You bought us salads? I thought I told you to get me a pastrami on rye?"

"Sorry. Aunt Maureen made me promise."

"I should've known you two would be plotting behind my back. Where's the dressing?"

I handed him a couple of packets of Italian dressing.

"Jeez. No Thousand Island?"

"Do they even make that anymore?"

"At least you could get Ranch. Damn."

After listening to Uncle Mike gripe about his salad through lunch, I was ready for O'Rourke.

We called again on the burner phone we'd gotten from DiNatale. Uncle Mike put the phone on speaker and placed it in the middle of the table.

"O'Rourke," O'Rourke answered as before. "What can I do for you, Mr. O'Connell?"

"Hi Pat, how you doing? We've had an interesting morning, and we wanted to get your take on some issues," Uncle Mike said.

"I'll help as much as I can."

"First thing this morning we were met by a woman named Shelly Urban from Seamless Dataminers about a past due bill owed by Team Player," Uncle Mike said.

"Yes, I can tell you about that," O'Rourke said. "Mr. Zino said if I ever paid that invoice, he'd cut my nuts off."

"What was the dispute about?"

"Seamless gave us crappy information. We contracted for skip tracing data on the accounts we have with bad addresses and bad phone numbers. We have some skip tracing software in-house, but we don't have the time or manpower to do in-depth skip tracing."

"Why did you use Seamless in the first place?"

"We've been using them for years," O'Rourke said. "They have all the databases and focus on skip tracing full time. This was the first time they failed us."

"Why did they drop the ball?" I asked.

"I'm not sure. Seamless tells us the accounts are just crappy. But I cherry picked a number of them and did my own skip tracing work. They simply didn't do their job."

"What did they say to that?" I asked.

"They denied it," O'Rourke said.

Uncle Mike cleared his throat. "We met Mr. Jalbert, the president of the Debt Exchange."

"Jalbert and Mr. Zino had a falling out," O'Rourke said, eager to offer information. "Team Player was supposed to get all this Globex Bank business through Jalbert's network. After our fiasco with Seamless and our failure to meet the goal for Globex, Jalbert told us that Globex wanted to go in a different direction."

"So Globex fired Team Player?" Uncle Mike asked

"That's correct."

"We're meeting with 2ndBetOnDebt this afternoon," I said. "Anything special we should watch for?"

"You need to come through for us with them. We get Globex accounts through Second Bet as well as a lot of other placements."

"We heard that only a few select agencies get business from them," I said.

"Yes, we're one of the few. Yesterday, Linda Roberts at Second Bet told me that Team Player is on the verge of being suspended. Mr. Zino has had arguments with Ms.

Roberts in the past. I'd talk to Mr. Zino about it, but as you know, Mr. Zino has serious health issues and can't be disturbed under any circumstances."

"We'll do everything we can," I said.

"I don't mind telling you, I'm worried," O'Rourke said. "Mr. Zino told me not to worry about anything and to hire more staff, and that's what I've been doing, but I really don't see it. We've lost the Jalbert network for Globex, and we're on the ropes with Second Bet. Mr. Zino said he had some irons in the fire and that he's giving a speech that will handle things, but I'm not so sure."

"I plan to give the speech," I said.

"What's it about? If I may ask," O'Rourke said.

I looked at Uncle Mike. He mouthed a variety of cuss words and gave me a "what the fuck" look.

What was the speech about? O'Rourke was my one hope to bail me out. Maybe I could dance a jig or tell a few jokes when I stood up in front of that crowd on Wednesday. "Zino told us to keep it confidential."

"Okay. I hear you guys are the experts, so I'm probably worrying about nothing. I'll continue ramping up, but I hope things go well at your meeting with Second Bet. I'm counting on you. We need the business."

We hung up.

I looked at Uncle Mike. "You know any good speechwriters?"

"It's you and me. We're the speechwriters. Let's write it right now."

"Good idea. We can always modify it later if we need to."

Uncle Mike pulled out a pad of paper. "Everybody seems to know Zino. His opinion must carry a lot of weight, or Jalbert wouldn't be so concerned."

"We know that Jalbert is setting up shop in certain states after a collection agency is fired by Globex Bank."

"And stealing their employees," Uncle Mike said, jotting down some notes. "This reminds me of a union election we had a few years ago. All these rumors were circulating through the rank and file about one of the candidates for president. He was a bum and everyone knew it. But it took one of our old respected members to get up and say what was on everyone's mind. He had the courage to shove all the dirty laundry in everybody's face. If not for his speech, the bum would've been reelected."

"Perfect. We need to approach it the same way. Jalbert is a bum. Globex Bank needs to wake up."

Uncle Mike scribbled. "This damn speech is writing itself."

16

OUR MEETING WITH 2NDBETONDEBT WAS SCHEDULED FOR two o'clock. I'd seen a sign near the registration desk that Second Bet was holding its meetings in another of the small private rooms along a corridor outside the exhibit hall. Uncle Mike and I walked over at our appointed time and knocked. We didn't hear anything, so we opened the door to the room. Several people sat on one side of the table and one person sat across from them.

"We're here for Team Player," I said.

One of the three people on the side of the table facing the door said, "Sorry, give us a few more minutes."

I looked at the man seated across from the trio. He looked up at me with gritted teeth and shook his head. It was clear the man was having a rough time. I closed the door on the inquisition.

We stepped back into the hall. "I'm not sure we can fake our way through this one." The background research I'd done on the Debt Exchange and those companies on our list for today didn't seem like enough. The Second Bet website described the company's mercurial rise in the debt-buying industry and showed pictures of row upon row of collectors seated at computer stations, but said nothing about how it treated its outside vendors. I'd be forced to rely on the fact I was a new hire at Team Player as an excuse for my ignorance.

"You're right," Uncle Mike said. "There's a lot at stake for Team Player at this meeting, according to O'Rourke. But let's think this through for a second. As I understand it, Second Bet is in direct competition with Jalbert for those Globex accounts. If Zino's speech is against Jalbert's Globex deal, then Second Bet should be loving Team Player and Zino, right?"

"Right, but O'Rourke told us Linda Roberts of Second Bet is threatening to suspend placements. Why would they do that if Zino and Second Bet should be allies against the common enemy, Jalbert?"

"I don't know. I guess we'll find out," Uncle Mike said.

"Let's make it clear that Zino didn't have the time to brief us on everything."

Uncle Mike nodded. "Good. That way, when we ask a bunch of dumb questions, they won't throw us out."

The man who had sat alone on one side of the table emerged from the room. As he walked past us, he tried to tuck in his shirttail and mumbled cuss words under his breath. "I hope you make out better than I did," he said.

We walked inside. Before I could introduce us to the trio on the other side of the table, one of the three stood and gave us a polite smile.

"Please, have a seat, gentlemen. I'm Linda Roberts, head of Agency Placements at 2ndBetOnDebt. I understand—" She brushed back her long brown hair with a swipe of her hand and glanced down at her notes "I understand that Eddie'O'Connell, a recent hire at Team Player, and Mike'O'Connell, a collection manager at Team Player, are present today." She didn't bother to introduce the man seated to her right, or the woman seated to her left.

I didn't see any court reporter in the room, but I had the feeling we were on trial. Maybe someone was secretly watching the meeting.

"I understand Zino has the flu?"

"That's right," I said. We sat down. The other two each wrote something in their notebooks.

I began to sweat.

Robert's tight smile disappeared. "Maybe Mr. Zino isn't here for a reason."

"Yeah," Uncle Mike leaned across the table. "He's hospitalized. But just between us."

Roberts nodded.

"Mr. Zino has suffered from complications. He has pneumonia," Uncle Mike said.

"I'm so sorry. Please give him our best," Roberts said softly, with a look of genuine concern. Then she straightened and said: "When I met with Mr. Zino last Friday at our offices—" She stopped, then started again. "I will go ahead and assume you'll be able to talk with Zino and advise him on what we discuss? Do you two need notepads to take notes?"

I shrugged. "Sure. We'll fill in Mr. Zino later. We're just last-minute replacements."

"Yeah," Uncle Mike said. "Mr. Zino took ill rather suddenly and didn't have time to give us all the particulars."

The woman to the left of Roberts slid a hotel notepad across the table to me.

"I'll take one, too, if there's no charge," Uncle Mike said.

The man to Roberts's right slid another pad across the table to Uncle Mike.

Roberts opened a folder and looked to either side. Neither of the other two looked up. The silent moment signaled the polite chitchat, if you could call it that, had come to a grinding halt.

"Let me bring everyone up to speed." Roberts took a short breath as if Zino's illness was a serious stumbling block and tried her patience. "When Mr. Zino and I met at our offices last Friday, I told him I'd reevaluate Team Player's prior performance."

She got right to the point and ran things like an army general. The employees on either side of her kept their heads down, as if she might order them to the chopping block at any moment. Of all the people I'd met today, she seemed the most likely to see through me. My antennae went up.

She said, "Zino wants to maintain Team Player's relationship with us, isn't that correct?"

"Yes," I said.

She continued: "Our company has taken on many of the responsibilities for the collection of its purchased accounts in-house. The number of collectors has been increased almost tenfold at Second Bet since it first partnered with Team Player years ago. This has allowed us to reduce our reliance upon outside vendors. For example, Second Bet now has its own network of attorneys doing legal collection work in a number of states in order to get to garnishment that much faster. So, any renewal of our relationship with Team Player might seem to contradict policy. However…"

She hesitated a moment, as if to organize her thoughts. I wasn't going to fill the gap. She was on a roll.

She clicked the pen in her hand a number of times as if something wasn't quite right. "Sometimes special circumstances may mandate that we reconsider."

At that moment, a man dressed in golfing attire walked through the door as if he owned the place. Maybe there was a schedule mix up. But the man smiled and nodded toward Roberts. Roberts and the two others stood up. We stood and joined them at attention. I took a second look and recognized the tanned face of the man.

"Eddie, Mike," Roberts said, "I'd like you both to meet the CEO of our company, Landis Tanner."

"I've met Eddie," Tanner said. He nodded to me and then stepped toward Uncle Mike.

Uncle Mike introduced himself.

Roberts sat and stared at me. I knew she wanted to ask how I'd met Tanner, but unless she asked, I wasn't going to tell her. She was the busybody corporate type who wanted to know everything and it might teach her something to be in the dark for once.

Uncle Mike glanced my way. We knew that Tanner was buddies with Eliot Scullion, the keynote speaker, and that both Tanner and Scullion placed million-dollar bets on the 49ers and lost. Tanner had also been the star attraction at last night's slugfest with DiNatale and his boys. What we hadn't known until now was that Tanner was also in charge of Second Bet. This conference became more interesting by the minute.

Of course, when Tanner said we'd met before, he was referring to the WagerEasy pre-Super Bowl party. He didn't know I had been a witness to last night's ass-kicking. He was walking stiffly and stopped at one point and rubbed his side. Then he grimaced, took a deep breath, and stumbled off to a corner of the room. His breathing came in short bursts.

"Just pretend I'm not here," Tanner said, leaning over a chair.

Roberts pursed her lips. It was as if the principal had come into the classroom to check on the teacher as she explained reality 101 to us.

Roberts made a few rage-filled scratches in her notebook and took a deep breath. She must've been waiting for Tanner. "Eddie, it's my understanding you're going to give Zino's speech scheduled for Wednesday?"

"That's right." News of my speech had traveled fast through the conference. Although I liked Uncle Mike's draft of the speech, I might need to reserve an early flight Wednesday back to Chicago.

"You know about Jalbert's deal with Globex?" she asked.

"Sure. Yes, I know about the deal." I looked toward Tanner. His smile had disappeared.

Roberts said, "At one point, Second Bet was forced to sever its relationship with Jalbert. He can't be trusted. He'll do whatever it takes to get ahead."

"Like what?" Uncle Mike asked.

Her lips formed a thin line, and she clicked the pen again. "Let's just say Second Bet and Jalbert have a long history. As I was saying." She took a deep breath. She didn't tolerate questions from the class. "Second Bet has always maintained a strong relationship with Globex. They are one of our biggest, if not our biggest, client."

"I understand," I said.

"Yes, well." She shook her head slightly, as if I might be the dumbest student ever. "We have had numerous meetings with Globex. I've met with Globex myself and there are many people at the bank who want to maintain the status quo. They're not so sure Jalbert can handle the business. Jalbert must be able to collect enough on the accounts he purchases to be able to buy accounts the following month and the month after that. This may cause issues with his investors because the returns he's promised are, shall we say, overly optimistic? The ramp-up costs are high in this business."

I looked at Tanner. Roberts seemed to be saying this to remind Tanner that Second Bet held the "nuts" in this little poker game and any speech I planned to give for Zino wouldn't matter. But maybe I was getting ahead of myself.

I doodled something on the notepad to look busy while I tried to read Tanner. How did it feel to lose a million, then get the shit beat out of you? Uncle Mike and I figured Tanner must owe money to the mob.

Roberts smiled like a hungry predator. "Our company can no longer turn a blind eye to Team Player's method of collection. Team Player has missed goal the last several months. We therefore have no choice but to suspend the placement of accounts to Team Player."

I couldn't believe it. The one meeting where O'Rourke needed our help and Team Player was getting fired.

Uncle Mike raised his hand. Roberts nodded in his direction.

"What do you mean—method of collection?" Uncle Mike asked.

"Yes, by all means, let's address Team Player's unique method of collections," Roberts said. "Typically, an agency does not request backup documentation on one of our purchased credit card accounts unless the debtor disputes the account in writing. Yet, Team Player requests backup documents on more accounts than any of our other agencies. Why? We sent our auditors to review Team Player files and talk to the staff involved. I'm not sure, Mr. O'Connell, if you participated in any of those discussions."

Uncle Mike shook his head.

"How about you, Eddie?"

I shook my head as well. Maybe "Operations" wouldn't be a sufficient excuse.

Roberts cleared her throat. She didn't click the pen. "It appears that the backup documents, which our company must pay extra to obtain from the debt seller, are not requested due to a written dispute by the debtor. They are requested by Team Player on a regular basis."

"This is good for me to know," Tanner said with a wide smile. "I've never heard of anyone doing what Team Player does."

Tanner acted as if he was learning everything about Team Player for the first time at this meeting. Was this the way corporations worked? The CEO walks into a meeting and hears something critical about an important vendor for the first time? I decided the answer was most likely "no." Tanner probably knew all about Team Player's method of collection, but was only acting as if it was the first time. It must be part of the game, a game of who has the power and who gets fired.

Roberts continued, "Zino has directed his staff to review the backup documentation and determine how the credit card balance was incurred. If the balance was based upon the purchase of groceries or medical expenses, the account is—how shall I say it—treated with loving care. If Team Player deems such purchases to be necessary and essential, the accounts are then shuttled over to a separate queue. Even accounts that are suit-ready, where the debtors have good jobs and are candidates for wage garnishment, are placed in this limbo status."

I was impressed by Zino. The Deacon gave the little guy a break.

"Second Bet is not a welfare agency," Tanner said. "The debtors incurred a loan from the credit card company to make these purchases and haven't paid it back. Plain and simple."

Roberts nodded in the direction of the CEO. "Zino regularly sets up payment plans that will take up to ten years to repay on these loving care accounts and that's without interest. Zino acts as if these are his accounts, not those of Second Bet."

"And that's why Team Player has been missing goal?" I asked.

Roberts clicked her pen. "Yes, you are new, aren't you?"

Tanner snickered. The two assistants looked up at me and shook their head with pity.

"Goal is of the utmost importance," Roberts said. "You can put that in your speech. No charge."

Tanner coughed. "Second Bet demands a high level of performance from its partners." He took a step to the side, still holding onto the back of the chair, and stretched in pain. "It's why we can afford to purchase the debt of Globex at a higher rate."

"We have demands from Globex," Roberts said. "We can't meet those demands if Zino insists on providing generous treatment to certain debtors."

"From what I hear," Tanner said, "Team Player can't count on Jalbert to forward the Globex accounts to Team Player, yet Team Player can't afford to lose the Globex business. Team Player's best chance is to work with us." Tanner stopped for a moment to let this sink in. He seemed to be saying screw you and checkmate. "If Team Player works its way through the suspension and garnishes the wages of these particular debtors, which have been given loving care as Ms. Roberts says, maybe we can start working together again."

If we were going to go down in flames, I might as well try to bring them down with us.

"You know what you should think about," I said. "I'm in an interesting position. I'm new to all this, but I'll have the chance to discuss my speech with Mr. Jalbert and Ms. Lundstrom at dinner tonight."

Tanner, holding onto the chair with both hands for support, bent over at the waist as if he'd just been hit in the gut again.

Roberts began clicking the pen. I lost count of the clicks. The other two assistants stopped taking notes and looked first at Tanner, then at Roberts, and back again.

"I thought we could count on your loyalty after all these years," Roberts said through tight lips.

I could've said: "what about your fucking loyalty," but I held back for the sake of Team Player and the corporate good of debt and mankind.

"Now hold on, Linda," Tanner said in a calm voice. "Let's take another long look at the situation. I think we might need to know what goes on at this dinner Jalbert has planned."

———

After the meeting with Second Debt, when we were out of earshot of others, we did our post-meeting handicapping.

"Eddie," Uncle Mike said, clapping me on the back. "You did great. I thought Team Player was sunk and then you casually mention how it's your speech and that we're meeting with Jalbert and Lundstrom tonight."

I laughed. "Did you see Tanner?"

"Yeah, he looked like he was ready to puke."

"Roberts was pissed. For the moment, they backed off suspending Team Player, but I don't trust them."

Uncle Mike checked our agenda. "Our next meeting isn't for another hour. Let's get a snack. That salad wasn't enough. We just need to keep each of these companies in play. That way, they'll continue talking to us."

"What I wonder about is how the Deacon could stomach this."

"It doesn't sound like he did stomach it. He refused to follow their rules. According to Roberts, he treated certain accounts differently than others."

"I would've figured the Deacon to be tough as nails on collection." I could understand why the Deacon argued with Roberts and why he didn't want to follow their strict rules, but what was Zino's plan?

"Zino told O'Rourke the speech would handle everything. I'll check again with DiNatale about the Deacon's laptop."

We had tried to get access to the Deacon's laptop and cell phone previously, but DiNatale said he'd have to check with Burrascano. "I like the speech we drafted, but I hope we can find out more before I have to step up to the podium on

Wednesday." We took the escalator down to the casino where we could find a sandwich place. I glanced at my cell. Arlene had returned my call while we were in the Second Bet meeting.

"I got a call back from Arlene," I said.

"You can't tell her the Deacon was murdered," Uncle Mike whispered. "We promised Burrascano."

"I know."

Uncle Mike shook his head. "Tell her the Deacon had to delay our meeting."

"Yeah. What else can I say?" I called Arlene back and got her voice mail. I was relieved. It would give me more time to work on my story about the Deacon. I left a message.

"We have to think about tonight's dinner," Uncle Mike said. "The speech we drafted will bring Jalbert down a few notches, but maybe we'll learn more tonight."

"The speech is excellent leverage," I said. "Maybe Jalbert will offer me a job."

"You? I'm the collection manager. You're just an MBA grad with no real-life experience."

"How about a side bet?"

"No way. I'm not betting with a card shark."

"I liked the way Roberts cozied up to us after the meeting."

"Yeah, she wants to know everything Lundstrom says at dinner." Uncle Mike said. "I assume Roberts has her own contacts at Globex and will use whatever she hears against Lundstrom."

"How does it feel to be a double agent after only one day?" I asked.

"I feel used."

17

WE MET JENNIFER HADLOW FROM GUSHER DEBT BROKERS in the sports book after our last meeting. Caesars didn't do anything in a subdued way, and the sports book took up a prominent place in the casino. If you were walking from the lobby to The Colosseum or the Roman Forum Shops located in the indoor mall, you couldn't miss the odds board. The black background of the odds board made the bright lights of the odds on today's games sizzle.

It had been a full day, and it would be good to sit down in one of the cushioned high-backed chairs. Yesterday, these were choice seats for the Super Bowl. Today, only a few seats were occupied by dedicated horse players.

Hadlow sat near the back row. To our left, a swarm of activity buzzed around the sports bar. I had house money in my pocket from my Super Bowl win, but I needed to talk to Hadlow. I wanted to find out everything I could about the

Deacon, but we also wanted to hear more about the infighting at the Debt Exchange conference.

We ordered a beer from one of the cocktail servers and settled into our seats.

"Any update on Tony?" Hadlow asked, brushing back a lock of her silver hair.

"We called the nurse's station. One nurse wouldn't talk to me about his condition due to HIPPA so I called back later and talked to another nurse. His fever is still a concern," Uncle Mike said.

"Darn it. I wished I could call him, but he hates phone calls. Do me a favor. The next time you talk to him, tell him you talked to me, will you? Ask him to call me."

Could Hadlow be the Deacon's love interest? She was the right age for a guy like Zino in his mid-seventies. She was complaining about Zino not calling her. "Why doesn't Mr. Zino like phone calls?" I asked.

She shrugged, and then a warm smile lit her face. "He just assumes the call will be trouble. As if he's expecting bad news. Someone asking for details on something at work. 'They should learn to handle it themselves,' he always says."

"The work was getting to him?" I asked.

"You're new. You don't know what it's like yet. But Mike and I know, don't we Mike?"

Uncle Mike nodded. "It's a grind. Monthly pressure to make goal."

"I assume that you, being new, want to know everything you can about the owner. But I don't want to tell you anything that would hurt Tony at the office. Some things he tells me in confidence."

"Don't worry about that," Uncle Mike said.

"That's right. Mr. Zino is a legend and a mystery to some of us. But we don't want to know any personal stuff," I said.

"Good, just so we're clear on that," Hadlow said. "Tony and I were here at the height of the debt-buying craze. You'd walk down the aisles of the exhibit hall back then and you could barely move. It was so crowded. The conference was jam-packed with people. Most of them were mom and pop types, hoping they found a business that would be their ticket to the top. Every portfolio I had to resell, I had multiple people bidding."

"This was when?" I asked.

"The late nineties," she said.

"You two—you and Tony—are survivors," Uncle Mike said.

"You're damn right we are," she said with a laugh that I found contagious. "No wonder we're so damn tired. That's why we've talked about getting out of the rat race. Tony said he always wanted to travel. Maybe find a little place in Tuscany, sip a glass of wine and watch the sun set. It's a good dream."

"I don't see why you can't do it," I said. "You've both worked hard." I wished the dream could happen. It made me that much more determined to find the Deacon's murderer.

I spotted Nicole and waved her over.

Uncle Mike and I stood. Nicole gave me a hug.

"It's been a long time, Mr. O'Connell." Nicole stepped past me and received one of Uncle Mike's bear hugs.

"You're looking good, Nicole," Uncle Mike said. "You're even prettier than the last time we met. I think sports betting agrees with you."

"Thanks, Mr. O'Connell." She patted his robust middle. "Retirement seems to agree with you."

Uncle Mike laughed. "I'm forced to try a lot of new microbrews at O'Connell's."

I introduced Nicole to Jennifer Hadlow.

"You're the poker pro," Hadlow said.

"That's me. It keeps me busy."

"She's also doing a cable show on sports betting called The Sports Betting Insiders," I added. "She picked the Chiefs in the Super Bowl."

"Wow. That's you? I've seen the show. You're great," Hadlow said. "A lot of people weren't happy with the result of the Super Bowl. I got here late yesterday and 49er fans were everywhere."

"Thanks, Jennie. I guess the 49er fans will have to wait for next year." Nicole whispered in my ear. "Eddie, have you got a minute?"

"What is it?" We stepped a few paces back from the row of seats, off to one side.

"See the race coming up at Thornton? My dad gave me a horse."

I expected Nicole to tell me about her decision to play Scullion in heads-up poker, not a harness race from Thornton

Racetrack. Her dad still trained a string of horses and had plenty of contacts. His picks could be good as gold.

"Eddie, can you place the bet for me?" she asked.

I assumed Caesars might not take a bet from Nicole on a horse from Chicago. The job of a sports book manager was to identify sharp bettors and determine whether to take their action. Maybe she'd burned the sports book once too often or maybe the manager would refuse her action due to her celebrity status. She slipped a wad of C-notes into my hand and whispered the number of the horse into my ear.

"I'll be glad to go up. Mind if I make a bet for Uncle Mike and Jennifer?"

She glanced around. "Sure. Just keep it quiet." The bar nearby might have a few folks watching and listening.

I checked out the number nine horse at Thornton Racetrack in Chicago. The horse was at nineteen-to-one at the track. Nicole's wager would not affect the track odds, since Caesars would book the bet. Maybe Nicole's dad had a part of Nicole's wager. Five minutes to post. "On the nose?" I whispered.

"Right. Let your uncle and the lady know the nine will either win or be nowhere." She tugged on my arm. "They aren't high rollers, right?"

"No. Uncle Mike is probably good for a sawbuck."

She nodded.

I explained the bet on the next race to Uncle Mike and Hadlow. They each bet a sawbuck, as predicted.

I walked up to the row of bored ticket sellers and got a harness program. Then I stood off to the side and studied the race. I searched the row of flat screens above the ticket sellers for the race from Chicago. I scratched the back of my head and walked up like I wasn't sure I was in the right place.

I made the bets, throwing down some of the money I won on KC in the Super Bowl together with Nicole's wager and the sawbucks from Uncle Mike and Hadlow, a total of more than seven hundred dollars.

"I won on KC yesterday and the nine is a hunch play," I told the ticket seller.

The ticket seller shook his head, pulled out the harness program and turned to the race. A few years ago, the ticket seller might check with the sports book manager on one of my bets. But I was a stranger these days, a sucker playing the harness. "Super Rocket. I get it. But let me get your name. You're staying here?"

I told him I was a guest and showed him my key card.

He nodded and punched my ticket on the nine horse at Thornton Racetrack.

I checked my ticket and then looked up at the screen. A Chicago snowstorm clouded the telecast of the harness race. The snow blew in a lazy, horizontal direction across the screen, a genial blizzard by Chicago standards, but I could barely make out the horses as they warmed up.

I walked back from the windows to Nicole. "Got it."

"Good."

"I won't ask you about the horse. It is what it is. What about your heads-up with Scullion?" I asked.

She raised her pinched thumb and forefinger toward her eye and parted her fingers a quarter inch. "I'm this close. Every pro I talked to so far wants in. But I'm waiting to hear from Wit."

"You'll need Wit's backing." Wit was the unofficial leader of the pros when it came time to decide whether to back a player in a heads-up match. "Do you know enough about Scullion and his game?" I asked.

"Some pros say he's a loser who plays too aggressive. Others tell me to 'watch it,' Scullion is being coached by Hans Becker."

Becker was a German pro who had a torrid record in Europe, but was new on the American scene.

"Maybe it's not worth the risk."

"What do you mean?" She seemed hurt.

I shrugged. "You said yourself you want out of the poker life and you've got the chance to do it with your show. If you lose, maybe you could lose the show."

The way I saw it, the only question about her switch from poker to sports betting analyst was why she hadn't done it sooner. We always knew that poker wouldn't last. It was a high-wire act with too much risk. Everyone could hit a losing streak, and playing through them could be a grind. The onslaught of new, younger players, with thousands of hours playing on their home computer, was changing the makeup of poker and some players didn't like it. Since I'd been out of the loop, I wasn't exactly an expert on the subject.

Her lips turned downward. "I didn't think of all the factors. Right now, I'm the top dog with the pro poker background. Losing to a non-pro like Scullion would get lots of publicity. I'd be a joke and I've got basketball coming up. Not my strong suit."

"If you play Scullion, it's a gamble. Something to consider."

"I want to do what I want. I hate being tied to my bankroll and how the cards are falling. You know what it's like with the pros. Each day it gets tougher and tougher. Lots of new faces."

I kept watch on the harness race from Thornton.

"How long has Scullion's coaching been going on?" I asked. "A guy like Scullion is a busy boy doing deals." The guy I'd observed yesterday had a huge ego. He didn't seem like the type to take instructions.

"A few months, they tell me. No one has seen Scullion play since he began getting coached."

"A pro acts intuitively," I said. "A guy getting coached has to think through what he's been told and at the same time keep his nerves in check."

Nicole glanced across the room at the wide screen of the harness race. There wasn't a lot of action around the country on a Monday night. "You've got a good point. Plus, I don't like the guy. Did you see the way he urged on his friend to bet on the Super Bowl?"

"The way he struggled over the bet, it was clear Tanner has a problem," I said.

"I'd like to show Scullion there are some things money can't buy," Nicole said. "Scullion wouldn't have picked me to play heads up in a million years, if not for my sports betting show."

"If he wins, you know he'll plaster it all over social media just to feed his ego."

"The bastard. If I win, I'll be another pro taking advantage of an amateur. The only thing I get out of it is money."

"Poker is like that."

"I won't have another chance like this one."

"Maybe it's time to move on," I said. "Pay the mortgage like a lot of hard-working people."

"God, do you hear what you're saying? You and me used to play poker to all hours, go to the blackjack table and then craps."

"Right. The next afternoon in the sports book. It was all about the action."

"Speaking of action, here they come."

I looked up at the snowy Thornton harness race. Uncle Mike looked back at me as if to remind me he had ten bucks on this horse and it better be worth it.

The pacers moved up to the mobile starting gate. The nine horse field fanned out across the track for the start. The starter car with the gate attached accelerated, signaling the start, each driver scrambling for position. The nine horse, Super Rocket, tore out from the outside post, got out front, then dove into the clubhouse turn and veered over toward the rail to take first position in the mile-long contest.

As the horses settled into single file headed into the backstretch, the horse in second place, behind the nine horse, went off stride. The driver immediately pulled away from the rail, but the snafu caused the horses in line behind to take up slightly and lose momentum, giving the nine horse a four or five length cushion. It was tough enough to pass horses in the accumulating snow, but next to impossible to do it from far behind.

Nicole tugged on my arm. "Every other horse is running for second."

It was the kind of race every horse player dreams about: a nineteen-to-one shot with an easy lead in the snow. "The nine just needs to finish." I'd seen a horse in this position still lose. They could go off stride or stop running.

"No worries. The nine is a rocket sled. C'mon, Super Rocket," Nicole yelled.

Uncle Mike and Hadlow were caught up in the excitement and yelling as well. A few horse players looked back at us. It had been a quiet study hall until this race.

Of course, it had occurred to me the race might be fixed, but right now I was enjoying the ride. Super Rocket raced down the stretch several lengths in front of a pack that seemed to have little interest in making up the ground they'd lost.

The nine breezed to the finish line. Uncle Mike threw a fist in the air. I grabbed Nicole in a bear hug. Hadlow stood and clapped.

Nicole looked me in the eye. "It's just the way I always remember winning with you."

I kissed her, or she kissed me. Romance in the sports book seemed out of place, but we didn't care. We were winners.

"You have stuff going on tonight with work?" She whispered in my ear.

"Yeah."

"Maybe after?"

18

FELIPE'S WAS LOCATED JUST OUTSIDE THE BELLAGIO, PAST A few shops and ten yards down a hall. If you continued down the hall past Felipe's, you would eventually find the light rail. By the time you found the rail stop, you could've walked to the next casino.

Uncle Mike and I walked up to the restaurant entrance, flush with cash from our win.

Jalbert sat at the end of a long table, the guests already seated.

I took in the scene. The restaurant's bar was crowded with A-list customers, reinforcements who had arrived a day late for the Super Bowl. They'd probably heard about the shooting at Caesars which lent an air of danger to their visit, a little intrigue and grit to go with the corporate meetings, shopping and slots.

Near Jalbert's table, a jazz trio, consisting of a piano player, bass, and guitar, tried their best to blanket the place in sound. The smells of grilled seafood and garlic wafted through the expansive room. The kitchen, encased by glass walls, smack in the middle of the restaurant, gyrated with the action of chefs grilling and plating, and pointing and shaking their heads at the waiters arranging plates on trays in full view of the ravenous, drunken throng.

My newly minted "other" would be on full display tonight. At dinner, I'd play the recent MBA grad, so new to the job I hadn't yet been pictured on the company's website. I assumed that the guy I pretended to be had dreamed of this day and probably dreaded it at the same time. I'd had my head buried in a textbook for a couple of years or more, studying balance sheets and business strategies of other great CEOs, but now I was out in the real world ready to showcase my knowledge. A guy like me had to view the dinner as a grand career opportunity, a chance to shake hands, network, and learn all the little things I could use to advance. I cringed. I hoped my "other" would appreciate the ass-kissing.

We forged a path around crowded tables, dodged waiters who cut past with trays of seafood and drinks, and maneuvered around customers shuffling toward the bar. Jalbert stood and waved as we approached. I waved back and spotted a couple of open seats at the far end of the table for twelve, at the opposite end of the table from Jalbert. In those safe seats, Uncle Mike and I could view the proceedings without being asked business questions that might reveal our imposter status.

But Jalbert must've seen where we were headed, and gave us several frantic waves, gesturing toward his end of the table. People near Jalbert got up and moved down the table, opening up two seats for us. Jalbert's face reddened as he shuffled his guests around the table. My alter ego smiled and nodded, in love with the chance to network with Jalbert, the playmaker.

Then, as I got to the table, I spotted a familiar face. A man in an expensive looking dark pinstripe suit with a white shirt, open at the collar, sipped from what I bet was a bourbon and water. Scullion.

When you wager a million and win, you look like a genius. When you bet a million and lose, you're a first-class chump. I'd slow-play any mention of Scullion's losing Super Bowl wager and keep it quiet for the moment.

Scullion was talking with a woman seated to his right, an attractive middle-aged woman with short blond hair. She was seated to the left of Jalbert, who occupied the seat at the end of the table.

Jalbert continued to stand. "Eddie, Mike, allow me to introduce you to Ingrid Lundstrom of Globex Bank." He was barely able to contain his enthusiasm as he turned toward the woman with the short blond hair.

Lundstrom nodded at us and smiled. She remained seated and sat directly across from me. I'd been assigned the seat to the immediate right of Jalbert.

Lundstrom wore a red sweater with white reindeer on it, a gold chain necklace draped around her neck. I reached over and shook her hand. I received a firm handshake in return.

"Gentlemen," she said as we sat down. "How nice of you to fill in for Tony. I hope he gets better soon. The flu is terrible this year, so I'm relieved that he's getting expert medical attention."

"Just between us," Uncle Mike said, waiting for their full attention. "Mr. Zino has a complication from the flu. He has pneumonia."

Lundstrom, Scullion, and Jalbert expressed their sympathies.

There was an awkward moment and then Jalbert continued with more introductions to those around the table, but with the noise and jazz combo it was impossible for any of us to do more than give a short wave or nod and smile back and forth.

Jalbert took his seat. "I'm also proud to have our conference keynote speaker with us tonight, Eliot Scullion."

Scullion sat across from Uncle Mike. He smiled and nodded to us.

Before I could say that we'd met, the hedge fund celebrity said, "I've met Eddie." He examined Uncle Mike. "And you are Mike O'Connell, Eddie's uncle? You must be proud of your nephew. I hear he's recently received his MBA?" Scullion spoke fast, like a guy with too many things on his mind.

"That's right," Uncle Mike said. "He keeps his nose to the grindstone." Uncle Mike beamed in my direction.

Uncle Mike had it easy. All he had to do was to play the Team Player collection manager, a role he'd slipped into as easily as a comfortable pair of old bedroom slippers. Uncle Mike matched anyone's idea of a collection manager. He was gruff, menacing, battle-hardened. Upon learning of Uncle Mike's position, the debt-buying execs seemed to give him a wide berth, either because they didn't want to tarnish themselves by associating with a veteran of the collection trenches, or, as I'd heard today, because they were slightly in awe of the magical numbers a good collection manager could produce.

"How do you know Eddie?" Lundstrom asked Scullion.

Scullion's jaw jutted forward and then he smiled, a less inebriated smile than the one I'd witnessed yesterday. "It so happens that Eddie is good friends with Nicole Nicoletti."

"The poker player you were telling us about?" Lundstrom asked.

Scullion nodded. "The two of them are from Chicago and may have some history. Eddie was very helpful." The way he mentioned "history" told everyone that Nicole and I had been more than friends.

Uncle Mike kicked me in the shins.

Lundstrom clutched her gold necklace and seemed to reevaluate my character. "Helpful? How?"

Scullion watched for my reaction. "As I said earlier, I made a Super Bowl bet with Ms. Nicoletti. If the 49ers won, she'd play me heads-up. We hadn't discussed what would happen if the 49ers lost, and then Eddie clarified the wager. If the 49ers lost, Nicole could decide not to play me heads-up, and I'd pay one hundred thousand."

"One hundred thousand? I may have to call you for investment advice." Lundstrom grabbed her cocktail and sipped.

"And you agreed to those terms?" Jalbert asked.

"Absolutely," Scullion quickly explained. "No problem. I've already paid Ms. Nicoletti. I am confident Nicole will decide to play me heads-up and I'll get my hundred K back, plus plenty more. The other pros will back Nicole against me, an amateur, because I'm considered dead money. But I plan to turn the tables on her and her colleagues."

Lundstrom's fingertips found the curve of her smooth jawline. "Nicely done, Eddie."

The man to Uncle Mike's right had been listening in on our conversation. He had a bushy mustache and was one of the few men at the table with a bow tie. He let out a low whistle. "One hundred grand. Now that's a bet."

Jalbert rattled the ice cubes in his empty glass. "Good work, Eddie. Let's get you two some drinks. I think we're ready for another round." He raised his glass in the direction of the waiter, who caught the signal and rushed over.

"Not for me, Stefan," Lundstrom said. "I'll switch to wine. I have a conference call early tomorrow with the higher-ups back in New York at the crack of dawn. I think they make a special effort to schedule an early conference call just to make my life hell when I'm in Vegas."

Uncle Mike and I knew better than to drink the hard stuff when we had to watch every word we said, and ordered beers. Could Jalbert or anyone from the conference have orchestrated Zino's murder? Then one of Uncle Mike's lectures echoed. Follow the path of the investigation and the facts, and above all, remain patient.

"I suppose one hundred K might seem like a lot," I said. I wanted to tease Scullion with the line and see what Scullion might do. I wanted to imply that I planned to mention his wayward wager of one million. Perhaps he'd already discussed it with Jalbert and Lundstrom, but I doubted it.

I also doubted if Scullion wanted me, a fresh MBA grad, to enliven the conversation with a rehash of yesterday. Not only had Scullion bet one million, he'd also wagered one million on behalf of his good buddy, Tanner, CEO of Second Bet, and, as I understood it, Jalbert's bitter rival. Casual friends didn't usually place one-million-dollar wagers for another, at least in my experience. How closely were Scullion and Tanner working together?

I decided to wait and evaluate Mr. Scullion more closely.

Jalbert and Lundstrom studied the wine list. Uncle Mike and the man with the bushy mustache to his right began discussing jazz, one of Uncle Mike's favorite subjects. I received a quick introduction to Horace.

While Uncle Mike and Horace bonded over jazz, Scullion cupped a hand and motioned me toward him. I leaned forward. "Eddie," Scullion said. "I'm getting concerned. I haven't heard from Nicole since I paid off the hundred grand."

I liked the fact Scullion would come to me with his concerns. It meant he figured I could play a role in facilitating his heads-up play with Nicole, and at the same time, stay quiet about his million-dollar chump bet. The hedge funder needed me.

I tried my best to generate a look of concern. "I'm not sure yet about Nicole's intentions." I wanted to keep him dangling. "I just left her in the sports book."

Scullion leaned closer. "You just left her? What did she say?"

"Not much. I guess Nicole is considering her options. People have schedules and commitments. You didn't give the pros a lot of notice, I'm afraid."

Scullion scratched his perfectly groomed gray hair and seemed to make an effort to appear unconcerned. "You're right. I'm a spur-of-the-moment guy. I should've planned all this out. I'm sure Nicole has lots on her plate. She has personal appearances and the poker tour."

"I hear you've been taking lessons with Hans Becker?"

"Yes. He's opened my eyes, Eddie. He's given me a grasp of poker on a whole other level and I can't wait to test it out."

I almost offered to play Scullion heads-up myself. I'd heard guys say that before—"I got a whole new grasp of poker"—and they'd drop a massive chunk of their bankroll trying to prove it to themselves. There were no shortcuts in poker, although playing thousands of hours on your home computer might qualify. But you couldn't "suddenly grasp it" like switching on a light bulb.

I had to be careful. Scullion was probably feeding me bullshit. Most likely ninety percent of what he said was intended to feed his ego and the other ten percent was probably meant to manipulate me. I had to remember the type of person I was dealing with, a man who came pre-packaged with ruthless cunning.

I wanted to see if Scullion might tell me his new strategy. "Hans is aggressive. Some say overly aggressive."

Scullion pursed his lips. "Maybe."

I had to give Scullion credit. He could put his ego on "pause" when needed.

Jalbert and Lundstrom had straightened out the all-important decision about the choice of wine, and the band was taking a break. Jalbert had ordered another round of drinks and several seafood tower appetizers. I needed to find out why we sat at the choice end of the table. Once everyone began to dig into shrimp, crab legs and oysters on the half shell, I'd never get their attention. This was my opportunity to ask Lundstrom what the "deal" meant to Globex.

"Ms. Lundstrom," I said. I wasn't comfortable with "Ingrid." "I'm told that you like the Globex deal with Jalbert's company?"

Jalbert's question at our morning meeting needed to be addressed: "what's your take on the issues?" Uncle Mike and I also had Second Bet wanting us to spy on their behalf.

Lundstrom stiffened. Scullion scowled, but Jalbert's face lit up. "That's right," Jalbert said. "Eddie wants to do deals, big deals. Like the ones he studied in school. He's fired up."

I wasn't sure where Jalbert got the idea I wanted to do "big deals." I assumed it was his way to make me appear to be a rookie they could dazzle with corporate glitz. I accepted my shitty role and smiled like an idiot.

Lundstrom's sharp blue eyes penetrated the lower depths a new graduate like me inhabited. "You look kind of old for grad school. Were you one of those who needed a do-over?"

"No, a lot of my class had work experience before they went to grad school," I said. "We also had to save money for tuition." My lie felt real, always a positive sign. It meant I was slipping comfortably into my role.

"Commendable," she said with a note of reluctance. "Stefan told me you're familiar with the deal. By selling our charged off portfolio exclusively to Jalbert's group, coupled with the placement of our prime forward flow accounts, we establish the kind of loyalty and synergy the bank craves."

She waited a moment and glanced at me and Uncle Mike. Satisfied that what she said had sunk in through our upper cortex, she continued. "Many people at Globex have spent hours on the analytics and they've concluded the deal will be good for the bank." The word "good" rolled off her tongue as if it was a pronouncement. "Globex Bank has so many other money-making opportunities in various markets around the world that its bad debt has become, what with regulation and politically motivated government fines, nothing more than a big pain in the neck."

Based upon the look of one hundred percent approval from Jalbert and Scullion, it was indisputable that the bank's welfare must be of concern to us all. A surge of responsibility pulsated through me on the bank's behalf, a sick feeling that I quickly doused with a sip of my beer.

"Sounds good to me," Uncle Mike said, raising his glass in a toast. No one joined him.

Lundstrom's gaze didn't leave me. "I need you to talk with Zino." She meant talk sense to Zino. She rubbed the back of her neck with one hand as if the whole idea of Zino gave her a migraine. "The deal will benefit many companies in the Debt Exchange. We have worked long and hard to make this happen. I know Stefan has staked his reputation and that of his company on this deal."

"Eddie," Jalbert said. "You'll find that some companies in the Debt Exchange don't approve of the deal. Second Bet has campaigned hard against our deal. But it's the future."

I was getting the hard sell, and I was being temporarily accepted as an insider. I nodded like a grateful pup receiving a doggie treat.

Lundstrom held her chin in the air. "At the end of the day, the bank's decision boils down to what I think is best for the bank, not what's best for companies like Second Bet. That company is intent upon being the dominant player in the debt-buying industry. That won't be good for the bank. Perhaps, at first, Second Bet will offer us an enticing bone or two, but in the long run, when they've stomped the competition into the ground, they'll demand to buy the bank's debt for a song. There are two things the bank can't tolerate—getting screwed and shitty headlines. Above all, the bank avoids controversy."

I was prepared to swear allegiance to the bank. Headlines might flush the bank from its safe haven in the shadows.

The waiter brought another round of drinks, while another member of the staff presented the bottle of wine to Jalbert and Lundstrom. They approved, and the bottle was opened. Lundstrom tasted the wine and smiled. "Excellent. Send me a case," she said with a laugh, allowing her glass to be filled.

Jalbert took a healthy swig of his drink and waited to see if Lundstrom had more to say. When she didn't, Jalbert began, "You see, Eddie, my company and those I've handpicked to join us will bring experience to the table that Tanner can't match." Jalbert glanced at Lundstrom and then at Scullion to be sure they were on board. "Each company in my network is intimately familiar with their geographic region and the particular problems debtors might be facing. Maybe there was a localized flood or storm that caused a missed payment. You have to be ready to work with the debtors on that. The better partner we can be for Globex, the sooner the bank can move on to more enterprising ventures. Tanner is trying to expand all over the U.S., but his company simply can't offer the same localized expertise."

It all sounded so cozy—partnering, giving debtors a break when they faced a disaster, allowing the bank to focus on making more money—it gave me heartburn.

Scullion had been listening closely and picked up his fresh glass. "Second Bet's profit projections depend on Globex accounts."

"Tanner and Roberts won't go down without a fight," Jalbert said.

What was Scullion's interest in all this? He was one of these hedge fund types who seemed to know everything before it happened. How did Scullion plan to cash in? Maybe he was here to spy on me for Tanner.

I shrugged like the fresh grad without a clue. "I guess Zino is against the deal because Team Player is no longer one of your chosen partners?" I looked at Jalbert.

Jalbert sipped from his cocktail. His silence seemed out of character.

Lundstrom shifted in her chair and folded her arms. "I'm sure Team Player will be asked to join Jalbert's team once their collection numbers improve."

"That's right," Jalbert said, setting down his glass. "We have an upcoming audit scheduled at Team Player and at the offices of other proposed partners."

Jalbert made it sound like being audited was the greatest opportunity ever. No doubt Jalbert would find something in the numbers to flunk Team Player.

Lundstrom rubbed her neck again as if the expensive wine hadn't done its job on her migraine. "Eddie, I'm sure Mike can tell you that Globex has accounts at Team Player that were placed some time ago. These accounts produce a good stream of revenue for Team Player."

I didn't need an MBA to know the importance of the term "revenue."

Lundstrom continued, talking slowly so I could understand. "But we're not quite seeing the level of performance we would expect to see from these accounts or the level of performance that Jalbert has achieved. Rather than pull the accounts from Zino and sever our relationship, we prefer to give Team Player additional time to bring its performance up to Jalbert's level. This upcoming audit should provide us with the data we need."

The underlying meaning of what Lundstrom said was clear—play ball or Globex will pull the old Globex accounts Team Player relies upon as revenue.

"We've been working hard at Team Player," I said. "The bank's accounts have top priority."

How did Zino swallow this? Zino's speech was titled, "The Pitfalls of Expansion." I'd find a controversy for Globex and pour gasoline on the fire. Hell, I'd give the bank a bonfire.

"I know many people don't like our approach," Jalbert said. One of the seafood towers had been placed at the other end of the table. The jazz band was back. "Linda Roberts has visited the bank, isn't that right, Ingrid?"

Lundstrom grimaced. "I get calls from her daily. She's a thorn in my side. She visited the bank twice this month. Both Tanner and Roberts have dropped in. Bank employees are beginning to make jokes."

A second seafood tower arrived at our end of the table. Jalbert was beating Second Bet at its own game and I admired him for it. But Zino's speech remained a threat. Jalbert had screwed over a number of agencies as he expanded his operations, and I intended to highlight that fact in my speech.

Uncle Mike and Horace each grabbed a crab leg off the giant pile of seafood. Lundstrom picked a cocktail shrimp with two fingers off the pile. Scullion went for one of the oysters on the half shell. Jalbert looked down the table and asked if anyone needed anything.

How much had Jalbert invested? He had state attorneys general at the table. That meant ponying up money for lobbying and campaign contributions. Add to that the cost of the expansion and the cost to out-maneuver a company like Second Bet on the verge of an IPO, and Jalbert must be "in deep."

When a person had bet it all and stood to lose it all, sometimes the only option could be murder.

19

WE'D PLANNED TO WORK OVERTIME TONIGHT. AFTER THE sumptuous dinner with Jalbert, we would meet up with DiNatale and pay a visit to Karmazin. Uncle Mike and I went upstairs to our rooms to change.

We were alone in the elevator.

"Can you believe that?" I asked. "Oh, my God, I'm a nobody and I'm being wined and dined like I'm the prince of Wall Street or something."

Uncle Mike laughed with me. "We pulled it off, damn."

"I'm talking to the keynote speaker like we're old buddies," I said. "Shit, I don't care if he's a billionaire or not. If he's got a crappy fifty million, it's more than I'll ever see."

"Goddamn, one of the top people at Globex Bank was explaining all this stuff to us. I'm sitting there watching you and praying that you keep a straight face and don't say anything stupid about the collection business."

"I know," I said. "A couple of times I almost slipped. But I kept it together. Jalbert must have it made. He's connected. Why is he taking the time to bring us into his little web? That's what I kept asking. It's got to be the speech. What else is there?"

"We've got to keep playing these people. The killer is going to slip up, I'm telling you," Uncle Mike said.

"Scullion is a master at this." I felt the adrenaline running through me. "He's sitting there as cool as a pair of loaded dice, and all the time he's buddies with Tanner. He knows I know it, too. Anybody could see that he and Tanner were old buddies at the pre-Super Bowl Party. Damn, what self-control."

"This dinner shows us what's at stake," Uncle Mike said.

"Forcing us to take chances," I said. "We always end up playing this dangerous game."

We got off the elevator and walked to my room. Once inside, we continued to rehash the events.

"I'm glad Jalbert picked up the tab," Uncle Mike said. "I watched when they handed Jalbert the bill. He didn't bat an eyelash. I give the guy credit. I would've keeled over."

"I guess you have to spend money to make money," I said.

"What did we learn tonight?" Uncle Mike asked.

"I've got to admire Jalbert for taking on Tanner and Second Bet. Jalbert must be in hock up to his ears. He's opening offices in other states."

"I heard Scullion talking to you about the heads-up match with Nicole," Uncle Mike said.

"He says Hans has given him a new grasp of poker."

"Jeesus. I wish he'd sit in on one of our nickel dime games. What did you think of Lundstrom?"

I held my nose and conjured up my best banker imitation. "I believe I'll have some wine. I'm talking to the Globex Board tomorrow morning and I'd prefer not to have a raging hangover."

Uncle Mike cracked up. "Here we are drinking a couple of beers instead of cocktails. They must've thought we were a couple of yokels from the sticks."

We laughed even harder.

"I'll try to be serious," I said, taking a deep breath. "Lundstrom likes Jalbert a whole lot, and she seems to have the bank's interest at heart. She made an excellent point about competition. If Second Bet gets a monopoly on debt buying, Globex will be stuck. What about Horace? You talked to him for a while."

"Horace is quite the character. He used to work for Seamless Dataminers. He was fired. He didn't want to go into it."

"You think Seamless could be a key to this?"

"Yup. According to O'Rourke, Seamless supplied Team Player with crappy data. That would make Seamless an ally of Jalbert in all this. But here is Horace at Jalbert's fancy dinner. No other skip tracing reps were there."

"Interesting."

"Horace wants to meet us tomorrow. He now works for a competitor of Seamless called End the Chase. Horace is looking for new clients."

"Good. The more industry people we talk to, the better." My cell buzzed. It was Arlene. "I better take it. We've been playing phone tag."

"Right. Put her on speaker," Uncle Mike said.

We exchanged greetings, and we each apologized for the missed calls.

"Eddie, Mike, I just wanted an update," Arlene said.

"Of course," I said. "We're getting the stall from the Deacon."

"You gave him my offer?"

"Yes, it was more than reasonable." I thought her offer of ten grand was enough for the Deacon to feel we had "skin in the game."

"What's his problem? Does he want more money?"

I couldn't blame Arlene for being put out. "The Deacon hasn't come back with a counter. I think we just need to be patient."

"I should've expected this kind of treatment from him. He knows he's got me over a barrel and wants to keep me hanging."

"Hi, Arlene, it's Mike. The Deacon heard about your scrapbook. We believe that's why he contacted you."

"Good," Arlene said with a note of triumph. "Keep that pile of crap safe, gentlemen. I knew that would get his attention. Tell him I'll use it, too, if I have to."

"Hopefully, it won't come to that," I said.

"The Deacon has been a thorn in my side for years. I hated the sight of him. Whenever he showed up at the house, I knew he and Porter would be off on one of those jobs. As I've said, at the time, I didn't know what those jobs included. I was a love-struck idiot, wet behind the ears. Porter and I would fight and he'd call me a spoiled brat. I'd cry and blame everything on the Deacon. The Deacon would just laugh. He was so smug. I swear he kept Porter out of town longer just to spite me."

"Maybe the Deacon's using the same delay tactics again to get you to meet his demands." Uncle Mike looked at me and shrugged. I hated lying to Arlene and so did Uncle Mike, but what choice did we have? "We have a tentative time for another meeting tomorrow."

"I won't hold my breath. I don't need this. I really don't." She sighed and her voice became soft. "I've read everything in the scrapbook. Be careful, gentlemen. Don't forget who you're dealing with. We'll talk tomorrow."

20

LATER THAT NIGHT, WE STOOD OUTSIDE CAESARS WAITING for DiNatale's limo.

Uncle Mike blew smoke toward the back end of a cab headed out to the airport. "It still makes me uneasy having DiNatale drive us around Vegas."

"Me, too. I'm also not sure about meeting Karmazin as employees of Team Player."

"I agree," Uncle Mike said. "But the way O'Rourke explained it to us made our collection call seem like business as usual."

I didn't know what we'd have done without O'Rourke's input on the finer points of Team Player's business. "I never thought of it before. When a wise guy makes a juice loan on the street, does he sit up nights counting payments and calculating interest? Hell, no. That's what Team Player is for."

"Just the thought of a wise guy doing bookkeeping cracks me up."

"Zino was a genius. All the pieces of the puzzle are coming together. Team Player collects and sends the stream to the wise guy, and he can focus on other money-making ventures. It's not until the loan is seriously delinquent that the wise guy has to bother with it."

"Right. As reps of Team Player, we're making a collection call. Plain and simple. Only we'll have DiNatale and his boys sitting outside the office."

"You think DiNatale will settle for that?"

"When I talked with DiNatale, he seemed to understand. It's customary that the debtor deal with Team Player up front."

"If I was Karmazin, I'd try to be sure the past due amount gets paid so DiNatale and others don't get involved."

"The Russian is in a tough spot and we want to keep him there."

DiNatale's limo pulled up, and we got in.

"Where is everybody?" I didn't see DiNatale's guys.

"They'll meet us there," DiNatale said. "I like them to be sure none of Karmazin's guys are hanging around."

"Right," Uncle Mike said. "Like an ambush."

DiNatale laughed. "I'd like to keep this simple."

We took DiNatale's limo to the parking garage of The Kremlin Casino. Like last night, the parking garage was dark and unattended. I noticed one of DiNatale's boys standing near the entrance to the casino.

DiNatale made a call on his cell. "Hey, Blade, everything

good?" DiNatale turned to Uncle Mike. "We're good. Karmazin has had too much time already. Don't cut him any slack."

If it was up to DiNatale, Karmazin might already be hanging from a meat hook, but that didn't get the account current. Killing the Russian would also cut off the pipeline to the Russian oligarchs everyone suspected of bankrolling Karmazin.

Why the oligarchs had allowed Karmazin, probably a strawman, to borrow money from Zino, a man with possible mob connections, was another question. But it was a question Uncle Mike and I weren't worried about. Maybe Karmazin thought he could handle the casino on his own, and when he ran into money problems, the oligarchs left him to figure things out. Maybe cutting off funds was a way for the oligarchs to let Karmazin know who was in charge.

Karmazin might not even know he'd stepped into the mob's crosshairs over the murder of the Deacon. Since the Deacon's murder remained a secret, Karmazin might just be a clueless sap who owed the wrong people at the wrong time. Whatever the Russian's real story might be, we'd try to unearth his version. It might almost be fun.

"Remember," DiNatale said, leading us to the executive elevator at the back of the casino, "me and the boys will be sitting in the waiting room outside, so if anything gets out of hand just let us know."

Uncle Mike and I looked at each other. Sure, we'd call out for assistance and DiNatale and his crew would run in and blast everyone in sight, including us.

One of DiNatale's boys, a rail thin man with a long scar down the length of his face, spoke up. "Karmazin has three of his guys in the office."

"Good to know, Blade. Be ready," DiNatale said.

Six of us crammed into the elevator to the third floor. Inside the offices, Karmazin's men and DiNatale's men stood on opposite sides of the room, eying each other like the place was a saloon in the old west. They all lit cigarettes and Uncle Mike relit his stogie. Uncle Mike and I were searched and then escorted into Karmazin's office.

Left alone, we examined the Russian's Spartan office. There weren't any family pictures or trophies or other memorabilia, just a big desk and a chair. A long table and chairs sat along one wall. It appeared to be the office of a guy about to leave town.

Uncle Mike and I knew better than to say a word. The camera up in the corner of the room near the back door told us we were being watched.

The back door opened and Karmazin walked in. He looked a lot older than I remembered from WagerEasy's pre-Super Bowl party.

His brown hair was wavy and out of control. He was unshaven and wore a stained blue oxford shirt; the shirttails hanging out. There were dark circles beneath his eyes. He shuffled into the room, his wide shoulders almost skimming the edges of the doorjamb.

"Ah hell," he said without a trace of a Russian accent. "I get a visit from the collection agency, aren't I lucky?"

Uncle Mike took the lead and introduced us. Karmazin shrugged and gave us each a limp handshake.

"You won't believe this shit, but I got the money. I fucking got the money," he repeated, sitting back down in his leather desk chair and leaning back. He rubbed his eyes with both hands and then massaged his forehead with his fingertips. He reeked of alcohol.

"We were supposed to meet last night," Uncle Mike said. "What the hell happened?"

"Yesterday? Ah yesterday. Yesterday I was fucked." He flicked the switch on the intercom. "Bring me a bottle of water." He turned back to us. "You want to talk about yesterday or today?"

"Yesterday," Uncle Mike said, on the edge of his seat.

We wanted to know what Karmazin was up to during the drive-by murder of the Deacon.

"Okay, okay," the Russian said with a calming wave. "I could've met you yesterday, but I was not a pretty sight. By the end of the day, I was blind drunk. I've got my home country to think about, so vodka it was. You have to smoke that thing in here?"

"Yeah," Uncle Mike said, puffing hard on the cigar.

One of Karmazin's men, a short man with greasy black hair, brought in a bottle of water, followed by Blade.

"Thanks, Ilya," Karmazin told his man, grabbing the water bottle with a shaky hand. "That will be all. Unless you guys want anything?"

"Nope," Uncle Mike said, blowing cigar smoke across the desk.

After the two men had walked out and Karmazin had slugged down half the bottle of water and wiped his lips with the back of his hand, he leaned across the empty desk. "It was hell, guys. I was in hell. I had the Deacon here and my countrymen back in Russia. I could run. Make a mad dash to my death, because one of the two would find me, and when they did find me, I'd wished I was dead. Better to drink and enjoy my last few hours."

He talked fast for a guy with a pounding hangover. I'd hate to hear him gab when he was sober.

I noticed how Uncle Mike listened carefully to the bullshit Karmazin fed us. Then I recalled what Uncle Mike had said about how he'd collected accounts when he worked part-time at Team Player. "You listen. You win them over," he'd said. "You make their problem your problem and work to find a solution."

"I was fucking nuts for buying this rundown shithole," Karmazin continued. "It's not the Bellagio, it's not even the old Imperial. It's the fucking Burger King of Vegas. I offered a discount on the rooms. I offered loose slots. I tried everything. I fell behind on payments to my countrymen and vendors, so I borrowed from Zino. I heard the Deacon would get involved if I didn't pay. Everyone told me not to do it. It was the option of last resort. You'll end up in the desert, everyone told me."

He shook his round head, squinted, and scratched at the stubble on his chin. "So, what do I do? Besides working my way through another bottle of the best vodka at the bar downstairs, I decide to bet everything. I decided to throw caution to the winds and do what sports books and bookies are told not to do—I went one-sided on the Super Bowl. The odds yesterday at The Kremlin on the 49ers were the best odds on the Strip. I even advertised on sports radio. We had them lined up at the sports book all day. Those California motherfuckers couldn't wait to get in here and bet, laughing and giggling at the dumb Russian. Every other sports book was putting limits on their action or nipping at the spread or moneyline, but I went all-in on the Chiefs because I had nothing to lose."

Uncle Mike grinned. "You're crazy. I can't believe you did that."

"Everybody stayed and drank and gambled like they were already winners. They bet prop bets all day, too. They wanted to stay and see the Russian take it up the ass. I drank one toast after another. They bought me drinks all day. We took more and more action."

Karmazin leaned back and belched. "Now my fucking head is ready to explode."

"You must've made a killing," I said.

"That's right. The best part? You should've seen those Californicators' faces when KC went ahead. The sports book was like a morgue. I was drinking with them, telling them how sorry I was for them and their team. Boo-hoo. At the same time my insides are ready to jump out of my chest. It's all like a dream, a bizarre, wild dream."

If Karmazin could go one-sided on the Super Bowl, maybe he was crazy enough to find the Deacon and orchestrate a drive-by shooting. The Russian was mad.

"So, you can pay us?" Uncle Mike asked. "Then what are we here for?"

Karmazin shook his head and held out his hands. "That's just it. I need a couple of days. I've got money flowing upstream and downstream—"

"What are you talking about?" Uncle Mike demanded.

"I'm telling you; I've got money in several different places and I've got to arrange things."

"Look," Uncle Mike said, standing up and leaning over the desk. "I don't make house calls, and if and when I do, I don't leave without funds being transferred."

Karmazin met Uncle Mike's stare. The Russian swallowed hard and his tongue swept his cracked lips. "I've got to have some time."

"Time for what?"

Where was that "understanding collector" Uncle Mike had boasted to me about?

"Stop yelling," Karmazin pleaded.

"Jesus Christ, we've got two groups of guys sitting out in the waiting room ready to go to war and you need a fucking accountant?"

"Stop yelling, please."

"What am I supposed to tell my client? You need time to do—what?"

Karmazin stood and screamed back. "My fucking head, goddamnit!"

"I don't care!"

"A couple of days!"

Uncle Mike pointed a finger in the Russian's face. "You got twenty-four hours! That's it. Then you take your chances."

Uncle Mike turned around and marched out of the room. Karmazin's head dropped, his arms stiff, still leaning on the table. I got up and left.

In the elevator on the way down to the parking garage, our entourage was silent. DiNatale's men stared at their shoes. DiNatale scratched at the mass of oily curls at the back of his head.

When the elevator stopped, DiNatale turned around and stared at me and then at Uncle Mike. "Remind me not to owe you fuckers any money."

21

THAT NIGHT, I SAT DOWN IN MY HOTEL ROOM AND TEXTED Nicole. She was playing in a cash game and would let me know if she could get away.

I pulled out Arlene's scrapbook from the room safe. When we learned the Deacon had been murdered, I had retrieved the scrapbook from the safe deposit box at the bank.

Usually, I'd be reading a crime novel. I'd picked up the reading habit when I was a kid. When I worked as a stock boy at O'Connell's in my early teens, I'd sit on the basement stairs behind the bar and read.

I kept myself busy at home and steered clear of action. But here in Vegas, where the poker room and the table games were right downstairs, it wasn't so easy. I had winnings in my pocket from the Super Bowl and Super Rocket that I could parlay into the makings of a serious bankroll.

Instead, I sat down with Arlene's scrapbook. There were handwritten notes, pages of single-spaced type from a manual typewriter circa the last century, complete with White-Out and coffee rings, brown, dried-out newspaper clippings, train schedules, and racing programs. One report detailed a bookie's discussion of a night partying with the Deacon. Some of the pages were filled with witness reports of crimes reportedly committed by Porter and the Deacon on behalf of the mob. Pages were stapled together even though each report was from a different investigator on a different date. Some of the pages were simply filler inserted by a private investigator in order to pad the fee charged to Arlene. It was a mess.

I read each page anyway. I owed the Deacon a long look at any history I could find.

Many of the reports detailed other strange ways of the pair. A number of alleged incidents involved mob associates who had testified against the mob and then entered the federal witness protection program. Porter and the Deacon would follow the informant through a network of contacts they'd set up across the country. It was a network that included a private army of bartenders, petty criminals, bookies and gamblers. Ultimately, Porter and the Deacon would stake out a certain restaurant known to serve a certain dish the informant couldn't live without, or a nearby ballpark or racetrack.

I imagined the informant walking back into the locker room after a round of golf to find Porter and the Deacon waiting. Did they immediately execute the murder contract? Did they pull their guns? The answer, according to the scrapbook, was "no."

"Hey, pal," Porter might say. "We've been looking all over for you."

"What do you know," the Deacon might say. "We never thought we'd run into you here. Where was the last place we saw you?"

"The courtroom," Porter would say.

"That's right," the Deacon would nod. "A courtroom. Spilling your guts to the jury and everyone else. You know, some guys are doing serious time because of you."

"Now don't say anything," Porter would advise their quarry. "Lies upset us."

The Deacon, according to reports, might happen to have a four iron in his hands. "I like the feel of this club. Do you mind if I take it with me? I use it for practice."

"My buddy likes to stay in practice," Porter would say. "Why don't we go someplace where we can talk? You like to talk."

"Or you can start yelling for the cops," the Deacon would hold up the blade of the four iron and run a finger along the grooves.

"Let's not do anything we'll regret," Porter would've said.

They had become emboldened over the years. The local cops would turn a blind eye to a "squealer."

"You could run. But we're watching you 24/7. We're going to a lot of trouble." Porter "the Pastor," Pearson reportedly said. There were pictures of his mugshot in the file and a few of him with Arlene. He looked like a regular guy.

One witness said that one of the men had just smiled and said, "We'll let you know what we want. You can't hide." Or, perhaps the witness had heard the line in a movie and decided it made a good story to tell investigators and reporters hungry for facts.

Around midnight, I heard a soft knock on my door. Then the door opened.

It was Nicole. Earlier, I'd given her one of my hotel key cards.

"Hello there."

"Want some company?" she asked.

She didn't wait for an answer. We tossed the notion of "let's take things slowly," along with our clothes, into the discard pile.

———

Later, Nicole and I were lying together in bed.

"I've wondered what your investigation is about. I know you can't tell me, but whatever it's about, all I can say is, thank God. Isn't this great?"

"Yes, it is."

"Did you think we'd find each other again? Just last year we were both in serious or semi-serious relationships and then—"

"Perfect timing."

She ran her hand along my chest. "Is it a coincidence? Or fate?"

"When I heard the investigation was in Vegas, I thought this might happen. Or rather, hoped."

"I give you credit. When you left, I thought, well that's it. Then you'd call me every other month or so to stay in touch. I'd be down and be thinking how crummy things were, and then I'd get a call from you."

"We had a special time." I wished I was better at explaining what I meant. I wasn't one who "got in touch with his feelings." I simply tried to do what was right. If I'd gotten the right cards that night years ago, I might've stayed in Vegas. Luck should never determine anything.

"It was special. I never thought this could happen—that we'd be back together again. I'd written us off. But that's how I look at things sometimes. When I bought my house, I figured that closes the previous chapters of my life, and now I'm moving on."

The house meant she'd set down roots. "You grew up in Chicago. It's a great town." I didn't think Vegas would ever be the right place for me.

"My dad and I haven't made any progress. The less we see of each other, the better."

"You don't have to see him."

"There's so much happening in Vegas. There's never a dull moment."

"Let's keep it that way," I said, pulling her toward me.

22

THE NEXT DAY, I BROUGHT THE COFFEE AND BREAKFAST sandwiches to Uncle Mike's room. Uncle Mike cleared a spot on the table. He had a room with a kitchenette, while I had the typical pair of queen beds, a desk, and a dresser. When it came time for Uncle Mike to secure accommodations, Burrascano had let it be known that Uncle Mike deserved only the very best.

"Big surprise that you wanted coffee in your room," I said, placing the breakfast stuff on the counter.

Uncle Mike took the lid off the cup and blew on the steaming hot brew. "What do you mean?"

I laughed. "What about your habit of smoking outside the hotel?"

"Oh," Uncle Mike shook his head. "A drive-by shooting has a way of curing you of that morning cigar. Besides, we need to call Irv."

Irv had founded an accounting firm in Chicago that had grown to six offices in major cities throughout the United States. On our jobs for Burrascano, we needed someone who could follow the money, and Irv's firm had proven invaluable.

"What else do we have on the agenda for today?" Nicole had ridden down the elevator with me for coffee. She would drive back to her house and get ready for the taping of today's episode of *The Sports Betting Insiders* at the Bellagio. I'd given her Marini's college basketball picks for tonight.

Uncle Mike walked over, opened the curtains, and stretched his arms above his head. "Another beautiful day in the desert." He scanned the surroundings from the tenth-floor perch.

"Inside the casino, I forget about what it's like outside," I said.

"You need to get out more. Meet people."

"Like Karmazin?"

Uncle Mike yawned. "I bet he drank half of California under the table Sunday."

"What did you think of him?"

"A couple of things. Karmazin didn't know that Zino and the Deacon are the same guy. That tells us nobody knows, outside of Burrascano and his inner circle."

"Karmazin was afraid of the Deacon, that's for sure."

Uncle Mike sipped from his coffee. "What good does it do for Karmazin to kill Zino? He'd still owe the money. He'd continue to believe the Deacon would come after him. Or the mob would come after him. The debt isn't going away."

"You didn't cut him any slack. What happened to that understanding collector who plays the counselor and lets the debtor cry on their shoulder?"

Uncle Mike grunted. "When you've got guys like Vic DiNatale sitting on the other side of the door, and you're collecting from a shady character connected to the Russian mob, you better put on one hell of a show."

"So, you're scratching Karmazin off the list?"

"No, the guy's an actor. Maybe I read him wrong. The Russian mob could be using him to get to the Deacon. We'll know in twenty-four hours. If he pays, then we'll scratch him off the list, but not before."

I was hoping for progress, and progress meant scratching people off our list, until I was left with one suspect I could focus upon. Leaving Karmazin on the list even temporarily aggravated the hell out of me.

Uncle Mike unwrapped one of the breakfast sandwiches. "What have we got here? Bacon and egg? Nice."

"Don't get used to it. Aunt Maureen wants you to eat right on this trip." I sipped from my coffee. "I'm trying to get a handle on Zino. At first, I think of Zino as a good guy running Team Player. He's buddies with lots of people here at the conference. Team Player provides cover for illegal bookies as well as being a legit business. But these bookies are being phased out of business due to the legalization of sports betting. I keep thinking of what Hadlow told us—how she and Zino dreamed of retiring to Tuscany."

"Right," Uncle Mike said, his mouth full. "The shell company that made the loan to Karmazin was Tuscan Acceptance."

"Correct. So, at first, I think of Zino as a guy at the end of the road, slowly slipping into obscurity. Then what do we find out? He's got a loan to Karmazin, connected possibly to the Russian mob and oligarchs, where the past due amount alone is four hundred K. What is the total loan amount—a couple million at least? That's just one loan. How much in total does Zino have out there on the street?"

"Maybe the money loaned by Zino to Karmazin came from some crooked union pension fund. We don't know."

"The Feds have cracked down on the misuse of pension funds."

"You hope."

I sipped my coffee. I'd eaten my sandwich downstairs, but watching Uncle Mike eat made me hungry all over again. "I'm just saying that Zino might be a bigger player than we think."

"When we met the Deacon, he acted as if his alter ego was in mothballs. He'd gotten plastic surgery. Then, we find out about the cozy Zino alias. I think your first impression was right. I think the Deacon wants to slip off to Tuscany and retire."

"I'm just not so sure anymore. Maybe the Deacon wasn't killed."

"You heard Burrascano. DiNatale wasn't acting. No way," Uncle Mike said. "Plus, we saw the birthmark above the knee. Also, I don't think Burrascano would pay us if the Deacon was pulling a con."

"Yes, you're right." It made sense. The mob hated to spend money. Arlene was still in the dark. I felt lousy about that. "What am I going to say to Arlene today?"

"Tell her the Deacon gave us a counter."

"How much?"

"I don't know. Make up a number."

"I wonder what the Deacon actually knew about Porter's disappearance." Arlene's scrapbook had left me with more questions than answers.

"Let's talk about what we need to do next. Forget about the Deacon for the time being."

"There's so much we don't know."

I thought again of the scrapbook.

"I know what you're thinking about. When you think of the Deacon, you think of your mom. Move on," Uncle Mike said. "Let's work on today. Don't forget, we're meeting Horace later."

Maybe Uncle Mike was right. "You said Horace is a character?" I got up and walked over to the windows and caught sight of a plane headed out across the mountains, the wings glistening beneath the desert sun.

"Yeah, he's a good guy. We both talked about jazz. His dad was a big jazz fan and played piano in a trio for years. Horace said he was named after Horace Silver, the jazz great." Uncle Mike took the final bite of his egg, bacon, and bagel sandwich.

"Aren't you taking this collection manager role a little too far?"

Uncle Mike talked and chewed. "A good collection manager is always looking for another skip tracing tool."

"I can't take it."

"Hey, in another life, I could've been a collection manager, you never know. Besides, I'm curious. Let's take a look at the software, then we can ask other people at the conference for their opinion. Talking shop always helps break the ice. We also need to talk with those friends of Zino who are pissed off about Jalbert's Globex deal."

Uncle Mike wadded up the wrapping paper from his sandwich, launched a set-shot at the trash can, and missed. "Okay, it's about time for our call." It was eleven o'clock Chicago time. Uncle Mike grabbed his cell. "You have the list?"

Irv answered on the first ring. "Hi Mike, hey Eddie," he said. I could picture the bald accountant pacing behind his desk inside the firm's luxurious offices located on the 86th floor in a glittering new building in downtown Chicago.

"Hi Irv," Uncle Mike said over the cell's speaker phone. "How's the family?"

The two exchanged pleasantries. Irv's grandson was now an active two-year-old chasing around after a miniature soccer ball. Irv had a video we were forced to watch—twice. Based on the two-year-old's moves, I had the kid pegged as a future accountant.

"Okay, I'm sure Eddie wants us to get down to business," Irv said. "I've got the troops organized and ready to go. They can't wait. What is it this time?"

The troops were about twenty volunteer accountants. They loved to dig into shell companies and the dealings of white-collar criminals, and understood the type of work we did. When he was a detective on the force, Uncle Mike had gotten Irv's son out of prison by proving he'd been wrongfully convicted. Irv's son now practiced general medicine for the Red Cross in Nigeria. Irv couldn't do enough for us.

"It's the debt-buying industry, Irv," Uncle Mike said.

"Oh yeah? That can be big business. Wall Street darlings. Who is involved?" Irv seemed to be champing at the bit.

"I've got a list," I said. I gave him Stefan Jalbert's Vortex Corporation and explained Jalbert's deal to buy the charged off accounts from Globex Bank. I described the competition of Tanner and 2ndBetOnDebt for the Globex Bank business. I included Sergei Karmazin, The Kremlin Casino, Eliot Scullion, and Team Player Collection Agency.

"Jeez, Eddie," Uncle Mike said. "Why don't you give him the phone book?"

"That's quite a list. I heard about the upcoming IPO of 2ndBetOnDebt," Irv said. "That might be a good starting point. Lots to look into. It's the chance for investors to reap their rewards." Irv always followed the money. "Stock options for employees are a big deal as well."

I thought of Linda Roberts and her zeal to collect as much as possible on Second Bet's accounts and her daily calls to Globex. What did she have in stock options? We told Irv about the friction over Jalbert's Globex deal.

"These companies are all jockeying for position to buy debt," Irv said in a flurry of words, as if his mind was three steps ahead of his speech. "Debt used to be sold at auction, but that got out of hand. The banks didn't want their debt falling into the hands of buyers they hadn't vetted."

"You're familiar with the business?" Uncle Mike asked.

"Yes, we had lots of debt buying by some of our entrepreneurial clients in the past, but that has dropped off in recent years. You'll want to know who is working with whom. The collection business is all about relationships, but so is any business, for that matter. It's the same for our accounting business. People want to meet face to face and know the person who works on their books and their returns so they can sleep at night. However, like any friendship or relationship, misunderstandings can occur and bad feelings result. At the end of the day, relationships can make or break careers."

Uncle Mike pulled out one of his cigars and began to unwrap it. The tempo of his words matched the slow progress of the stubborn cellophane he tried to unwrap. "The same is true in the police department. If I'd worked more on relationships, maybe I'd still be on the force. Right now, we're attending the Debt Exchange Conference in Vegas."

"They had that shooting at Caesars," Irv said.

"Yeah," Uncle Mike said. "We kept our heads down."

"Damn," Irv said. "You guys are always in the middle of something." He laughed, a quick brittle laugh that he customarily cut short to avoid losing too much of his time. "I know, I know. You need it yesterday."

"Right again, Irv," Uncle Mike said.

23

WHILE WE WERE TALKING TO IRV, I RECEIVED A CALL FROM Nicole. When we finished with Irv, I called her back.

"Eddie, have you got some time?" Nicole asked.

"What is it?"

"I really need to see you. Can you come to my house?"

From the tone of her voice, I knew there was a problem. "Sure. I'll be right over." I hung up and turned to Uncle Mike. "I need to run over to Nicole's. She sounds flustered about something." It was so unlike Nicole.

"Go ahead. We aren't scheduled to meet with Horace until ten-thirty. I've got a bet with Jennie as to whether or not the two of you will make it work this time." Uncle Mike smiled, slapping me on the back.

"What side did you take?"

"She took Chicago, and I took Vegas. I'll go downstairs with you. Hopefully, by now, it's worth the risk to light up my cigar outside."

When I got to Nicole's house, I ran up to the front door and knocked.

Nicole answered. She had on a red leather vest, black slacks, and her hair was done as if she was about to step in front of the TV cameras.

"Hi," she said, giving me a quick hug. "I'm glad you could make it."

TV Nicole had an air of confidence. I was struck by her eyes. They were alive and alert and angry. She could predict winners. "Damn, you're beautiful."

"You said that last night, but I don't mind hearing it again." She gave me a sad smile. "I'm supposed to be at the casino in twenty minutes to tape our next show. I just heard a little while ago. They say it could be over. That's why I called."

"What?"

"I'm not totally sure yet. I'm in shock. I need to vent." She pulled me close and gave me a tight hug. "I'm glad I can count on you."

She pushed me away and slapped her right fist into the palm of her left and began to walk toward the kitchen. "I couldn't go to the casino right away. Not until I talked to someone first." She pulled off her vest and threw it at the sofa.

I was confused, but I had a feeling she'd fill me in before long.

"We worked so hard. We were a team." She paced about like a caged panther. "I don't know if I'm coming or going right now." She took a deep breath. "I think the show might be over. *The Sports Betting Insiders* might be history."

"What? Didn't you say they wanted you to do basketball? The show was doing great."

"It's not that," she said. "WagerEasy is backing out. I don't think any other sports betting operator will sponsor it. The rumor is Franzen will be fired."

"What? Franzen just held that successful pre-Super Bowl party."

Nicole should be riding high. She'd picked the winner of the Super Bowl on a national broadcast. Nicole and the show should be more popular than ever. Why would WagerEasy dump the show? My anger flared.

"I don't get it."

"Me neither," she said, glaring down at her cell phone. "I've called Franzen about ten times and she's not calling me back. I'm worried and pissed. I was thinking about going over there, but I'm in no condition to drive. I'm a wreck. I'd like to scratch someone's eyes out." Nicole had a temper. I'd need to stay calm to get her to do the same. I couldn't blame her, though; the sports betting show was her pride and joy.

"Maybe we should go over and talk to her before you get too upset. It might just be a misunderstanding. Do you know where she lives?"

"Yes. I gave her a ride a couple of times when her car was in the shop." She found her purse and dug into it. She pulled out her keys. "Maybe I have no choice now but to play Scullion heads-up."

"Now wait a minute," I said, stopping at the door. "Playing this guy heads-up shouldn't be something you feel pressured to do."

"You don't think I can beat that shithead? I'm a pro." She had her hands on her hips.

Just when I had the situation under control, I had to light the fuse again. "Take it easy. All I'm saying is it's unneeded pressure right now. When you put yourself under pressure, you always rise to the occasion. But too much pressure isn't good for anyone."

"Have you been talking to Wit? Why haven't I heard from him?"

"No, I haven't been talking to Wit or anyone else," I said.

"You just think I can't handle it."

"Of course, I think you'll beat him. I'm just saying you have alternatives here."

"Like what? Play the slots?"

"No," I tried to hunt for the best diplomatic way to suggest a waiting period. "You can ease back into poker full time. You don't have to play heads-up right now."

"Why don't you call my mortgage company and tell them how I'm easing up? I'm sure they'll say, 'sure, go ahead, take your time, sweetie, while we foreclose on your ass.' Responsibility is not your thing. You don't understand why others take on responsibility."

I didn't appreciate being the two-year-old in the conversation. "Fine. Let's drive over and see Franzen. Maybe she can clear this up."

Nicole swiped back her long hair. "Sorry. I'm probably making a big deal out of nothing. Let's talk to Franzen. It's just that a guy like Scullion is my chance to make a big score and have some breathing room until I can get a gig on another show. I can't tell him to wait. My moment of celebrity is now. Once that fades, I won't get another chance. Fish like Scullion don't grow on trees."

"Let me talk to Wit with you."

"Would you? He's always respected you. You were like the son he never had. The last time I saw him, he asked about you. Can you meet him today? We're scheduled for a late lunch around two o'clock."

Like other pros, Wit played in marathon cash games until three or four o'clock in the morning. His breakfast was a late lunch for most people.

"I'll make time." I'd have to be careful. Wit could read me like the back of a cereal box—sugar-coated Eddie bullshit in a box, he'd say. If I wasn't one hundred and ten percent behind Nicole's heads-up match, Wit would never commit and then no one would back her. I could hear the old pro now in that deep drawl of his. "Eddie, you know Nicole better than anyone, and if you aren't on board, there must be a problem."

"Thanks, Eddie." This time she threw her arms around my neck and gave me the kind of kiss that wouldn't help us get answers from Franzen anytime soon. Nicole could hit the "turbo" switch when she got in the mood.

"Okay, okay," I said, reluctantly stepping back. "Let's go to Franzen's."

I drove Nicole's car to Franzen's house as Nicole barked instructions at me. She'd been so proud of her show and her successful picks. Her fans would miss her and she'd miss her fans. If, in fact, WagerEasy had dropped out and no other operator picked up the show, Nicole would be starting from the beginning again. My hands tightened their grip on the steering wheel.

"My agent tells me these shows aren't easy to find, at least ones that paid as well as The Sports Betting Insiders," Nicole said, rubbing her forehead. "Am I going to have to rely on my cut from daddy's track bets? A fix if I ever saw one. Fuck me. I'll be blackballed in every sports book in the city if I keep giving in to him. Turn at the next right."

I agreed. She would be blackballed if she kept making bets on what seemed like fixed races running in Chicago. But instead of agreeing with her, I tried my best to talk her off the rocky ledge. "You'll come out of this okay. A lot of people saw your broadcasts. I'm sure social media will be buzzing."

"Thanks. Left up here. Fuck social media. A pack of piranha."

I had the same thoughts about social media, but kept them to myself. We drove into a blue-collar neighborhood with apartments. Franzen lived on the second floor of an apartment building a few blocks from an out-of-date shopping center. The parking lot was almost empty. I reminded myself that today was Tuesday, a working day.

We walked up the stairs and knocked on the door. Someone flipped the curtains inside, but I didn't tell Nicole. No one answered the door.

"C'mon, Nicole," I said. "Maybe Franzen will be at the casino."

"Bullshit." Nicole pounded harder. "Carla," she called out, "open up."

"Take it easy, will you? A neighbor might call the cops." I put my arm around Nicole. "Let's go. The time probably isn't right. If Carla was fired, it will be a tough time for her."

"We were friends, Eddie. At least I thought Carla and I were friends. What the fuck?"

"C'mon," I told her. But she kept pounding.

The door opened a crack. Franzen stood in the doorway in a bathrobe, her hair sticking out in a dozen directions, and a cigarette dangling from her lips.

"What?" Franzen demanded.

"I want answers," Nicole said.

"Can we come in?" I asked. I didn't think we should have a screaming match outside on the landing.

"No, you can't come in," Franzen said. "And I have nothing to say. You called me how many times and I didn't answer, doesn't that tell you anything?"

"It tells me you're avoiding me," Nicole said.

"You got that right," Franzen said.

"Lower your voices," I said. "You two are friends. Remember that."

"Our ratings got better and better. People were betting like crazy with WagerEasy at the party," Nicole said.

"I can't talk about their record profits," Franzen deadpanned.

"Why are they pulling the plug?" I asked.

Franzen shrugged. "Sometimes companies expand too fast." She held up one finger, asking us to wait a second. She came back with a package. "Take a look. I had to sign this in return for my severance money."

I took an inch of paperwork out of the mailer. It was a nondisclosure.

"What the hell is that?" Nicole asked, taking a step back, as if the mailer held a clump of poisonous snakes.

Franzen exhaled smoke. "I'm a single mother. It won't be easy for me to find another job in this town. I worked for the enemy—one of those bastard operators trying to steal casino business. Now WagerEasy has left me high and dry. I can't fight the NDA, I'm fucked."

"We can take it to court," Nicole said.

Franzen shook her head. "Sorry. You have to pick your battles in this world, and this is one I can't fight."

Nicole turned to me as if somebody had appointed me an arbitrator. "Eddie, can't we—"

"She's right," I said. "Sorry, Nicole." I wished I could stuff the NDA down the throat of the nearest WagerEasy boss.

"Then I'll play Scullion heads-up," Nicole said.

Franzen froze. "You're playing Scullion?" She took back the mailer I handed her. A sour look crossed her face. "I hope you whip his ass."

24

I GOT BACK LATE FOR OUR MEETING WITH HORACE IN THE
exhibit hall. Nicole and I had driven to the casino together. She
wanted to check in with the studio employees and thank them
for all their hard work over the past two years. It was a classy
thing to do and, much to my relief, she was beginning to get
her temper under control.

Uncle Mike stood near the coffee setup inside the exhibit
hall.

"You're late," he said, looking at his watch. "How's
Nicole?"

I told him about the abrupt end of the sports betting show
and everything else that had occurred. I also told him how I
hated to see a guy like Scullion get his way and I didn't like the
fact Nicole felt compelled to play him.

"You think Wit'll agree to the match and get the other
pros to back her?" Uncle Mike asked.

"It will kill Nicole if they don't." The camaraderie between players had grown over the years. I'd been a part of it for some time and respected each of the players.

"You're going to try to convince Wit Witkowski, the dean of the poker pros?"

"Right." I grabbed a paper cup and got coffee from one of the tanks. We took a few steps back from the table for privacy. The conference sessions were on break and the attendees began to stream into the exhibit hall.

Uncle Mike rubbed his chin. "Let me get this straight. You told me it might not be the best thing right now for Nicole to play heads-up, but you're going to talk to Wit?"

"I know. What can I say? I'm on her side—one hundred and ten percent."

"Bullshit. I know you'd like to drop in on WagerEasy and strangle somebody, but you can't. And you can't go to Wit on Nicole's behalf when you don't think she's ready. She could lose a lot of money. I'm talking about a lot of money. And so could her backers."

"That's what heads-up is about."

"No, it's not. It's about a poker pro sticking it to some egotistical rich asshole, whose balls have swelled up to the size of melons and is in dire need of having somebody kick him squarely in the crotch."

"When will Nicole be ready? I thought about it some more since I first talked with her. When are we ready to take on a tough challenge, maybe the toughest challenge of all? It's certainly the biggest challenge of Nicole's poker life so far. She's not just playing in the World Series where you lose ten grand and get knocked out. The other pros will be backing her. It says a lot."

Uncle Mike stabbed at me with his index finger. "You are complicit, don't you see? You know she's under intense pressure and now might not be the right time. Yet you're going to use your friendship with Wit to convince him and the other pros to go ahead with this cockamamie idea."

"You have to strike when the opportunity is pounding on your door."

"Jeesus. Now I've heard everything."

"We're looking for a killer. Aren't we playing a murderer heads-up? Or doesn't that count?"

"It's not the same thing."

I could see this was a one-sided argument. I was the nephew, the kid who was always in trouble and in need of a lecture. "Fine. Where is our meeting with Horace?"

"Third aisle over."

Uncle Mike wasn't going to give an inch, and I had the same stubborn streak.

We walked past booths at the end of the aisle. Hadlow's company, Gusher Acceptance, featured a backdrop of an oil derrick gushing a torrent of dollar bills into the sky. "Be your own boss," the display proclaimed. Hadlow was fast-talking a couple of prospects in an attempt to sell what little debt she had left in her meager inventory.

Another booth hawked collection software. It was staffed by two leggy Vegas models offering brochures and a warm smile, and had attracted a large crowd.

As we passed a booth for a process service company, I leaned over to Uncle Mike. "What about these skip tracing companies? I know they find people, but–"

"But you'd like to know what the hell it's about. Well, I'll tell you." He stood with his hands on his hips. "When I worked at Team Player we sent over a batch of accounts and I can see by the dumb look on your face, you don't know what I'm talking about. A batch is say a thousand accounts with something in common—the same placement date, the same creditor or maybe they're batched up because they're all small balance accounts."

"A thousand accounts? What the hell?"

"A lot of people owe money. It's a funny world outside the casino walls—people have to make money and buy things and then they get canned and go into debt. It's sort of like what's happening to Nicole. Except she's got a dumbass knight in shining armor."

"Let's skip the shitty comments."

"People fall through the cracks. They fall off the edge of the world, I don't know. A collection company keeps looking for them. Maybe the debtor hits the lotto or marries some rich asshole, I don't know. But shit happens. All of a sudden, the skip tracing company gets a phone number or an address or something and viola—the debtor is found and agrees to pay the debt. Maybe they need to clean up their credit to buy a house or something. It's life."

"So, you keep hunting and hunting and the skip tracing company scours all these databases to find people."

"You got it, Sherlock. Voter's registration, small business licenses, driver's licenses, the list of databases goes on and on. Or they skip trace for a job or bank account. Back in the good old days, people got in a covered wagon and moved west. Now, there's nowhere to go."

We walked over to the third aisle. The fourth booth down the aisle was packed with people. It was the End the Chase booth with a backdrop display of a green Steve McQueen Mustang in flight at the crest of a hilltop street in San Francisco. Everybody, it seemed, needed skip tracing.

Uncle Mike shook his head. "We can't look at software in this circus."

"I don't see Horace."

We got the attention of one of the busy staff. Uncle Mike told her we had an appointment and gave her his name.

She checked a list. "Mr. Smith has set up a computer station in one of the ante-rooms down the hall." She handed us a piece of paper with a diagram and a room number. "I don't know why we need a diagram. It's just down the hall."

"Thanks." Uncle Mike turned to me. "Can you spare the time for this?"

"C'mon." I was getting pissed off at his attitude.

We walked on in silence. Down the hall, I spotted the meeting room for 2ndBetOnDebt. Inside, I assumed Linda Roberts and her gang were beating up another one of their vendors. Outside the room, a couple of nervous attendees awaited their turn for the inquisition.

One of them waved as we walked by. "Hey, you guys are with Team Player?"

We nodded and a distinguished man with white hair came over. "My name is Jim Brandt. I'm a friend of Tony Zino. How's he doing?"

This wasn't the first time we'd been approached by one of Zino's friends. We went through the introductions and told him about Zino's condition. Like one of those fish stories, every time we talked about Zino's flu, it got worse. We told Brandt that Tony's fever was higher; he was on fluids, and the doctors were concerned.

Brandt shook his head. "Damn. Tony and I have known each other for years. He's like family. My agency works the Northeast, so when debtors move to the Midwest, we'll send the accounts over to Team Player, and vice versa. I understand you had dinner last night with Jalbert?"

"That's right," Uncle Mike said. "Felipe's. I'm still stuffed."

"You know what Jalbert is trying to do, don't you? We were all supposed to be part of his little network and now we're getting shut out. Jalbert is moving into the Northeast. He just hired my longtime paralegal Darcy. He's out to screw Zino as well. He'll be trying to hire you next."

"We've heard about his tactics," Uncle Mike said. "You can count on us."

Brandt looked at Uncle Mike and then at me. "Zino is scheduled to give a speech tomorrow after the keynote. We're all looking forward to it."

"Eddie will be giving the speech," Uncle Mike said.

I nodded. The way Brandt talked about Jalbert muscling into his territory, I felt our draft of the speech had a good chance of rallying the troops and getting Globex to reconsider.

One of the reps from Second Bet stood outside the meeting room and called for Brandt.

"I'm being paged," Brandt said. He scowled as if he knew what kind of grilling he'd get inside the room from Roberts. "Nice meeting you."

We walked on to Room 110, which, according to the diagram, was at the end of the hall.

Uncle Mike knocked on the door. There was no answer. "I guess we better let him know we're here. You can be the one to apologize for being late."

He opened the door, and we walked in. There was a computer on the table, a whiteboard on the wall with a diagram, coffee cups, and a stack of brochures, but no Horace.

"Maybe he stepped out for a minute," I said. The back door to the room was ajar. I leaned over the table. The computer screen was black. The chair had been pushed back against the wall as if somebody had run out in a hurry. Then I saw the blood splatter on the keyboard and Horace's body on the floor.

25

WE IMMEDIATELY CALLED 911 AND STEPPED OUT OF THE room. I called to the people standing outside the Second Bet meeting room and told them what had happened. Uncle Mike got on the phone to Detective Woodyard. We needed to establish a time frame of when we arrived for the meeting with Horace and make sure we had witnesses who could corroborate the time of our arrival at Room 110. I thanked God for our random talk with Brandt. The last thing we needed was to be placed on a list of suspects for the murder of Horace Smith.

"The killer tried to set us up," Uncle Mike said as we stood in the hall, waiting for the police.

My adrenaline had spiked with the discovery of a dead body. The ensuing utter chaos throughout the conference area added to my high blood pressure. Uncle Mike seemed to take the murder in stride like it was just another Tuesday. I took several deep breaths.

I'd seen dead bodies on previous jobs. Uncle Mike and his partner had me drive along with them when they worked murder cases for the Chicago police. By now, I should be a pro. Maybe if I thought through what Horace's murder meant for our investigation of the murder of the Deacon, I could focus on the business at hand.

I'd been worried that our undercover work for Team Player might be the wrong place to look for a killer. A conference about collections didn't seem like a place for murder. Now it was clear my concerns were unfounded. Horace's murder confirmed the killer was, in fact, linked to the Debt Exchange. Yet, it still didn't sit well with me. Maybe I was obsessed with the Deacon. I couldn't quite swallow the idea that the Deacon had been killed as his alias, Zino.

"Yes, the killer tried to set us up," I said. "What could Horace have told us that the murderer didn't want us to know?"

"Good point. Horace must've known something."

Caesars security personnel arrived and secured the area. They had us wait outside the exhibit hall to be questioned by the police. When the police showed up, they immediately had everyone vacate the exhibit hall as well as the entire floor.

We left this investigation to the police. Fortunately, Uncle Mike's previous contact with Detective Woodyard helped us. Not only would Uncle Mike's relationship with the detective keep us off the suspect list, it would also allow us to obtain information on Horace's murder. We would cooperate with the detective and the detective would cooperate with us. I wanted to know if the gun used to kill Horace was the same one that killed the Deacon.

We told the detective about Horace's appointment schedule the staff person had at the End the Chase booth. Who was Horace scheduled to see before our meeting?

Detective Woodyard seemed eager to follow up on this lead, but I didn't think our killer would be stupid enough to put their name on a list. Our killer had orchestrated a drive-by shooting to nail the Deacon aka Zino in what appeared to be a personal vendetta. The killer was feeling the pressure from us, but he was crafty.

We also filled in Woodyard on the type of work Horace did.

"I'm sorry you guys have to go through this," Woodyard said. He bit his upper lip as if he was about to say something. Maybe he was beginning to wonder why murders kept popping up during our stay at Caesars.

Uncle Mike took a deep breath. "As I said before, I'd appreciate it if you'd keep my prior experience between us."

The detective had played poker with Uncle Mike and his retired buddies from Chicago, and that's why we'd been granted the chance to view the Deacon's body at the coroner's office. I assumed that Uncle Mike had been introduced as a former homicide detective to everyone at the poker game.

"You mean your prior experience as a cop?" Woodyard slipped his pen back into the breast pocket of his suit coat. "Why is that?"

"I'm retired and working as a collection manager for one of these agencies, and I'd like to keep that quiet."

Woodyard nodded. "I can understand that. Sometimes people treat us cops like the enemy. I don't know why—I guess that's just the way people are. Don't worry, Mike, your secret will continue to be safe with me."

As the detective and his staff got busy with the hopeless grunt work of finding out who was where and when, and who had the opportunity to shoot Horace in the back of the head as he explained the many features of the End the Chase software, we got busy on our end. I called Shelly Urban from Seamless Dataminers and told her Team Player wanted to set up payments on their past due invoice.

Urban was ecstatic and said she'd meet us right away. After some discussion, we arranged to meet her outside near the parking garage so Uncle Mike could smoke his stogie without having people stare at him. It turned out that Urban was also a smoker and appreciated the bonding opportunity. I'd be the clean lung guy sucking up second-hand smoke.

Outside, once the two of them lit up, Urban got down to business. She wore a similar business suit to the one she wore yesterday and smiled at us like we were old friends. "What arrangements can you make on the past due balance?"

I wanted to get her interest and cooperation, but the last thing I wanted was for Team Player to pay Seamless.

"We were talking about five hundred per month without interest."

"That's a non-starter," she said with a laugh. "You'll need to do better than that."

Uncle Mike said, "We've got other concerns."

"You may have heard about Horace's murder?" I asked. The valet station was mobbed with police cars and emergency vehicles. Once every ten minutes a lone taxi left the valet station and drove past toward the boulevard. The usual valet traffic had been drastically reduced to a trickle. After witnessing Sunday's drive-by shooting, I found it hard not to examine every vehicle.

She took a deep drag on the cigarette. "Everyone's talking about Horace."

"We discovered the body."

She shrugged and puffed away. "If you would've made arrangements sooner on the invoice, you wouldn't need to look at End the Chase or talk with Horace."

"Horace told us he used to work with you," I continued. "He left under a cloud and blamed you."

"What?" She laughed as her fingers pulled back the bangs of her short red hair.

"We could point the cops to you, but we don't want to do that. We just want to get things resolved."

"Resolved? Do you want to pay the damn twenty-thousand-dollar invoice or not?" Her face reddened.

"You want the hassle of talking with the cops?" I asked.

She shook her head. "The cops will find out, anyway. It's no secret that Horace and I both worked at Seamless. If

Horace blamed me, so what? I don't know what that fool told people."

"Well, if you don't help us, we won't help you get your invoice paid."

"Who is Team Player going to use—End the Chase? They've only been around six months. They'll be in scramble mode now that Horace is dead. Seamless has been around for fifteen years."

"What if End the Chase got Jalbert's business?" I asked.

Her mouth dropped open. "I don't get it."

"Horace was sitting with us at dinner last night with Jalbert and Lundstrom." I seemed to be hitting a soft spot. I assumed that Jalbert's little network pulled a lot of weight at Seamless Dataminers. Jalbert was probably their biggest client. "There were state attorneys general at the table. Eliot Scullion was there."

"That goddamn son of a bitch. Horace didn't think the rules applied to him. Now I'm left to clean up his mess."

"It's our understanding Jalbert gets good data from Seamless and everyone else like Team Player got crap."

She stared me down. "You'll have to prove that."

"I need to have someone skipped. Can you do that for me?"

Her head dropped. "I don't know where you got all this. You can get fired for that."

"Is that why Horace was fired?" I asked. Her ensuing silence told me I was probably right.

Uncle Mike couldn't hold back any longer. "You're in this up to your chin, young lady."

"I have to talk with my employer." She pulled out another cigarette and pointed it at me. "I'll smoke this in the casino, thank you. Goodbye."

"We're not done with you," I called after her.

26

WE STOOD IN THE SMOKER'S SECTION OUTSIDE CAESARS. I continued to examine each vehicle that left the valet stand as well as the flow of police and emergency personnel. The curious crowd walked past a few yards away, some of them pointing to the bullet holes out front. The statues had been removed from their vestibules.

We were alone in the smoking station and could talk openly.

"Ms. Urban wasn't happy with Jalbert," Uncle Mike said.

"I can't blame her. Seamless gave good data to Jalbert and bad info to everyone else. It makes Jalbert look like a shining star to Globex Bank. Then Jalbert has the gall to invite Horace, now employed by Seamless' competitor, End the Chase, to Jalbert's big Monday night conference kickoff dinner."

"Do we know why Seamless had fired him?"

"I think Horace may have been terminated due to a rules violation," I said.

"You don't think Horace is the one who made sure that Seamless sent crappy info to everyone except Jalbert?"

"Maybe, but I don't think so. Based on Urban's reactions to what we said, I think Seamless agreed to be in cahoots with Jalbert. I think Horace violated other rules."

"We have the killer going after Horace." Uncle Mike said. "The question is why? If Horace was going around telling people the secrets of Seamless—that they gave Jalbert good data and everyone else crappy info—then maybe Jalbert killed Horace to shut him up? Horace could jeopardize Jalbert's scheme to expand."

"Why did Jalbert invite Horace to dinner? To give him a boost by allowing him to talk with new clients like us? You can catch more flies with honey."

Uncle Mike puffed on his cigar. "Maybe it turns out the dinner invite isn't good enough for Horace. He doesn't shut up. Horace is so pissed off at Seamless that he continues to spread rumors. It worked, too. We saw the crowd around the End the Chase booth."

"Horace didn't think he was vulnerable," I said. "He reserved that room outside the exhibit hall. The killer could easily have entered through the back door, asked Horace a couple of questions about the software, shot Horace, and slipped out the back door again."

"Where does that back door lead?"

"It's supposed to be for employees only, but I saw others using it."

"I'll ask Woodyard for a diagram of the premises."

"Jalbert called me and left a message while we were talking with Urban," I said. "He wants to meet us as soon as possible."

"No shit. I like it when people get nervous after a murder and want to meet right away. Jalbert is making himself an interesting suspect."

"I can't wait for Jalbert's job offer."

"Forget it. I'm the one who'll get the job offer. I'm the collection manager. I can collect accounts in and around Chicago, hire staff, and get those numbers right out of the box. What can you do? Hang up your grad school diploma?"

I laughed. "I'm the one giving the speech. I'm the guy he has to win over."

"You MBA grads are ruthless," Uncle Mike snickered. "Plus, you cost real money. I'm available for a decent raise and flimsy bonus, plus I'll do all the heavy lifting."

"For imposters, we're doing alright. But seriously, what are we going to tell Jalbert if he does offer one of us a job?"

Uncle Mike looked at me with his cop face, the one that signaled discipline when I was growing up. "Take it, for Christ's sake. Then string Jalbert along and fuck him over."

If Jalbert was the killer, that strategy might just get him to make a dumb move. "Good plan."

Uncle Mike got down to the stub of his stogie. "Linda Roberts stopped by earlier when I was waiting for you. She and Tanner also want to meet this afternoon."

"Don't tell me, they want to hear all about Jalbert's dinner?"

"Yup."

Uncle Mike extinguished his cigar in the ashtray. "They also want to use us and then fuck us over at the same time."

"Yes, Tanner's motto seems to be 'screw you and checkmate.' I have to meet with Nicole and Wit about the heads-up match between Scullion and Nicole. Then we can track down Jalbert," I said.

"I wouldn't want to be in your shoes. I wash my hands of the whole heads-up thing. You know I only want what's best for you and Nicole, right? If she does play Scullion, I hope she beats the pants off him."

"Thanks."

"Don't forget, we owe Arlene a call," Uncle Mike said.

"I'm dreading it, but I won't forget."

I only had a few minutes to get to my late lunch meeting with Nicole and Wit. I hadn't seen Wit in a few years, and other than a few emails back and forth, we hadn't talked for a long time. Maybe I wouldn't have any influence with the dean of the poker pros and all my arguing with Uncle Mike about what I planned to do was nothing more than a useless exercise.

———

Inside a café at Bellagio, I was led to Wit's table by the hostess. The place was crowded, but Wit sat alone in a far corner away from the windows surrounded by potted plants.

Everyone wanted a seat by the windows to view the fountains, and I assumed Wit, a long time Vegas resident, could care less about the regular fountain show out front.

Wit stood, and we exchanged a warm handshake. He looked good for a man in his late seventies who had made a career out of poker. I noticed his hair had thinned out even more, and his eyes seemed tired. He always said that poker kept him sharp, but everyone had their limits.

I took a seat across from him. "Where is Nicole? She was supposed to meet me here."

His hand shook as he brought the cup of coffee to his lips and sipped. "Eddie, I wanted to talk to you alone. I'm glad Nicole came to me before she officially agrees to play this high roller heads-up. That's the right thing to do. I heard about WagerEasy pulling out. It means the end of Nicole's sports betting show and leaves her high and dry. I don't think her head is in the right place, know what I mean? She's been playing poker for fun with her fans. That screws up your game."

The waitress brought Wit's breakfast, a stack of pancakes, two eggs sunny side up, and a side of bacon. She refilled his coffee cup and asked me if I wanted anything. I told her no.

I leaned across the table. "Nicole will be playing Eliot Scullion, a businessman. He's a nobody at poker. What does it say about the pros around here if you can't back one of your own against somebody like him?"

Wit took off his trademark fedora and placed it on the table. Then he picked up his knife and fork and cut into the stack of flapjacks. "As an unknown, he's that much more dangerous. He's working with Hans Becker. Don't sell Hans short. The guy has turned out to be one hell of a tutor. The players he's worked with the last few years have shown vast improvement."

"This isn't the Wit I remember. You used to say the only way to be a good poker pro is to put in years around the table playing against the best. You wrote a book about it. Well, Nicole has been around that table for years."

He brought a forkful of the flapjacks dripping with syrup to his mouth. "Not lately. She hasn't."

"What about all these math robots that play on the internet twelve to fourteen hours a day? I suppose that qualifies them as pros? Is that all it takes?"

He picked up a strip of bacon and pointed it at me. "If that's all it took, I'd quit."

"Exactly. Nicole shouldn't be punished because she's been a celebrity. She's brought the kind of publicity the pros need. The purses for poker tournaments have increased quite a bit thanks to her."

Wit eyed me with that glassy stare that had taken down a lot of big pots over the years. "You've got a vested interest in Nicole. I shouldn't even be talking to you."

"I'm not denying that. Nicole and I broke up a few years ago, but we're still close. Maybe we'll get back together, I don't know. I'll put my cards on the table on that score."

Wit nodded. "I'm glad to hear you say that, Eddie. I've known you a long time. I liked your style from the very first time you showed up in the high-end cash games. It impressed me when you decided it was time to leave and get your act together. It takes a lot of guts to start over. It meant leaving Nicole."

"Sure, it wasn't easy to dig myself out of the hole." If he knew I still felt the pull of the craps table, poker and the horses as well as sports, Wit might not be giving me such a glowing assessment. Maybe Wit did sense it. If so, he'd know how much I wished it was me who would be playing Scullion heads-up.

"But you did it. You got out of that hole and learned some valuable lessons. I understand you're here for one of those business conferences. A little birdie told me you got an MBA. Good for you. I never thought you could do it. I thought we were both cut from the same cloth— compulsive gamblers. Your past experience should tell you what's at stake. You, of all people, know what a delicate thing a player's bankroll can be."

If Wit knew I was playing an imposter tracking down a killer, he'd toss that breakfast plate in my face. A player's bankroll was his most prized possession. For an imposter like me to ask a player to place their bankroll in jeopardy made me realize I was right on the edge of risking everything. It wasn't my bankroll, but so much more. Maybe I was risking too much for Nicole.

No, Nicole could do it. She deserved the chance.

"I talked with Scullion. He said Hans has given him a whole new grasp of poker."

"Shit, he said that?" Wit asked, bending over the table abruptly at the waist like somebody stuck him with a shiv.

"Look Eddie, if you can honestly say Nicole is ready and if you'll vouch for her, then I'll do it."

It meant I'd be an outcast in Vegas if Nicole lost. The burden would be on my shoulders, maybe even more so than Nicole. All the leverage and good will I'd accumulated in the past and treasured more than anything would be lost. Wit knew how to put someone to the test and I knew I couldn't hesitate one second or he'd see right through me.

"You bet I'll vouch for her. Tell everyone. Because everyone will be thanking me and congratulating Nicole when she wins."

27

AFTER MY TALK WITH WIT AT BELLAGIO, I MET UP WITH
Uncle Mike at Caesars. We hustled over to the conference hall,
but everything was shut down by the police due to the
investigation of Horace's murder.

My cell buzzed. "Eddie, this is Stefan Jalbert." I heard lots
of talk and laughter in the background, and Jalbert had to raise
his voice. "I'm in the bar near the lobby. It's crowded. Can you
join us?"

"Sure, what's it about?"

"We've been discussing those issues you brought up the
other night. We can talk more when you get here."

I told him I'd be over in a few minutes and turned to
Uncle Mike. "That was Jalbert. I told you I'd be the one to get
the job offer. It's the speech—it was my nightmare before and
now it's my lotto ticket."

Uncle Mike shook his head. "You better ask for an employment contract because you'll be fired the day after the speech and Team Player will never rehire you."

"Team Player won't want me?"

"I'll see to it," he laughed.

"How do you want to play this?" We had a position of leverage and we had to keep the killer off balance.

"You're the one getting the job, right? That means I get all the fun."

It meant we'd milk this opportunity for all it was worth. The killer was feeling the pressure. They'd killed Horace to cover their tracks involving the murder of Zino. The killer might know or guess by now that we were imposters.

The bar near the lobby was packed. Almost everyone in the bar crowd wore a conference nametag and sport coat. Maybe the crowd had been subdued at first when they'd learned the news of Horace's murder, but after a toast to Horace and a few more drinks, the noise must've gradually increased to what it was right now, nearing the decibel level of a Saturday night at O'Connell's.

Jalbert sat at a prominent corner table, a stack of files on his right, a laptop directly in front, and a martini to his left. Ingrid Lundstrom sat erect to his left. She pulled a red sweater tight around her shoulders as she greeted me with a smile.

Jalbert stood as we approached. "Eddie, we saved you a seat."

Uncle Mike and I looked around. There weren't any other empty seats.

"We need to talk with Eddie," Jalbert said to Uncle Mike. "But they might have extra chairs in back."

Uncle Mike shrugged and walked toward a waiter.

"We had to improvise," Jalbert said, touching the deep scar above his lip. "There's no telling when the conference area and exhibit hall can be reopened. That means no open bar. We'll have to buy our own drinks. What would you like?"

"Whatever Ms. Lundstrom is having," I said, getting comfortable in the chair. I couldn't help but notice the number of people looking our way.

"Gin and tonic," Lundstrom said, raising her glass. "Eddie, the bank needs to move quickly."

Lundstrom's furrowed brow and serious expression conveyed the importance of the moment. The bank's needs were her monumental concern, and I had to respect that.

Jalbert leaned toward me. "It's too bad about Horace. But there have been rumors about drugs."

"I hadn't heard." I resented the rumors which I assumed were unfounded, but in my current role, I had to let it pass.

"I can't afford to wait for Zino and the audit of Team Player," Jalbert continued. "I need people I can count on from the start. We need you in charge of my Chicago branch. Your experience in Operations will be invaluable."

Jalbert had gotten right to the point and offered me the job at his new Chicago branch. Team Player had been written out of the Globex deal. I kept a straight face.

"Since Zino will have me blackballed from the industry and probably refuse to give me a reference, I'll need at least a five-year contract." I tried to appear to be a sincere young man who wanted security.

Jalbert's smile widened. "What did I tell you, Ingrid? He reminds me of myself."

The comment made me sick, but that was the territory of the imposter.

"He looks out for number one," Lundstrom said. "But I wouldn't worry, Eddie. Tony is too nice to have you blackballed. Unfortunately, Tony's numbers dropped in the last quarter and Stefan's company out-collects every other agency. The bank needs full compliance and performance, and Stefan has recruited only the best, most proven personnel to head up each new location." She nodded toward me as a way to indicate I'd be in good hands with Stefan.

"You'll be a part of the expansion, Eddie," Jalbert said as he dug into the stack of folders. "Zino's absence at the conference could not be more crucial."

Or convenient, I wanted to add, but utilized all that self-restraint I'm known for.

Lundstrom sipped from her gin and tonic. "You're getting in on the ground floor."

"I have to give that speech for Zino tomorrow. He knows a lot about expansion and the trouble it can cause." I couldn't resist reminding them of the power I held with the speech.

"That damn speech," Lundstrom muttered under her breath.

"Don't even talk about it," Jalbert said. He shuffled manila folders and pulled one out. "I have an employment contract right here. I think you'll find it suitable." He handed it to me.

I left them in suspense while I perused the contract, nodding several times. "The salary is okay, but this is only a six-month contract." The salary was about ten times what I reported to the IRS on a yearly basis.

Jalbert pulled another document out of the file. "We can change that. Here is your speech for tomorrow."

"You haven't missed any details." I couldn't wait to see what kind of speech Jalbert would want me to give.

"Did you make the changes in the speech that the bank wanted, Stefan?" Lundstrom asked.

"Yes, I believe those were inserted." He studied the document and then handed it to me.

A hand gripped my shoulder as I began reading the speech, a speech that would make a politician proud, since it seemed to say absolutely nothing. I looked up.

It was Brandt, the friend of Zino we'd met earlier, when we were on our way to see Horace. Brandt's statement to the police had kept Uncle Mike and I off the suspect list for Horace's murder. I wanted to thank the guy, but the way he sneered at me made me think he wanted to fight instead.

"So, Eddie," Brandt hissed, "I see you've found a place at the royal table. Congratulations."

"They wrote Zino's speech for me," I said.

"Hey, everyone," Brandt called. "Come over here."

Brandt's friends, who were also Zino's friends, huddled around. People saw the crowd and gathered in a circle around the huddle. I always enjoyed being the center of attention.

But I wasn't the center of attention. Ingrid Lundstrom rose from her seat like the Queen of Collections and nodded toward each person around us. Lundstrom smiled and stepped toward Brandt.

Lundstrom gave Brandt a warm hug.

"Ingrid, so good to see you," Brandt said.

Others reacted the same way Brandt did, hugging Lundstrom and almost bowing before her. I couldn't believe this. A love-fest was happening before my eyes when I needed a riot. Lundstrom came up with more sweet talk for each of them. They were swooning over each other.

Lundstrom preached to Brandt. "The bank has concerns, Jim. You've missed goal for two straight months on your existing portfolio. Can you tell us what's going on?"

Brandt's face flushed. He went through a rambling list of things they were doing to contact debtors and improve collections. Why didn't he mention how Jalbert was moving into his region and had hired Darcy?

Lundstrom smiled. "Oh good. That's so good to hear. The bank will like that. You see, everyone, the bank has to weed out underperformers, not only on an annual basis, but on a quarterly basis as well. Only the top performers will be retained and rewarded with market share. Those that continue to underperform will have their accounts recalled."

If accounts were recalled, I assumed the staff could read a magazine until they were laid off. Lundstrom pulled on a lock of her blonde hair and tugged at the lapel of her blouse. She was businesslike and played her role to perfection. Any poker player would fear her.

What I saw was magic. It was the power of the big banks in full force, and Lundstrom wielded that power like a sorceress.

She sipped from a fresh gin and tonic. "For too long, the bank has had to rely on an old boy's network. These good old boys expected bank business as a matter of right, rather than as a matter of performance, and the bank suffered. The bank needs to work with only the best-of-class, if it wants to win in its space."

It boggled my mind that people stood and nodded. Win what? I could only conclude these people must be under Lundstrom's spell.

Lundstrom turned and looked down at me. "Eddie is learning. He's learning that you need to dedicate yourself. The bank has been my life. No family. No diversions. On Sunday, I'm working on special projects. I look for people like Stefan who are equally dedicated. People who want to make the bank their life."

I swallowed hard to keep from cracking up or throwing up. Thank God, I had my bartender job at O'Connell's to rely on.

Lundstrom turned back to Brandt with a look of heartfelt concern. "I heard Darcy left."

Brandt nodded and cleared his throat. "That's right. Darcy has been with me fourteen years. Our office was her first job out of school."

"Darcy always did such a great job. So responsive," Lundstrom said. "The bank simply loved her."

Uncle Mike slipped through the crowd. "Don't worry, Ms. Lundstrom. You and the bank can still love Darcy while she's working for Jalbert."

I expected people to cheer, but instead there was dead silence. Uncle Mike didn't seem to care. I could tell my uncle was about to go on a roll. I sat back and savored the moment.

"We all heard from Horace about Seamless Dataminers," Uncle Mike continued. "He told us that Seamless sent good skip tracing information on debtors to Jalbert, while the rest of us got crap."

We were out to make trouble. The conference would end tomorrow and we had a killer to shake loose.

Uncle Mike stood in front of the crowd. "Jalbert is hiring our people right in front of our nose, and the bank has us handcuffed. I'm not going to stand for it and neither is Mr. Zino. Mr. Zino is in the hospital. They're taking advantage of the situation. Mr. Zino has been good to me for a lot of years, and I'm not going to let it happen."

A rumble of what sounded to me like indignation rippled through the crowd. The word "cheater" and "Jalbert" had become coupled.

"Please, everyone," Lundstrom said, gesturing toward Uncle Mike. "This man is merely a collection manager."

"I don't care if I'm a dishwasher," Uncle Mike said with a look of pure disgust. "Jalbert is going to audit us? Naturally, he's going to say Team Player can't cut it." He grabbed the employment contract out of my hands and waved it around.

"Jalbert is trying to hire one of our employees right under our nose."

"That's confidential," Jalbert said, standing up and trying to pluck it out of the air. Uncle Mike shoved an elbow close to his nose to keep him at bay.

"You're placing Team Player's existing portfolio in jeopardy," Lundstrom said, her arms crossed. "Don't be led astray by this—this collection manager." She uttered the word "collection manager" as if it were on a par with a mangy dog.

Uncle Mike's face had turned a shade of red. I began to wonder if his years of frustration fighting bureaucratic corruption at the police department had come to the forefront as he ranted.

"Team Player doesn't care about the bank's precious existing accounts, Ms. Lundstrom," Uncle Mike said. "Team Player is not going down without a fight. C'mon, everybody. Hang together. We all know the Seamless data was crap. We all know what Jalbert is up to. He's hiring our best employees. If the bank sells all its accounts to Jalbert, and he expands into our territory, where does that leave us?"

Jalbert stood. "I won't stand here and be falsely accused—"

"Good," Uncle Mike shouted back. "I don't want to be part of your cheater's network. All we want is an even playing field and if the bank won't give it to us after all these years, then the bank will suffer, believe me," Uncle

Mike pointed to Lundstrom as if she was the bank. "Because Jalbert can't expand and handle it all on his own."

Uncle Mike extended his arms over his head and ripped the employment contract into little pieces and threw them up in the air like confetti raining down over Jalbert's head.

Brandt started to clap. Others began to clap with him. Somebody in the back whistled.

"Take your accounts," somebody yelled.

"Shove it," someone else shouted out.

Without looking behind her, Lundstrom took a step back and almost stumbled.

Jalbert walked around the table and was heading toward Uncle Mike. I stepped in front of Jalbert.

"Get out of the way, Eddie." Jalbert grabbed me by the shoulders and tried to shove me out of the way. I had my feet planted and held my ground.

Jalbert threw a wild roundhouse right in my direction. I blocked it. He squared off to fight. Everything around me faded away. It was just him and me. My years in the gym took over, and the footwork took over. My Golden Gloves boxing experience came to the forefront. Jalbert threw another wild right that I dodged.

I could hear Uncle Mike shouting something. I think he even tugged on my sleeve. Nothing could sway me. I wanted a piece of this fucker. Bad.

I moved to my left and let Jalbert throw his right again. I moved fast to the right and clipped him on the side of the face with a setup punch. He ran at me, his arms wide to tackle me.

I slipped away and connected with a right to the head. Jalbert lost his balance and did a belly flop onto a table of drinks.

Uncle Mike got in front of me. "That's enough, Eddie."

I wanted to finish it. Uncle Mike grabbed hold of me. Others stepped in and took hold of Jalbert.

"Eddie, that's enough," Uncle Mike repeated.

28

After the near riot in the bar, Uncle Mike and I walked through the casino in the general direction of Caesars sports book.

"I thought the plan was for me to accept the employment contract," I said.

"Sorry about that. I improvised. I put myself in Zino's shoes and asked, what would Zino do? And that's what I did. I didn't know a fight would break out over it. You did good. Did you see the way people were looking at you after the fight?"

"No, I was thinking about a knockout in round two." Once I'd clicked into boxing mode, it wasn't easy to gear back down. The fight had been unexpected and short, which only added to my adrenaline overload. I'd walked out fast and didn't wait around to accept the congratulations being offered by Zino's friends.

"I think those people were in shock. They expected Jalbert to beat your ass."

What? "They expected that old man to beat me? You're kidding."

"He's built like a fireplug. Like me."

"Except for the baggage you're carrying around your mid-section."

Uncle Mike laughed. "Too true, too true. But if you keep feeding me salads, who knows?"

"You're behind about ten thousand salads."

"I got a text from Jennie to meet her in the sports book," Uncle Mike said. "The old gal is a lot of fun."

For Uncle Mike, labeling a woman around his age an "old gal" was one of the highest compliments he could bestow.

"That's fine with me." I always looked forward to talking with Hadlow. She was my one true link to the Deacon.

"Where's Nicole?" Uncle Mike asked. "Maybe she can meet us."

Uncle Mike was probably thinking about that ten-dollar winning bet he'd made. "I'll text her and let her know where we are. Her heads-up match starts tonight. Scullion insisted. She's meeting with Wit and the other pros to go over the percentages."

"High finance?" Uncle Mike asked. We stopped as I texted Nicole.

"The one thing Scullion has going for him is his bankroll. He'll try to muscle Nicole off hands with the amount of his bets. She'll need the ammunition to counter that."

"Right." Uncle Mike looked away.

I knew he was trying to avoid bringing up our previous argument over Nicole playing in the heads-up match and the fact I had talked to Wit. The heads-up match only added to my anxiety.

Uncle Mike nudged me. "Look who's waiting for us up ahead."

Tanner and Roberts gave us a wave. We continued walking toward them.

Tanner stepped into our path. "Have you two got a second?"

The four of us slipped into a vacant row of unpopular slot machines.

"We were in the bar just now," Tanner said, shaking our hands. "We wanted to congratulate you on your takedown of Jalbert. The video is everywhere."

Roberts gave us a dazzling smile and shook our hands as well. "Nice video. It will go viral. The Globex collection partner losing his shit. I've already talked with my contact at Globex. They've seen the video. They've also set up a call for tomorrow morning with Lundstrom. I think they'll institute a waiting period on Jalbert's deal."

"We don't need analyst reports when we've got Jalbert doing a belly flop," Tanner said.

The two of them high-fived and echoed corporate speech back and forth. They were almost giddy. You'd think they'd just hit the jackpot on one of the lonesome slots around us.

I recalled what Lundstrom had said. The bank hates two things—getting screwed and controversy.

"All Jalbert had in his corner was Lundstrom," Tanner said. "She was almost enough."

Roberts sighed. "Lundstrom got mad at Second Bet for no reason. A simple misunderstanding."

"Let's not have that happen again," Tanner told her.

"From now on, I'll be on the phone with Lundstrom every day," Roberts said.

"Unless they replace her," Tanner said. They laughed together again.

I hoped I could shift some of their appreciation over to Team Player. "You wanted to know about Jalbert's dinner, right? You also told us you were going to reevaluate the number of accounts you'd send Team Player on a monthly basis."

Tanner smiled. "We'd like to reevaluate Eddie, but we have policies and procedures."

"Besides," Roberts raised her eyebrows, "The dinner is irrelevant now that Jalbert is swinging and missing on social media."

Tanner held up the video on his cell. "He's down for the count. Jalbert lost his cool. The bank will hate that."

Roberts bowed slightly in our direction. "Good work, Eddie, Mike—you did our job for us and you'll have our everlasting gratitude."

"After the sale of Second Bet goes through next week, I'll use the same playbook with other industries. Thanks, guys," Tanner said.

They turned to leave, but I didn't want them to go on such a high note. "I just wanted to know, Mr. Tanner, how does it feel to lose a million on the Super Bowl? According to your friend Eliot, it was even more than that with prop bets."

Tanner swayed slightly and held his ribs.

"You're walking better today, Mr. Tanner," I called after them. The beating Tanner had taken from DiNatale and the boys had put a hitch in his giddyap.

"Those assholes," Uncle Mike muttered. "I can't believe those two. And to think Tanner will get rich off that IPO or the sale of the company or whatever he's planning. The next time DiNatale wants to use Tanner as a punching bag, maybe he'll let us join in."

I didn't intend to ridicule Tanner. If anyone was sensitive to the issue of losing money at gambling and going into debt, it was me. But we had to pressure the killer every chance we could. To get them to trip up, you had to make them angry or be an immoveable obstacle or both. We carried a bucketful of salt to rub in their wounds and always tried to stand in the way of our suspects.

Since we didn't know who the killer might be on our list of suspects, we tried to spread joy wherever we went.

"What do you think of Jalbert as a suspect?" I asked.

Uncle Mike stopped. "I like him more and more. If Globex reverses course, as Tanner and Roberts said, Jalbert might blame us. We'll have to be on our toes."

"He showed his violent streak," I said.

"Jalbert lost it, that's for sure. He could be the one, but it's the murder of Horace that keeps bothering me. What could Horace have told us?"

"Or what was Horace about to show us using his End the Chase software?" I'd been thinking along the same lines.

"Horace's murder tells us one important thing. We're on the right track with the Debt Exchange," Uncle Mike said. "Things will really start to heat up now."

29

WE WALKED TOWARD THE SPORTS BOOK AT CAESARS, THE
odds board listing tonight's sporting events and the flat screens
televising the horse races, gave me a warm invitation to sit and
handicap.

"Nicole texted back," I said. "She can't make it. She's still
working out percentages with Wit and the other pros."

"I want to see that match." Uncle Mike pointed to the
seats near the front. "There's Jennie. I feel like shit lying to her
about Zino."

"Me, too."

"We'll have to tell her when this is over."

"Or she'll end up like Arlene."

"I'm going to ease off on Zino's symptoms."

"Okay."

One person at the Debt Exchange who we didn't worry
about as a suspect was Jennifer Hadlow. We found her seated

alone in the sports book. She had saved us a couple of seats even though the entire row and most of the sports book was empty.

The fake Tony Zino, one of DiNatale's boys planted at the Vegas hospital room, had reported the delivery of a Get Well Basket and a mushy card with hand-drawn hearts signed: "Love, Jennie."

Hadlow was slumped down in her seat, looking at her cell phone. She seemed to be waiting for her old companion, and the vibe of loneliness made me wish I could tell her not to worry. Yet, the truth was even worse, and I got pissed off all over again.

"Hello, you two," Hadlow called as we took our seats and greeted her.

"Hi, Jennie," Uncle Mike said.

"How is Tony?" she asked.

"Some slight improvement," Uncle Mike said. "His fever dropped a notch or two."

"Oh, thank God. Let Tony know I'm praying for him." Hadlow took a moment to wipe a tear away and turned toward me. "I happened to be near the bar when the scuffle broke out."

I wasn't surprised to hear she was there. It seemed the entire conference had congregated around the bar.

Uncle Mike beamed like I'd won the middleweight championship or something. "How did you like my boy here? He still has the old reflexes."

"Congratulations, Eddie," Hadlow said.

I thanked her. Uncle Mike took the seat closest to Hadlow to talk. I sat next to my uncle and leaned back in the high-backed cushioned chair. The row of flat screens above the ticket sellers offered only slim pickings for horse racing this time of day, on a Tuesday in early February.

I glanced at the odds board for tonight's basketball games and looked for the games I'd given to Nicole in anticipation of her broadcast. Marini, my buddy at O'Connell's, liked the underdogs with the points in both the Penn State versus Michigan State game at East Lansing, and Duke versus Boston College in Boston. He also liked the "under" in both games.

There wasn't any reason to waste perfectly good picks. I ran up to place a couple of modest wagers on Marini's games.

"You're back," the ticket seller grumbled. "You almost cost me my job. Damn harness races. What do you want?"

I gave him my bets—hundred-dollar win bets on Penn State and Boston College, and the under in each game.

"You want a drink ticket, too, I suppose?"

"Yeah, that would be nice. Give me a few of those."

"Maybe you want the casino to comp your room, too?"

"No, I don't want to bankrupt the place."

He muttered a few cuss words, but I saw the hint of a smile. Standing all day taking bets was no easy job.

I walked back.

"Did you get another horse like Super Rocket from your girlfriend, Eddie?" Hadlow asked.

Uncle Mike tossed a crooked smile my way. "She used to be his girlfriend."

Hadlow shook her head. "No way. Nicole still has it bad. Women know these things. And you have it bad, too."

I couldn't argue with her and smiled.

"What did you bet on?" Uncle Mike asked.

"Those basketball games Marini gave me," I said.

Uncle Mike nodded. "Too bad Marini's picks won't be part of Nicole's broadcast."

"What happened?" Hadlow asked.

We told her how WagerEasy had pulled the plug on the show after the Super Bowl. We also told her that Nicole had requested some picks for tonight's game to use on her show and that my old friend Marini had supplied the picks.

"I like that," she said. "You guys wager smart. I wish when people walked into a casino, they weren't so damn stupid. They act as if they're supposed to lose, for gosh sake. It only makes the casino bolder—they want every penny you've got. Tony couldn't stand it. The corporate casinos are like the banks. Like Globex. They can't get enough. When you miss a credit card payment, they raise your already outlandish interest rate and tack on extra charges. Credit cards are the biggest scam ever. And then there's investment banking. I'll tell you; the banks have the power; they are the House. Their finger is in every pie."

I didn't want to argue with Hadlow. If I did, I might jinx Marini's picks. But there were plenty of times when I wagered like a dummy.

A wait person came by and asked for our drink orders. I pulled out our drink tickets.

"Thanks for the drink ticket, Eddie," Hadlow said. "Good for you. Don't let the casino get away with a thing. And from what I saw, you didn't let Globex get away with anything today, either. Good. Tony hates what the banks are up to."

"Credit cards. What else?" I asked.

Hadlow swiveled around and faced me. Uncle Mike scooted back. "Tony hated what the banks got away with in 2008. They just about ruined everyone financially and robbed us all blind. But no one went to jail. The government even bailed them out, and the banks gave bonuses to their employees."

It was clear Hadlow shared Tony's feelings.

"It's hard to believe," Uncle Mike said. "White-collar criminals who could care less about the money of hard-working depositors."

I understood why the Deacon would resent the favorable treatment given to white-collar fraudsters while his buddies did life sentences for RICO convictions. The Deacon's buddies knew they'd have to do time sooner or later, and probably deserved it, but the unfairness issue remained.

"You know what Tony really hates," Hadlow said. "He hates Second Bet. They want more and more garnishments. They don't care what kind of charges the consumer incurred on their credit card. It could be for medical treatment or food." Her voice grew anxious. "Maybe the cardholder had been laid off. People get sick or injured and don't have insurance. Compare that situation to the person who runs up their credit card balance on vacations and fancy restaurants, and refuses to pay. Tony goes against the mainstream of most of the people here. There has to be a better way, he says, and I agree with him."

"Zino wasn't one to abide by somebody else's rules, was he?" I asked.

"Don't get me wrong about Tony," Hadlow said. "My mother always said watch out for the man who's quick to judge and always thinks he's right. Tony's not like that."

Our drinks arrived, and I tipped the wait person extra to make up for the free drink tickets. "Tony isn't quick to judge?" I asked Hadlow. She was in the mood to talk about Tony, and I wanted to keep her going.

She sipped from her drink. "No, he takes his time and studies things. It's as if he's seen a lot worse things in his life and the little stuff at Team Player and the Debt Exchange doesn't seem to bother him too much. It's as if he's at that stage of life where he needs to take a breather."

Her voice had lost its edge over the banks and had slipped into a sentimental vibe.

"He's earned it," Uncle Mike said. "Look at Team Player and everything he's built."

Jennie took hold of Uncle Mike's arm. "Tony told me not to tell anyone, but I'll tell you if you can keep a secret."

We both agreed.

"It was one of the bad things in Tony's life. He told me a friend of his had disappeared. Actually disappeared, can you imagine?" Tears welled up in her blue eyes. "Tony told me, 'You know, Jennie, there's nothing worse.'"

I assumed the friend who had disappeared was Porter.

"They never found the friend?" Uncle Mike asked.

"No. I've asked Tony several times if there was any news, but there wasn't."

"Did he say who the friend was?" I asked.

Jennie shook her head. "No, never. It's a heartache for Tony. He always says, 'know your friends well.'"

She shared Zino's heartaches. What she said told me Zino came complete with opinions and wattage. He was angry about stuff, about the casinos, the banks, and the garnishment at all costs mentality of Second Bet.

I'd seen firsthand how Zino's enemies feared him and Zino's friends relied upon him. She'd given me an insight into the emotional core of Zino, his fire, his love, and what made him tick.

It made me take another look at Zino's murder. Maybe it wasn't about Team Player business. Maybe it was something personal.

My cell buzzed. It was Arlene.

I nudged Uncle Mike. "It's the office."

We excused ourselves and stepped over to an empty row at the back of the sports book.

"Good evening, guys," Arlene said. "Anything to report?"

"He's stalling again," I said.

"Why am I not surprised? More fun and games. What was the Deacon's excuse this time?"

Uncle Mike said, "All he said was that something came up, and he didn't have time to talk."

"Maybe I should just give up. One of my doctors gave me a prescription to help me forget. I don't know. A night with Porter and the frustration of the dreams is better than no Porter at all."

I wanted to tell her something. I wanted to tell her she wouldn't be paying for the investigation or our expenses, but I couldn't do that.

"The heart does grow fonder," she said. "If anyone should know that, it's me. Those long times Porter was away with the Deacon taught me well. Almost by magic, I began to treasure our time together and learned to accept being alone. Since we were childless, whenever Porter went away, I immersed myself in our investments. I was pretty damn good, too. Porter began to rely on me. We became a team. Even when Porter was gone, he was there with me."

Arlene's toughness in the business world had become legendary.

Uncle Mike coughed. "I'm in touch with the Deacon. We have another time set tomorrow."

"I know. One excuse after the next. Don't badger him too much. It will just play into his hands." She sighed. "But you can tell him my patience is wearing thin."

30

Later, Uncle Mike and I walked over to the Bellagio to watch the heads-up match between Nicole and Scullion. Uncle Mike had to stop by the men's room thanks to those beers he drank at the sports book.

As I walked past the Horseshoe Bar to the poker room, I spotted Jake. He saw me at the same time. He was a tall, thin man with curly black hair who was the bartender during the late evening shift.

My old poker days came rushing back to me.

"Hey, Eddie, where've you been? What've you got? Anything good?" It was the same way he'd greeted me before, but Jake acted as if we'd last talked only yesterday instead of years ago.

"Hi, Jake. No, I've got nothing good."

"The usual?" he asked, snapping the chewing gum to avoid smoking on the job.

"No, just a beer."

"Hurting?" If you were "hurting," Jake would give you a free drink. "Hurting" meant you were dipping deep into your bankroll.

"I'm not playing."

"Good. Glad to hear it. You must have something good. C'mon. Where've you been hanging out? I haven't seen you in a while." Jake's machine gun patter came at you fast.

"I moved back to Chicago."

"That's right." As he talked, he swiveled from one side of the Horseshoe Bar to the other, checking in with customers bent over video poker machines. "What's in Chicago? C'mon," he called out over his shoulder.

Jake used to watch us run from the poker room to the sports book and then back again. "We got a sprinter," he'd yell. He'd gotten himself a stopwatch to keep the gag going as if we were horses running a quarter mile workout. "You gotta do better than that," he'd say.

This was my prior life, hitting me like a slap in the face. Shit. Jake had been our navigator, our coach, and our teammate.

Jake stopped the tour of the bar and stared me down, wiping his hands with the bar towel. He was silent for at least five seconds, a world record.

"C'mon," Jake said. "I talk to people. They say you got an MBA."

"Yeah." What choice did I have? I had to keep up my cover. If I revealed my imposter status to Jake, I might as well set up a neon sign out on Las Vegas Boulevard.

"Damn. Good for you. You know it's not everyday somebody leaves this place and then comes back. And they don't come back as a tourist. You playing?" He glanced toward the poker room. If you hadn't been playing poker, then you were going to play poker. Otherwise, why were you here in the first place?

"No, Jake. No poker. I'm attending a conference."

He smiled and shook his head. "I'll be damned. A real-life escape artist. What'd you do? No more sprints? No more big wins, no more hurting days? How did you do it? You put out a manual on this? I could hand them out."

"No, no big deal." I was a traitor to the cause by not telling Jake the whole story. My move out of Vegas had been a big deal. It cost me Nicole and a way of life. Every day I told myself I'd changed for the better. But I didn't have an MBA hanging on the wall to prove it.

Jake smiled and nodded approval. "I'll be damned." He pointed an accusatory finger at me. "You're here to watch Nicole. She's playing some zillionaire heads-up. I hope she murders him."

"Right."

He washed a glass and wiped it to look busy, his eyes scoping out the bar. "I hear you helped set it up. You got Wit on board, that's what I heard?" He waited.

"Damn right. I told Wit what I thought, and he took it from there. He knows Nicole. We all know her."

"Good. Good for you. You come back here from Chicago and you're up to speed on Nicole? Well, I'll be damned."

I knew what Jake was really saying. He was saying that people were talking. "She'll kick his ass."

He snapped the gum. "You two are good for each other. Don't let her get away, you dumbass." He pointed his finger at me as an exclamation point. "Remember what I'm telling you."

———

We walked onto the packed poker floor. My focus was on the back left corner where Bobby's Room was located. The private room was a couple of steps up from the poker floor, enclosed by windows. There were two tables, and the room was reserved for the top pros. Guards stood at the entrance.

Inside the room, Nicole sat across from Scullion at one of the tables. The dealer sat in the middle. A small crowd stood inside the room, and a larger crowd stood outside the windows. We joined the crowd outside. We wouldn't be able to see the cards, but we'd be able to see who was raking in the chips.

From inside the room, Wit gave me a wave.

I turned to Uncle Mike. "I'm going inside. Wit wants me."

"I'm going with you. I wouldn't miss this."

We walked up to the entrance. The guard glanced toward Wit, got the nod, and allowed us to enter. We walked up and stood by Wit.

Nicole sat comfortably in her seat. She wore an oversized sweatshirt with a WagerEasy Sports Betting Insiders logo and a green visor pulled down low to shade her eyes. Maybe the sweatshirt was a cynical statement about the cancellation of the show.

Scullion sat ramrod straight on the edge of his chair. He wore a dark blue suit, sky-blue tie, and a white shirt. He looked like a guy hoping the bank would approve his loan.

Neither player acknowledged my presence or anything else around them. One hundred percent of their focus was upon the cards.

The dealer was a professional woman with long straight blond hair who didn't smile or talk.

Wit, wearing his trademark fedora, leaned over and whispered to us. "You guys haven't missed much. They just started. Still feeling each other out." He turned toward the man to his right. "You know Hans, don't you Eddie?"

"Sure." I shook hands with Hans Becker, the tutor hired by Scullion, and introduced him to Uncle Mike. Hans wore a tan suede blazer and sported sunglasses.

Hans flashed one of his movie star smiles my way and cracked his knuckles. "Thanks for your help arranging this game. I think Eliot will surprise you," he said in a thick German accent.

What had he cooked up with Scullion? It would have to be something extraordinary to rock Nicole off her game.

It was Scullion's turn for the dealer button. He threw in the small blind of five thousand, and Nicole threw in the big blind of ten thousand. The parties had agreed on the amount of the blinds. The blind was similar to an "ante" and generated action in Texas Hold 'em. The dealer, acting on behalf of Scullion, dealt first to Nicole.

The players could look at their two down cards or hole cards. Scullion, the dealer, had the first option to bet this hand

and then Nicole, the big blind, would act first after the flop, the turn, and the river. Heads-up rules differed somewhat from games of Texas Hold'em with more than two players.

We waited for Scullion to bet or check or fold. On TV, the viewer could see the players' hole cards, but we were not so lucky. It made it almost impossible to understand a player's strategy. The winner would show their hole cards if called, but the loser usually would not.

In heads-up, the players were extremely aggressive and played a lot of hands. A hand that one would normally fold in a game with four or five players might be a very playable hand in heads-up.

Scullion picked up a couple of chips from his impressive stacks and tossed in a ten grand opening bet into the middle like it was loose change.

Nicole waited for what seemed to be a prescribed amount of time. She liked to play to a certain rhythm. Finally, her hand moved slowly to her more modest stack of chips. The pros would resupply her if needed, but I hoped that wouldn't happen. She picked up chips carefully from one of the stacks and kept her eyes on Scullion the whole time. "Raise."

Scullion flashed a sly smile. Out of the corner of my eye, I saw Hans come close to shaking his head. Scullion called the thirty thousand dollar raise. I put Scullion on a high pair, a great hand in heads-up.

The flop, three community cards in the middle, came out—five of clubs, three of hearts, and ten of diamonds.

There was another round of betting. This time Nicole checked, Scullion bet thirty grand, and Nicole called.

The turn, one community card added to the middle, was a two of hearts. Scullion wasn't getting much help, unless he had tens. Nicole checked, Scullion raised, and Nicole re-raised. Scullion called. The crowd grew quiet.

"The first big hand tonight," Wit said.

The river or fifth street came out. It was a queen of hearts. Scullion's hand went quickly to his chips, a bit too quickly. This time, Hans, standing beside me, seemed to sigh. His student was an idiot.

Each player would use their two hole cards, together with the five cards in the middle, to make their best five card poker hand.

Nicole made another thirty-thousand-dollar bet. Scullion quickly raised the same amount. Nicole re-raised and Scullion called. I didn't count the mess of chips in the middle, but it was over a quarter of a million dollars.

"Have you got it?" Scullion asked.

Nicole flipped over a four and six of hearts—a flush. She'd had a straight on the turn.

Scullion's mouth hung open. "You raised right out of the box with a four-six?" He showed his hole cards—two queens, giving him a set or three of a kind with the queen in the middle.

Nicole said nothing and didn't acknowledge the queens. She merely reached out and pulled in the chips. Some of the pros outside the windows, unable to see the cards on the table, threw fists in the air when they saw Nicole collect the first big pot.

Scullion scratched his head. "When I lose, it spurs me on to find a way to win. Even when I lose, I win."

Nicole looked up at him, then returned to the business of stacking chips.

"Sorry about asking to call it quits early, but I have to give a keynote at a business conference tomorrow here in the hotel," Scullion said. "We'll start again tomorrow afternoon. I'm still on eastern time so late nights are difficult. If I knew what I know now, I would've never moved to New Jersey. I'm not a fan. I wish people had told me what it was like."

The dealer dealt the next hand, and Scullion continued to talk. Nicole didn't engage with him, so Scullion tried to make eye contact with the crowd.

"It's a great industry—debt buying," he continued. "People always run up those credit cards." He kept talking about the industry and himself. I assumed Nicole would find inflections in his speech that would telegraph what kind of hole cards he was playing.

Scullion bet and Nicole raised. Scullion folded.

For a second, I spotted Nicole's eyes beneath that visor when she stretched her neck back. Her eyes had grown cold. I knew those eyes. Her eyes had turned ice cold the day I'd left Vegas several years ago.

I hoped Nicole and I would get back together again. Hadlow was right. The only question seemed to be if it would be Vegas or Chicago. If Nicole lost the heads-up match, she'd want to move to Chicago. If she won, she'd stay in Vegas, no doubt about that. The question then would be if I'd move to Vegas.

A return to Vegas would mean a return to my old life, the one that flashed before me when I was talking with Jake. I didn't like that old version of me, the one who was out of control and in need of a navigator. I'd tried to conquer Vegas, and I'd lost. I knew a rematch would end with the same result.

The dealer dealt another hand, and it was Nicole's turn to go first. She checked. Scullion bet and Nicole raised. Scullion folded again.

"I looked for your show yesterday and then I heard it had been canceled. Too bad," Scullion said. "You had some good picks. I understand from some of the sports books managers on the Strip that your father trains horses in Chicago. I hear the sports books don't like taking your bets on his horses."

Wit nudged Hans. "What's your guy doing?"

"It gives him the façade of control," Hans explained. "It's mind boggling how his ego feeds his play. His power shines through and he's almost unbeatable."

Scullion went first and checked. Nicole bet and Scullion raised. Nicole folded.

"You know," Scullion continued, "I have a string of horses running at Belmont and Gulfstream in Florida. If your father is having trouble, he could move to Gulfstream in the winter and train a couple of my cheap claimers. You know, just to see how he does."

I wanted to leap across the felt and see how Scullion did with my right cross to his jaw.

People glanced at each other. Scullion's toxic insults had dumbfounded the crowd.

Scullion picked up his hole cards. "I've got some nice two-year-old fillies coming up. It would be a great opportunity for him to work on some quality stock for a change. Of course, he wouldn't be the trainer of record."

Wit leaned over to Hans. "What shines through is the fact he's an asshole."

Hans nodded.

Uncle Mike nudged me. "Sorry, Eddie." He showed me his phone.

I tried to read the text. It was about a meeting.

Uncle Mike whispered. "It's him." The look of utter disbelief on Uncle Mike's face shocked me.

"What?" I whispered back.

"Let's go," Uncle Mike whispered. "Now."

I read the text. It was from the Deacon.

31

THE TEXT SAID, "MEET AT THE SAME PLACE. FIFTEEN minutes." The amount of time provided told us the Deacon probably knew where we were. We left and took the walkway over the side street to Caesars.

"It's a text from the Deacon's phone," Uncle Mike said as we walked. "But I bet it's not the Deacon."

"What if they've been fucking with us?" Maybe Burrascano and the Deacon had sent us on a wild debt-buying goose chase.

"I don't think so. If this is who I think it is…"

I tried to pry more information from Uncle Mike, but failed. He didn't like to speculate; he liked facts. When we got to the Roman Forum shops in the underground mall, I asked, "Should we take the same precautions as before?"

"You bet."

Uncle Mike waited at the end of the hall while I surveyed the crowd. Then I made my way from the cover of one group of shoppers to another and from one store entrance to another, until I arrived at the same hall outside Walt's Collectibles, the one that led to the door marked "Employees Only."

A tall woman janitor leaned against the wall; one leg bent with her foot planted on the wall behind her. She was casually studying her phone and chewing gum. The janitor's cart sat between her and the main corridor. She wore a mall-regulation army-green uniform.

I looked around for the Deacon or someone like him. Then I noticed how she shook her head, her mouth set in a "give me a break" expression. She wore an earpiece.

I approached. "You texted us?"

"Yeah. Is Mike coming?"

I waved toward Uncle Mike and he walked down the hall, staying close to one wall.

"What's this about?" I asked her.

"Wait." She snapped the gum. "I don't want to say everything all over again."

She didn't wear any makeup and her hair was pulled back tight. Her hands were rough and dirty, her fingernails short. I'd have bet money she was, in fact, a janitor.

Uncle Mike arrived. She stood up straight and put her cell away.

"Mr. O'Connell," she said, shaking his hand, "my name is Claudia. I'm the one who texted you." She turned to me. "You're Eddie, the nephew?"

She shook my hand as well. There was strength in her hand that could only come from working out with weights. Beneath the baggy janitor outfit, I could see she was muscular and possibly armed.

"We won't meet again. Listen carefully." She kept watch on the hallway.

"You watched us that first night?" Uncle Mike asked.

Now I knew what Uncle Mike had meant when he said, "if this is who I think it is."

"Yes. I was also the one who followed Eddie into the parking garage of The Kremlin Sunday night. Eddie, you have a sixth sense. I usually never get noticed."

I nodded a thank you, but I had a million questions.

She spoke directly to Uncle Mike. "We don't have much time. We've been watching you. I'm one of the Deacon's team. He left a lot of loose ends when he was murdered. You met Karmazin yesterday. We've had him under surveillance. He was ready to run, but he hasn't. We don't think you need to worry about him."

"Wait a minute," I said. "Let's go back to Sunday night."

Claudia ignored me. "Horace's murder tells us you are on the right track. Believe me, we want the murderer more than anything."

Uncle Mike raised an index finger to interrupt her. "I know we've got some ground to cover. Do you think Zino was killed because of his actions at the conference, or do you think somebody was looking for the Deacon and found out about his alias?"

"You mean was he killed as Tony Zino or was he killed as the Deacon? That's the sixty-four-thousand-dollar question, isn't it Mr. O'Connell? We do know that the Deacon had received threats on his life. That's why he was worried about Arlene and her scrapbook, and that's why he made arrangements to meet you."

"He made arrangements to meet us?" Then I recalled how Burrascano urged Uncle Mike to meet with Arlene, and bring me, the newbie private investigator, along.

Claudia nodded.

"Was the Deacon planning to retire?" I asked.

"I don't know." She took a step back. "Here come some shoppers. Follow my lead."

The shoppers came closer and Claudia went into her act.

"The men's toilet is across the hall," she pointed. "If you're looking for the corridor to the Mirage, go back down the hall the way you came and turn left." The shoppers walked past us without turning in our direction.

Her ability to play her part impressed me and made me uneasy at the same time. When imposters meet another imposter, there's this awkward moment where you realize just how vulnerable you are and I didn't like the feeling.

She watched the shoppers pass by and then took a step closer. "Sunday night. You were right to follow DiNatale. You thought he'd visit Karmazin, I assume. Then DiNatale and his boys worked over Tanner. It's one of DiNatale's jobs to be sure Tanner places bets only with our people, our bookies."

I figured DiNatale had somebody witness Tanner betting with Scullion, but how could the mob hope to keep Tanner from betting on one of the many sports apps on his cell? "How can DiNatale or anyone be certain Tanner bets only with your bookies?"

Claudia nodded. "That's the genius of the Deacon. He found ways around legal sports betting. Tanner has a number of loans with our people. When he fell behind on payments, he was forced by the Deacon, through an intermediary of course, to sign self-exclusion paperwork that we distributed through channels. Tanner is unable to place bets through legal apps or the legal operators could lose their license or be fined."

Uncle Mike laughed. "Damn. That's brilliant. I guess the Deacon wasn't ready to coast into retirement."

It took me a second to absorb this news. The Deacon used state-authorized self-exclusion to "capture" a gambler's business. "Amazing. How much does Tanner owe?"

"You have your sources. We have ours," she said. "You do good work. I was the one cleaning up those bits of paper you threw all over the bar, Mr. O'Connell."

"Jalbert's contract?" Uncle Mike said. "Sorry about the paperwork."

"I have to get moving. I'm a temp and I've got to make my rounds," Claudia said. "We will help you as much as we can, but like you, we are working with the mob and outside the mob. The Deacon liked it that way. He used the mob when he needed backup and he could operate in the legit world at the same time. Only a few people know the Deacon has been murdered. Keep it that way. You should also know that men—other men, not one of our team—are following you."

"The men who killed the Deacon?" Uncle Mike asked.

"We believe so, but we aren't sure."

"You're using us as bait," I said.

Claudia grabbed hold of her cart and began to push it toward the exit door. "If you want to call it that. Remember, it's a matter of timing."

———

We walked into the men's room across the hall to back Claudia's cover story for those who might've been tailing us, and also to take a piss. Then we walked into Walt's Collectibles and hung out near a glass counter with baseball cards on display. We were alone.

"What the fuck," I said. "We're being used as bait?"

"Maybe we need to wear bullet-proof vests. We might get caught in the crossfire," Uncle Mike said.

"What did she mean 'it's a matter of timing'?"

"I don't know. And what about, 'You have your sources and we have ours'?"

What sources? "Could she be talking about Irv?"

"That reminds me. I got an email from Irv a little while ago." Uncle Mike studied his cell.

While he checked his cell, I looked for an email from Wit on Nicole's heads-up match—nothing. Maybe Scullion had lost enough and decided to quit. I hoped they'd all be partying at the bar by now.

"Irv is having a courier drop his report on the financial stuff to us tomorrow at seven. There goes my beauty sleep. Good old Irv."

"I still have that damn speech we drafted." The black cloud hanging over me had gotten so dark I could imagine the distant rumble of thunder.

"Forget about the speech. Let's think about what Claudia told us. What about this self-exclusion they forced Tanner to sign?"

"I considered the self-exclusion option for a while when I tried out gambler's anonymous."

"That went well." The edge to Uncle Mike's voice conveyed disappointment with his gambler nephew.

"Skip it." I didn't need to dredge up the old argument over my past gambling debts. "Every state has self-exclusion, I think. You sign up for it and the gambling operators have to honor it. They've got a list. If the self-excluded gambler sneaks into a casino and loses, the gambler gets his money back. The gambler can also be sued for trespass and has to forfeit any winnings. The casino or operator in the case of sports betting apps can get shut down or fined. Self-exclusion is big in Europe where sports betting and gambling has forced a lot of people into the poorhouse."

"Claudia was right. It's pure genius by the Deacon. Evil, but pure genius."

Uncle Mike called over the salesperson and asked to look at a baseball card on one of the shelves in the glass case. It was a White Sox player.

"Who is it?" I looked over Uncle Mike's shoulder.

"Luis Aparicio. Played for the 'Go-Go' White Sox back in the late fifties, early sixties. He was a base stealer. Led the league with fifty-six stolen bases in 1959. Little Louie—he's in the Hall of Fame."

"Great years for the Sox."

"Yeah. They won the pennant in 1959. Lost to the damn Dodgers in the World Series."

Buying something would substantiate the reason for our trip down the hall and the stop at Walt's.

Uncle Mike told the salesperson to wrap it up. Little Louie only cost my big spender uncle ten bucks.

We walked back into the hall outside Walt's.

"Let's get back to the investigation," Uncle Mike said. "Jalbert had motive to kill Zino. Zino is standing in the way of his deal with Globex. Zino has a speech called the Pitfalls of Expansion. Everybody is waiting for it. Even Lundstrom is afraid of the speech."

"Jalbert had a new version of the speech for me," I said. "Plus, Jalbert had motive to kill Horace. Now we find out that Tanner has major gambling debts with the mob. Maybe Tanner knew it was Zino who had ordered him into self-exclusion, and not the mob."

"Zino seemed to use DiNatale for the dirty work. That way, Team Player could stay behind the scenes and keep getting business from Tanner and Second Bet."

"Tanner is ready to cash in through a sale of his company or an IPO. I guess selling the company is faster, so that's probably what he'll do." Maybe Franzen knew about Tanner's self-exclusion. Maybe that was why she was tense when Scullion made the wagers on the Super Bowl. No, the bet wasn't made on Tanner's WagerEasy account, they were made on Scullion's account. WagerEasy shouldn't get into trouble for that. "If the killer is the type with lots of money to hire the shooters as a diversion so he can nail the Deacon on the front steps of Caesars, then he's got enough resources to find out things. Maybe Tanner did know Zino was behind his self-exclusion."

"I'm loving this case," Uncle Mike said. "There are so many variables. We need to talk to Tanner. Hey, look who's coming. Isn't that our buddy?"

DiNatale walked toward us.

32

VIC DINATALE KEPT LOOKING AROUND AS HE STRODE UP TO us. It was late on a Tuesday night and the number of shoppers had steadily dwindled.

"Hey guys," DiNatale said, shaking our hands like we were long-lost friends. "I'm glad I ran into you. I wanted to tell you something." He lowered his voice, standing so close his cologne nearly choked me. "That fucking Russian paid, brought his debt current. I never thought he'd do it. I figured Karmazin was jacking us around. But he believed you. You guys are good. You know, I've got some other deadbeats I'd like for you to get off my sheet. You want to give them a try? There's a commission in it."

"No thanks," Uncle Mike said. "My collection days are behind me."

"The way you threatened Karmazin had all of us thinking we'd have to shoot our way out of the joint." DiNatale laughed.

We laughed along with him.

DiNatale turned serious. "We need to keep you alive for the speech."

"What?" Uncle Mike said.

"Calm down," DiNatale lowered a hand.

Uncle Mike got in the mobster's face. "Keep us alive?"

"Easy. You'll be drooling into a cup when you're eighty years-old, don't worry. We just need to be careful."

"What about the speech?" I needed to know what Zino planned to say. Any morsel would help. How did DiNatale know about the speech in the first place?

"A hell of a lot of legwork went into tomorrow," DiNatale said. "Don't fuck it up."

"That's a big help."

DiNatale pulled a gun from the shoulder holster beneath his suit coat. "You're the sharp guy, you'll figure it out. You guys have guns, right?"

I took my gun out. "What the fuck, Vic?"

"You going to tell us what's going on?" Uncle Mike demanded.

"We spotted some guys." He pointed to the end of the hall, where it funneled into the main corridor.

I couldn't believe this. "You think they'll ambush us?"

DiNatale chuckled. "They're not down here to give you a bro hug. Stay the fuck away from me, too. You're the guys they want."

"Thanks." Now I knew why Claudia sent us a text to meet us down here. We were indeed bait; we just didn't know we were already hanging from the fishhook.

"Look at the bright side, Eddie," Uncle Mike said. "It's better we meet these bastards with our guns drawn than the way the Deacon got it—pinned down by a drive-by, fucking helpless."

Shots echoed down the corridor. DiNatale ran toward the wall to our left and kept moving toward the main corridor. We didn't have time to make a plan. A spray of bullets aimed at DiNatale forced us to run toward the right. We leaned against the wall.

"Let's go back," Uncle Mike said, tugging on my arm.

But the shooter got off a flurry of shots down the corridor, blocking our path. At the same time, a steel door the size of a two-car garage door dropped down across the entrance to Walt's.

The shooter was in the main corridor, outside a closed deli. A couple of the stone rectangular tables on the patio had been overturned on their side, one facing out toward us and another turned at a right angle facing the casino entrance. DiNatale was shooting in that direction. The shooter popped up from behind his tabletop fortress and we tucked into a spot along the wall behind a rectangular pillar.

Shots clipped the vertical structure that jutted out from the wall. We were exposed. I pulled my gun and shot back.

We couldn't run back to the restrooms. The shooter had a good angle. We had to keep moving. Another shooter blasted the hallway with an AK-47.

DiNatale's return fire forced the shooters to take cover. We scrambled down the wall to the next pillar. DiNatale had taken cover at the entrance to Tiffany's. We returned fire and ran toward the Gucci store, Uncle Mike limping along and cussing a blue streak.

What took only half a minute or less seemed like an eternity. The shooters hadn't been able to draw a bead on us. DiNatale had done a great job of keeping them busy.

"Wind sprints," Uncle Mike wheezed. "Too old for them." He dropped to a knee, gasping.

I tried to get a grasp of the situation. There wasn't time to identify where DiNatale's guys were or who was crouching behind the tables. If people are shooting at you, you shoot back.

Shoppers screamed and ran. A couple of security guards huddled in the entrance to a clothing store beside the deli. Some shoppers in the main corridor dove to the floor and snaked along toward a safe place. Shop until you drop had a new meaning.

"Jeesus," Uncle Mike said. "These guys got balls."

"You okay?"

"Yeah. But my leg won't handle another sprint."

The shooters unleashed a volley in our direction and one toward DiNatale. We ducked down behind the four-foot marble wall around the entrance. The bay windows and displays shattered. Glass broke around us. We used our arms to shield our faces.

"Go inside," I told Uncle Mike.

"No, DiNatale needs us." Uncle Mike fired at the table tops.

He was right. The three of us could keep the shooters busy. If one of us skipped out, all of us would be vulnerable. We had to keep peppering their fortress. Keep them contained.

Besides, I didn't want DiNatale to accuse us of not pulling our weight. No way.

We were pinned down, but we could afford to wait for reinforcements. DiNatale's boys should show up any minute. The police were on the way, too. I heard the faint echo of sirens through the Roman catacombs.

"We just need to wait it out." I said it to convince myself.

That helpless feeling overwhelmed me again. The same feeling I had when I was pinned down in the drive-by. Shit.

I twisted around. A man crouched among the Gucci bags inside the store. He wasn't shopping for the wife. He was inching closer and aiming a gun at my face.

I fired on impulse. The force of the bullet brought him to his feet. His face contorted in pain. He took a deep breath. He was a fighter. Slowly, his gun hand came up again. I fired another round into his chest. He collapsed.

Uncle Mike looked at me. "Damn, you got eyes in the back of your head."

Across the hall, Tiffany's took a barrage of bullets. DiNatale ducked down below identical four-foot-high marble walls that supported the bay windows. Inside, a man stepped around a counter with a gun.

"They planted another guy at the jewelry store," I said.

"I got him." Uncle Mike aimed and fired a few rounds over DiNatale's head into the shop, winging the man.

DiNatale glared at us. Then he turned around and saw the guy on the floor. DiNatale darted inside and unloaded several rounds.

There was a momentary lull. The killers had plenty of tricks and we didn't want to make any quick moves. I kept twisting around to be certain no one other than a couple of terrified salespeople occupied the Gucci store.

The deli shooters were also dodging shots from the direction of the casino. I assumed these were DiNatale's boys. That meant the corridor to our left was the only exit for the deli shooters. They took it.

"Vic, they're running," I called out.

DiNatale had reloaded. He left the dead man inside the store and ran to the store's entrance. He grabbed his cell phone.

Seconds later, men ran down the corridor and DiNatale followed them. I wanted to run after them, but Uncle Mike wouldn't be able to go far on his leg. I'd have to stay.

"I wish we could question one of those shooters," Uncle Mike said.

"Fat chance."

"Yeah, DiNatale was so pissed, he'll kill them for sure."

"He'll chase them into the desert if he has to."

The police and casino security began to swarm over the mall.

We left the Gucci store and followed others toward the casino. Uncle Mike limped along beside me. "I'm not loving this case as much as I did ten minutes ago."

33

BACK IN MY ROOM, I DIDN'T FLOP INTO BED EXHAUSTED. Instead, I sat upright in the chair with Arlene's scrapbook spread out on the desk.

Immediately after the shooting, Uncle Mike and I had joined the dazed shoppers and were herded away by security to await questioning. We spent a couple of hours talking with the detectives. Once they confirmed our story of self-defense with video footage from the Gucci store and talked with Detective Woodyard, we were released. We would contact Woodyard later to try to learn more details.

Uncle Mike had been impressed with everything about tonight's shootout—the devious strategy of the gunmen by planting shooters inside the shops; the way Claudia and DiNatale had sniffed out the ambush; and the fact I had eyes in the back of my head. Thank God, I'd turned just in time to see the shooter inside the store and fired before he did.

I made a cup of coffee and went over the draft of my speech for tomorrow. I added a few things about Jalbert's offer of an employment contract and Uncle Mike's answer on behalf of Team Player. When it came to the Debt Exchange, I had a lot of other things to worry about.

Like how did DiNatale know about the damn speech? I would've demanded answers, but he was busy running down shooters in the mall. Zino's close connection to the mob was a wildcard in the investigation.

I had to think through the facts of the investigation, get back on track, and take things in stride.

Horace's murder showed we were on the right track. Zino's murder must've been connected to the conference. But how? I sat down at the desk and took a sip of coffee.

Jalbert, our main suspect, could've killed Horace to shut him up about Seamless Dataminers. He might try to kill us, too, especially if that viral video of his belly flop ended up costing him the Globex deal.

Tanner, Jalbert's rival and enemy, had been forced by the mob to sign up for self-exclusion and could only bet with mob-controlled bookies. If Tanner had found out Zino was behind the forced self-exclusion, it could be a motive for murder.

Then there was Karmazin. He had brought his debt current, but I still didn't trust the Russian.

Uncle Mike and I were in the middle of it. The killer must be feeling the heat. Hell, it felt as if I could almost reach out and touch the murderer; we seemed that close.

My analysis of the current state of affairs was one of my old tricks. I used it to psyche myself out. I was in the stretch, just another sixteenth of a mile to go, and I'd be able to reach the finish line. I needed that second wind, a late kick. The conference would end tomorrow.

I grabbed a protein bar to go with the coffee. What must Nicole be going through? I'd tried to call her all night and she wouldn't call me back.

According to Wit, the game took a turn when Scullion started his nonstop table talk. Nicole and Scullion had ended up nearly even when Scullion's preset cutoff time of eight o'clock was reached. The game would resume tomorrow, but a poker pro should've made fast work of the egomaniac. It was an embarrassment in the making for Nicole and Wit was pissed.

The abrupt withdrawal of WagerEasy also remained a puzzle. They dropped the sponsorship of *The Sports Betting Insiders* and vacated a lucrative market in Vegas as if they were running from something. But what were they running from?

When I'd worked for WagerEasy, the home office back in London seemed to be stuffed shirts worried only about "tea time." They didn't get perturbed about anything. "Perturbed" was a word they'd actually used in company-wide memos. "Nothing for us to get perturbed about," they'd say.

I went to my laptop to email my former girlfriend, Tara. She was still in contact with people from WagerEasy and might know something.

I wanted my email to her to sound businesslike, but not too businesslike. Breakups were never easy, and I'd been forced to take a back seat to Tara's career. Being the second choice never went down easy.

Hi Tara

It's been a while. How are you doing? Uncle Mike and I are in Vegas. A friend of mine was recently laid off by WagerEasy (sound familiar?). She was working on The Sports Betting Insiders *cable show sponsored by WagerEasy. No one is talking. I understand WagerEasy not only ended the cable show but closed its office here in Vegas. I don't watch ratings, but I guess the cable show was successful. Can you find out why WagerEasy took these actions? Maybe one of your old friends knows something (Vivian?). I wouldn't bother you if it wasn't important.*

How are you doing in D.C.? Are you still running in 10K races and doing those killer workouts? Your mom said you're "adjusting." I hope that's good! I helped your mom move some furniture last week. She still drops by O'Connell's once a week for her card game with the ladies' group. She is always in good spirits, especially when she wins (which is most of the time).

Take care. Chicago misses you.

I read the email over again. I wasn't sure if I'd said too much or too little. It was certainly the longest email I ever wrote. She might put two and two together when she read that Uncle Mike and I were in Vegas, and figure we were on another job. If so, I hoped she'd look into WagerEasy right away.

Of course, it was the middle of the night in D.C., so I realistically couldn't expect any response until tomorrow.

Next, I wrote an email to Marini to thank him again for the college basketball picks. Both teams he'd given me had covered the spread. Penn State had won outright on the road. I also won on the "under" on each team. It was too bad that Nicole couldn't have given those picks to her fans as she'd planned. WagerEasy picked a great time to close up shop.

I'd avoided the poker room and the table games during my short time in Vegas, but I kept on winning. There must be something for me to learn from all this.

Then it was time to stop procrastinating and start my night's routine. I had to get back to Arlene's scrapbook and continue digging into the history of the Deacon and Porter and scrounge for clues from the past.

The pair had carried out contracts for the mob in various parts of the country, especially the east coast. I assumed the east coast mobs hired the Deacon and Porter from Chicago because outsiders might have an easier time getting close to a target. It would also be easier for outsiders to evade the police and slip away after the murder contract had been fulfilled.

I flipped over another faded page of single space type with odd margins and White-Out stamped "classified," and studied some handwritten paragraphs scribbled on the back of the page by an agent who had followed the Deacon and Porter down a street in Manhattan toward the Lincoln Tunnel.

34

AT SEVEN A.M. THE NEXT MORNING, I KNOCKED ON THE
door to Uncle Mike's room. He answered the door in a T-shirt
and a pair of baggy sweatpants. Clumps of hair around his ears
and the back of his head were sticking out in every direction.

"C'mon in." Uncle Mike shuffled toward the kitchenette.
"The courier just came a minute ago. Damn, I'm getting too
old for this."

I spied the package on the table. "How's the leg?"

"It feels like a lead pipe. You look like shit. Did you get
any sleep?"

"Not much."

"Still studying the scrapbook?" He inspected my tray.
"Bacon and egg sandwiches again?"

"Nope. Oatmeal. You can heat it up in the microwave."

"That's criminal." Uncle Mike trudged toward the
bathroom.

I placed the coffee and breakfast tray I'd bought downstairs on the table. "My work on that scrapbook will yield results. Just wait. Want me to open the package?"

"Keep up the hard work. Let's see what Irv came up with."

The package was about as anonymous as it could be—no sender or other identification, just a plain white banker's box. What I was opening could wreck a lot of careers at Irv's accounting firm if it fell into the wrong hands.

Irv had taken a huge risk on our behalf. A search warrant or other court involvement was usually required to obtain this type of information. Financial information conveyed by a client to their accountant would be considered privileged and confidential. If the financial maneuvers were in some way part of a criminal enterprise, disclosing the documents to third parties could be dynamite.

As much as the documents were cloaked in secrecy by the law, they were just as crucial to our investigation. It didn't matter who the suspect might be, a start-up, a partnership, or a company on the verge of an IPO, if a perpetrator had bet their entire bankroll, and that bankroll had been placed at risk, then they might do whatever it took to save it and sometimes that included murder.

At the Debt Exchange, we had a number of people betting their entire bankroll. Jalbert had made his big bet on the Globex deal. Tanner was betting that Jalbert's Globex deal wouldn't go through, so he could move forward with an IPO or a sale of the company. Tanner and those holding stock options would hit the jackpot. Others, like Scullion, or perhaps Zino, had probably invested in one of the companies.

My heart beat a little faster. My fingers weren't working right. Untying the package became an intricate task. I was a kid on Christmas morning. We needed answers.

I finally opened it and picked up the first couple of pages. "This is interesting." As I guessed, there was nothing in the paperwork to identify Irv or anyone in his firm.

Uncle Mike sat down at the table, put on his reading glasses, and took the lid off his coffee. He added the cream I'd brought. "What have we got?"

"Take a look at these summaries." The thick stack of underlying documents inside the banker's box made Arlene's scrapbook look like a dime novel. It would take hours to decipher what Irv had sent without the one-page synopsis.

The first rundown involved Jalbert. He'd been a minor league hockey player, raised near Quebec. Several times, the Maple Leafs had brought him up to the big show as a late season enforcer. The number of minutes he'd served in the penalty box had set some sort of record. After the late season fights, he'd be sent back down, never getting the opportunity to participate in a playoff game. He'd gotten divorced and was estranged from his kids. He'd carried on an extramarital affair with one of his staff and had been sued by the woman last year, resulting in a settlement. His company, Vortex, had several major investors, including Scullion.

"Irv and his staff are magicians," I said.

Uncle Mike bent over the summaries. "I wonder what skip tracing company he uses?"

"It says Jalbert was an enforcer in the NHL. No wonder people thought he'd kick my ass."

"Maybe you caught him on an off night."

"Thanks. Good thing we weren't on skates."

I picked up the one-pager on Tanner. He had a cocaine addiction that began fifteen to twenty years ago and had forced him to do several stints in rehab. He had signed up for self-exclusion for his gambling problem in California a year ago. He and two partners had started 2ndBetOnDebt in the mid-nineties by obtaining seed money from private investors. The partners incorporated shortly thereafter and were forced to file for bankruptcy. The private investors sued for fraud, resulting in a personal bankruptcy by Tanner. Since he claimed not to have any assets, the private investors decided not to pursue the fraud case in bankruptcy court. Tanner bought Second Bet out of bankruptcy for a song and started expanding the debt-buying operation by bidding outrageously high amounts on debt portfolios offered for sale by the top banks. The expansion attracted top Wall Street investors and hedge funds, including Scullion.

"I was hoping one of our suspects was an Eagle Scout and we could eliminate them," Uncle Mike said.

I handed Uncle Mike another summary. "It doesn't get any better."

In his teens, Scullion had gotten into trouble with the juvenile court and changed his name. In his early thirties, Scullion had faced domestic assault charges. He got divorced, and then landed a job on Wall Street. After four years on Wall Street, he started his own hedge fund and was sued by his prior Wall Street employer for a breach of his employment contract. A non-compete provision didn't allow him to contact prior clients. That case dragged on in the courts for several years and was settled. Scullion's hedge fund had recently joined up with a larger private equity group and had been under investigation by several state attorneys general.

I grabbed a bundle at the bottom of the box. It appeared to be an attorney's file, but all the names of the attorneys and the law firm had been redacted. "What do you make of this?"

Uncle Mike took it from me and began flipping pages. "It's all Latin to me. What is Irv doing to us?"

"It appears to be a law firm case file. They did a lot of work."

"Let's get Irv on the phone."

Uncle Mike pulled out his cell phone. He got in touch with Irv immediately. "Hey Irv, it's me and Eddie. You're on speaker in my hotel room."

"I thought you guys might call. I debated whether to call you."

"Is this an attorney's file in the bottom of the box?"

"Yeah, it is. It was weird, Mike. Out of the blue, we get this call. An attorney in town was working on this stuff for a guy named Zino who is connected to Team Player. The law firm brought it to us."

"Why?" I asked.

"They refused to say," Irv said. "When I reviewed it, I understood why."

35

UNCLE MIKE AND I STOOD NEAR THE COFFEE SETUP IN THE exhibit hall. Scullion's keynote speech was scheduled to start soon, and that meant my speech would follow.

Tanner walked up to us as if he'd been looking for us. "Hi guys, how are you doing today? I don't see Zino. Is he still in the hospital? I heard his condition was serious."

"I'm afraid so," I said. Did I detect a note of sarcasm in Tanner's comment?

Our dealings with Tanner had been consistent and jived with Irv's summary. Tanner boxed people in and then screwed them over. I liked Tanner best the first time I saw him—when DiNatale's boys took turns playing Rocky punching a side of beef.

"That's too bad about Zino. I guess there won't be any speech—"

"No, I've got something ready," I said. "Don't worry, I have kind words for Second Bet." Uncle Mike and I had spent a good chunk of the morning absorbing what we should say based on Irv's info.

"Good, good," Tanner said, trying to read me. "I'll stick around then. Did you hear the news?"

"No," Uncle Mike said. "We've been on a conference call all morning."

Tanner licked his lips and puffed out his chest. "Globex Bank signed on the dotted line with Second Bet. Everything is good. You haven't seen Jalbert, have you? I certainly would like to offer him my most sincere condolences. He put up a good fight. Oh well, this clears the way for our IPO, although we are considering something cheaper and faster. We have ongoing talks with a private equity group. We're making good progress on a sale of the company."

Tanner was so upbeat, I thought he'd do a jig.

"Very nice," I said. Although I felt like giving him another beating.

"You should be proud," Uncle Mike said.

"Don't worry, when you guys get your numbers up, Second Bet will be open to talk."

"Appreciate it," Uncle Mike said.

Tanner looked around and seemed to confirm that no one was eavesdropping on our conversation. "I'm about to be handed a blank check. Everything I've fought so hard for. I'm finally at the top of the mountain and I can stop groveling."

He took a deep breath. His chin jutted out. "You see guys," he pointed to his chest. "I'm owed. I'm owed lots of money because I bet big on these debt portfolios. Now I'm going to do more than enjoy myself. I'm going to make people pay. And I'm going to do the same thing in other industries."

Tanner was worked up in a high energy sweat over where he'd been and where he was going. We let him talk it out. When a guy feels like he's on top of the world, he'll tell you his life story.

"I've been pulled in a million and a half directions for so long, bidding on debt portfolios, hiring analysts, firing analysts, building a collection floor, and dealing with asshole collection agencies like you guys, who throw my accounts on the back burner after you cream it.

"I fired collectors almost as fast as I hired them. I signed leases on space with no idea how I'd pay the rent. I borrowed money and brought in investors to expand because expansion was the only option, the only way to attract more investors."

Tanner took another deep breath. "It was nothing more than a Ponzi Scheme. And now all my debts will be gone in one fell swoop and be someone else's worry. I don't know who the hell contributes to the pot of money handled by these private equity hedge fund outfits—mutual funds, teacher pensions, drug dealers—who the hell knows and who cares. But I'm thankful to each and every one of them."

Tanner reached out and shook our hands. "Maybe my luck will rub off on you guys. Can't wait for your speech, Eddie." He spotted someone in the passing crowd and walked off.

"How do you like that?" Uncle Mike said. "The guy is something else." Uncle Mike turned to me. "Are you ready for your performance?"

"Why not?" I shrugged. "Let's get into the ballroom. I want to hear Scullion's speech. Maybe he'll say something I can pass along to Nicole."

"She has the continuation of the heads-up match later today, right?" Uncle Mike started walking toward the exit from the exhibit hall. The ballroom was only a short walk.

"She needs to rally. I've called her a couple of times but she doesn't answer or call back."

"She'll do fine. She's a pro." Uncle Mike grabbed his cell. "It's Woodyard. I better take this. I'll catch up with you inside."

Uncle Mike wandered over toward a stretch of windows that looked out on an expansive deck. Numerous attendees stood at a respectful distance as they talked on cell phones.

We wanted to get some information about the shooters in the mall. The easiest way to get that information was through Woodyard. If we'd stayed at the scene all night, we would've gotten tied up with more questioning from detectives who might not be as easygoing as Detective Woodyard. With today's festivities on the front burner, we simply couldn't afford to sacrifice the time.

I followed the stream of people to the ballroom.

Someone tugged on my arm from behind. I turned and was hit by a cloud of cheap cologne.

"Hey, Eddie." DiNatale smirked.

"Vic, what the fuck?"

He pulled me aside. "We only got one of the bastards last night. The other guy got away. I want him bad. He ran faster and left his pal to make a stand."

"Fuck."

"We couldn't hang around. The cops were all over the place. If they hadn't shown up, we would've found the other one."

"Any idea who they were?"

"I tried to find a wallet on the gunman in Tiffany's but nothing. I'm glad you guys spotted him. Nice work. You guys saved my ass."

"You did nice work, too."

"Me and my boys will be in the ballroom. Maybe I'll recognize the guy we didn't get." DiNatale clapped me on the back and walked off, cell phone in hand.

Did DiNatale anticipate trouble in the ballroom? Why not? They'd shot up the valet stand out in front of Caesars with a drive-by and shot up the indoor mall like it was a shooting gallery. Any place seemed to be a good place for the killers.

DiNatale didn't mention my damn speech just now, but I'd bet the bank he was here to make sure I delivered it.

36

As people hunted for a seat, I walked up the aisle toward the front. One of the conference hosts spotted me and took me backstage. My chance to audition as a public speaker was only an hour away. The black cloud hung so low over my head that my shoulders drooped from the weight.

Scullion stood near a waist-high table backstage with a bottle of water in his hand. He seemed relaxed and stepped over to shake my hand despite the fact I clearly worked for Team Nicole.

"Eddie, I can't wait to hear Zino's speech." A sly smile tugged at the corners of his lips. "The sooner we give these talks, the sooner I can get back to the heads-up match. You heard, didn't you? We're almost back to even."

"Yeah, I heard. I also heard what you said about Nicole and her father."

"No offense intended. It's merely table talk. Talking is allowed. Talking works. Nicole has given me 'tells' in response to my rambling. Why not tell you? She'll never be able to change things up by this afternoon."

I wouldn't say anything to Nicole about what Scullion said. I assumed he was telling me this in hopes I'd tell Nicole and then throw her off her game with unnecessary bullshit.

"It's a social game," Scullion continued. "Just because Nicole doesn't want to talk, why should I be quiet? The crowd in Bobby's Room enjoys my quips. A little trash talk opens things up."

Jalbert walked up to us. As the president of the Debt Exchange, it was his job to introduce the keynote.

"Okay," Jalbert said. "Are you ready, Eliot?" Jalbert looked at me like I was horseshit on the bottom of his shoe. "You had your chance, Eddie. Instead, you tore up the contract."

I reminded myself of my suck-up status as the fresh MBA grad. "I didn't do it."

"You didn't do anything to stop it. In fact, you seemed to be enjoying Mike's show." Jalbert didn't mention our roughhousing afterward. Maybe he wanted to avoid round two.

"Mike has seniority. What could I do?"

Jalbert turned to Scullion. "Can you believe it, Eliot? I invite these two to dinner, and what gratitude do I get?"

"You had Horace there as well," I said.

"Eliot invited Horace," Jalbert said. "You think I'd invite that loudmouth? Horace spread all kinds of slander against me and against Seamless."

Scullion studied me intently, trying to guess the cards I was holding. "You and Mike found Horace's body, didn't you?"

"Trouble follows you two," Jalbert said.

"We were there to find out what End the Chase had to offer. You can never have enough skip tracing tools," I said, echoing Uncle Mike's collection manager motto. I rubbed the back of my neck and acted confused. "You know, Mr. Jalbert, I'm glad I didn't sign your employment contract."

"Why? Because you're an idiot?" Jalbert said.

"No, I'm not an idiot. I saw Mr. Tanner earlier, and he said that Globex Bank had signed a contract with Second Bet this morning."

"What?" Jalbert's face turned red. He took a step toward me. "I haven't heard that. You're lying."

I shrugged. "I didn't see the actual contract—"

"I haven't seen Ingrid all morning," Scullion said.

Jalbert rubbed the scar over his lip. "I haven't either. We were supposed to meet for breakfast."

One of the conference hosts hustled toward us. "Mr. Jalbert, the crowd is growing restless."

"Alright, damnit." Jalbert reached inside his sports coat and pulled out a slip of paper. His hands trembled. "Does everyone know about Globex but me?"

"We'll get it straightened out," Scullion said, smoothing out his hair and adjusting his tie.

Jalbert took a couple of shaky steps and then walked out onto the stage. He stood at the podium for an entire minute, staring out at the crowd. Maybe he was trying to determine if the crowd was talking about him and his failed Globex deal.

Scullion shook his head. "Poor schmuck. I'm going to miss those dinners." Scullion pulled out a few folded pages, which I assumed contained his speech. "Eddie, you might have to introduce yourself. I don't think you're too popular at the moment."

"It's my first conference and my first speech. I hope people don't expect too much." Sometimes I made myself ill with the imposter routine.

"We don't," Scullion stated flatly.

Jalbert finally stumbled through the introduction and Scullion took the stage to lengthy applause. Only in America was money worshipped on such a grand scale. Scullion nodded and waved, soaking up the adulation.

Jalbert skulked away to the opposite side of the stage.

Uncle Mike stepped through the door behind me marked "Employees Only."

The crowd settled down somewhat as Scullion held up two hands, requesting quiet.

"I love debt buying," Scullion shouted into the microphone. The crowd roared and rose to their feet again.

"What did Woodyard say?" I asked Uncle Mike.

"The shooters were Russians from out of town. Woodyard is at a dead end."

I told him how one of the gunmen eluded DiNatale.

"That guy will come looking for us."

"We wondered about Karmazin's payment," I said.

"Yeah. Karmazin probably arranged for the Russian shooters. It's like a Russian to repay you with money he got from a contract to kill you."

My cell buzzed. "I have to take this. It's Tara. Leave the door open so I can hear Scullion at the same time."

"Say hello to Tara for me."

I stepped through the back door into the hallway.

37

IN THE VACANT HALLWAY BEHIND THE BALLROOM, I answered Tara's call amid loud cheers and laughter from Scullion's opening joke.

"Hi, Tara."

"Hello, stranger. It's so good to hear from you."

"I'm sorry it had to be a work-related question—"

"No, no problem. Happy to help however I can. We should talk more often. It's my fault, too."

Her voice was strong and confident. I'd forgotten all the nuances and inflections in her voice and the time lapse unnerved me for a moment. "How are you getting along?"

"I'm still running and doing those killer workouts. How's your leg?"

"Fully recovered."

She paused a beat. "I met someone here in D.C."

"That's great." Tara's mom had told me the news. "I was worried you'd be lonely."

"Thanks."

I told her about Nicole.

"The poker player?" she said. "I'm so happy for you both. That's right, you're in Vegas."

"For a week or so."

"Thanks for helping my mom. She talks about you and Uncle Mike all the time."

"She's a regular at O'Connell's these days."

"She calls the tavern her second home, although she rarely drinks. A sherry once in a blue moon, maybe."

Scullion was giving the crowd his Horatio Alger story, starting with his childhood in Florida. It was enough to turn my stomach.

"Well, let me get to it. I know you're probably busy. I called Vivian as you suggested, but she didn't have anything. She put me in touch with Ms. Larsen. Can you believe that?"

Ms. Larsen had been in charge of the legal department at the branch office of WagerEasy in Chicago, where Tara and I had worked. Tara had not been on good terms with Larsen and neither was I. "You're kidding."

"It was truly amazing," Tara laughed. "She acted as if we were old buddies. She even laughed."

"I didn't know she could laugh. That's terrific. Ms. Larsen was under a lot of pressure at WagerEasy."

"She was. We all were. Now she works at a law firm involved with sports betting. They don't have WagerEasy as a client and, since WagerEasy laid off Ms. Larsen, there's no love lost. She was happy to tell me everything she knew. It hasn't become public yet."

"What is it?"

"She said someone had made a large Super Bowl bet at a WagerEasy function in Vegas."

"I was there." It was Scullion.

"You were? I guess the WagerEasy rep was present while the sports bettor contacted someone in New Jersey to place the bet," Tara continued.

"Okay."

"You don't know the legal stuff. Neither did I, but Ms. Larsen explained it to me. In fact, she made it sound like the juiciest gossip ever in the legal sports betting world. The sports bettor made the bet on his New Jersey account using a third party or proxy. The bettor was not in New Jersey at the time. A proxy bet like this is illegal and also against the policies of WagerEasy. The state gambling commission is looking into it and has frozen the man's account. WagerEasy could lose its license in New Jersey and be fined."

New Jersey was the first state to legalize and had brought the issue of sports betting legalization to the U.S. Supreme Court, and won. Sports betting in New Jersey had shot through the roof after legalization. New York hadn't legalized mobile betting, so throngs of sports bettors were crossing the state line to wager every weekend. New Jersey had hit the jackpot.

To lose New Jersey would be a disaster for WagerEasy. Now I understood why WagerEasy had closed its Vegas office and fired its manager.

"What about the bettor?" I asked.

"He'll come out smelling like a rose. Although his WagerEasy account was frozen for fifteen million, he'll likely get it all back. The sports bettor was the consumer and couldn't be expected to know all the legalities at the time. He's the victim. The WagerEasy rep on the scene allegedly gave tacit approval of the proxy bet. The sports bettor had wagered on the 49ers and lost, so he stands to be made whole."

"You mean he won't lose his Super Bowl bets?"

"That's the opinion of Ms. Larsen, although I guess the attorneys are having a field day. Here's the other part of the story. The sports bettor was the one who notified the state of the illegal proxy bet."

I tried to absorb the juicy gossip and legal gimmicks involved.

Tara laughed her signature laugh. "It's a stroke of brilliance."

38

IT WAS TIME.

I stumbled out to the podium to introduce myself. Of course, I wasn't introducing myself; I was introducing my imposter self, the Eddie O'Connell role I'd played all along. The fresh MBA grad that didn't know much about debt buying or Team Player, but was ambitious and impressionable. I'd used him as a weapon to gain information and as a shield to avoid suspicion. Now I used him to avoid simple stage fright, as an excuse to read words on a page instead of making eye contact or telling an opening joke.

What would I have done or said if the person walking up to the microphone in front of several hundred or more people was, in fact, me, rather than an imposter? I wasn't sure. I wasn't one of those who gave speeches. Maybe I'd held the floor at O'Connell's on a rowdy night now and then, but that didn't count.

"Let me introduce myself," I said into the microphone. I cleared my throat because I heard the crowd talking amongst themselves. "I'm new to the conference and new to Team Player. My name is Eddie O'Connell."

I made the mistake of looking up. The faces stared back. Rows and rows of faces. My throat turned dry. I began to sweat. I couldn't interpret the mood of the faces.

I spotted Uncle Mike in the front row with Hadlow. Uncle Mike nodded as if to say, "you can do this." He'd been there for me my entire life.

My eyes couldn't focus. I planned to read words on a page, a seemingly impossible task at the moment. I couldn't make myself turn away from the field of eyes staring back.

I imagined this was a poker game. The faces and the eyes were players, nothing more. I was accomplished at the art of watching one player specifically, while at the same time watching them all. What was their immediate reaction to the hidden hole cards? The emotion that flashed across players' faces ran the gambit of emotions from the joy of unwrapping an unexpected gift to outright disgust. I didn't need to look for tells. I could read their faces as easily as I could read a racing program.

My mood changed. I wasn't flabbergasted. I was in control. "You all know Tony Zino, my boss." I stopped. I had their attention. "He's in the hospital. He's recovering. We've been worried, but we're in touch and he sends along his best wishes to you all."

I wanted to tell them, "The Deacon can't be with you. All of what I'm about to tell you is the Deacon's work." But I didn't. It had been agreed that we wouldn't divulge the death of the Deacon and we'd stayed true to Burrascano's orders.

"I know some of you might have questions or comments," I said, reading from the wrinkled page with my handwritten notes. "Team Player's attorneys will be sending out all the reports and whatever lawyers do. I spent all morning with accountants and lawyers and I'm still not sure I understand everything."

I spotted Tanner and Roberts seated together. I stared straight at them—I wanted them to know I had the "nuts"—the hand I held was unbeatable. Tanner looked at his watch and glanced around like he was scouting for a quick exit. Roberts had her arms folded, her face set in attack mode. She would've "called," if we were playing an actual poker hand.

Scullion stood backstage to my left. I glanced over. I needed to include him in this hand—he couldn't sit out. He smiled, enjoying my outward case of nerves.

"Remember, I can't..." I hesitated and crinkled the paper into the microphone. "I can't answer questions. Mike O'Connell, also here from Team Player, can't answer questions. We've been advised by Team Player's attorneys not to answer questions. I repeat, we can't respond to questions. I'm just the messenger."

"We won't kill the messenger," someone yelled out. People laughed.

I smiled and waited for the laughter to die down.

"Mr. Zino's speech is titled 'The Pitfalls of Expansion.' I've asked Mr. Zino what he meant exactly, and he told me, 'Figure it out, dummy.'" The crowd rewarded me with a modest chuckle.

I pulled out another piece of paper and went through my crinkling routine. Uncle Mike and I had ripped up the speech we'd drafted after consulting with Irv this morning and replaced it with the stuff prepared by Zino's lawyers.

This was the moment where a player hesitated and followed the ritual of poker. I contemplated my next move—would I go "all-in" or not? The other players watched me closely. I wanted them to sweat.

"This is a prepared statement," I said, reading aloud. I stumbled and repeated myself a couple of times to let them know this wasn't me, it was some lawyer. "Team Player as assignee is in possession of convertible debentures. These debentures represent loans to Landis Tanner, and in return for the monies loaned to Mr. Tanner, he has pledged shares in 2ndBetOnDebt and its affiliated companies. The conversion provision of the debenture allows Team Player as assignee to convert the debentures into shares of 2ndBetOnDebt, which shares are owned by Tanner and were pledged to Team Player as assignee as security for the loan. The debenture contains customary, market standard covenants and allows for a conversion feature in the event of a breach of covenant. Notice of breach and demand for conversion has been given in accordance with the terms of the debenture."

I took a long look at the players in the room. They now understood I was "all-in." All the chips on the table were at risk.

I continued with the prepared statement. I raised the volume of my voice to showcase my imposter status, a nervous first-time player who couldn't wait to grab the chips out of the middle and stack them.

"This conversion of the debt to stock of 2ndBetOnDebt has given Team Player as assignee a majority interest in 2ndBetOnDebt."

Tanner most likely didn't know Team Player had obtained an assignment of the many loans he'd made with illegal bookies and illegal betting sites. Not one of these illegal bookies could refuse the mob or Burrascano, who must've been working on the Deacon's behalf to buy up every single loan.

It was a classic move by the mob—loan money to a compulsive gambler until he was forced to turn over his business to pay the debt. Only this move, orchestrated by the Deacon, had been accomplished over a period of time on a much grander scale. It boggled my mind. The law firm humming in the background had voluntarily turned over their file to Irv, probably on orders from Burrascano. It seemed lots of people knew about the upcoming speech, except for me and Uncle Mike.

"As collection agencies, I'm sure you know if you don't pay, you pay the piper. The piper today is Tony Zino and Team Player."

Tanner stood, his hands on his hips. "Is this some kind of stupid joke?"

DiNatale and a man the size of a vending machine walked down the aisle along the far wall near Tanner's section. Tanner glanced over.

"Your gambling debts caught up with you, Mr. Tanner," I said, almost as if I was apologizing. It was what MBA Eddie would do—try to smooth things over. "They also have informed me, the lawyers I mean, have informed me that these docs were all signed in Nevada and therefore they are as good as gold."

"This is bullshit," Tanner howled.

Roberts stood up and shoved Tanner. He lost his balance and hit the folding chair as he fell. "What the hell did you do?" She looked down at him on the floor. "You and your insane gambling."

"Million-dollar bets add up fast, Mr. Tanner," I said.

Brandt stood and began to slow clap. Several others, Zino's friends, also stood and joined in. Then it seemed the entire room was clapping in unison.

David, or in this case, the Deacon, had slain Goliath.

Tanner stood. "I've got something to say." He walked down the row, past people, to the aisle.

DiNatale stood with his hands on his hips. "Where do you think you're going, asshole?"

The ballroom turned silent.

"This is a hoax. Plain and simple. My attorneys—"

DiNatale slugged him in the gut. "You're not on the agenda."

Tanner doubled over, then dropped to his knees.

"Nice," Roberts squealed. "I've been wanting to do that."

The crowd roared. People high-fived.

Some people stood and shouted questions at me.

"What does Team Player plan to do?"

"When is Tony Zino coming back?"

I raised my hands, palms outward, to calm them down. "I don't know exactly how this will impact things. But I do know that Team Player has been ramping up."

I wanted to tell them that this was the Deacon's brand of justice, the Deacon acting from the grave. But I couldn't say any such thing.

"Remember, I'm just the messenger and this will all take time," I said. The Deacon's power play would shift the industry back to the way it was before. Quick profit would not be the end-all goal. Team Player wasn't about to go public.

I looked down from the stage at Uncle Mike and Jennifer Hadlow. They were laughing. Hadlow's company would be relevant again. The debtors who had been forced to use their credit cards for necessities would be handled with "loving care."

39

I GOT BACK TO MY ROOM TO CHANGE OUT OF MY "SPEECH clothes" and into something more casual.

I called Nicole again as I tied my shoes. It was my third try to get in touch with her.

"Eddie," Nicole answered. "I don't want to talk. Not now." Her voice was thin and high-pitched.

"Five minutes—"

"No."

"Just listen."

"I know what you're going to say."

"What?"

"You're going to say what the others are saying. Wit and all the others. You're going to say I should step aside and let another pro play Scullion."

"No—"

"I won't do it. No fucking way. Understand?"

"Good. I don't want you to."

"What?"

"Just listen to me for a minute."

"This better be good."

"It is." I talked fast.

———

As I finished changing clothes, there was a knock on the door. It was Uncle Mike.

"I see your housekeeping is up to its usual standards." The chair crammed into a slot between the bed and the window was covered with dirty clothes. "This place is a dump." He stared out the window. I had a good view of the parking garage.

"We can't all enjoy most-favored status with a suite."

He walked over to the desk covered with pages from Arlene's scrapbook. "What did you come up with?"

"Like I've said, the murder was personal. You don't need to go to all the trouble to arrange a drive-by just to kill a working stiff like Zino, the head of a collection agency. Zino you gun down in the men's toilet or in the hallway of the hotel. You wear your mask and walk away. But if you want to get somebody when they're helpless and shoot them in the face—"

"You're right. You better bring your 'A' game to kill the Deacon." Uncle Mike flipped pages of my notebook and my handwritten notes.

"The next question—how did the killer find the Deacon?"

"Another crucial question."

"I think it's connected to Horace's murder."

"How so?"

"I thought Scullion must've invited Horace to Jalbert's dinner. Jalbert wouldn't invite Horace. Horace was spreading rumors about Jalbert."

"Right." Uncle Mike sat down in the desk chair. "Horace was saying that Seamless provided good data on debtors to Jalbert and then gave everyone else crap."

"Correct. That's why Team Player didn't pay its invoice to Seamless. Well, when I was waiting backstage earlier, Jalbert confirmed the fact that he didn't invite Horace to dinner, it was Scullion."

"Makes sense. Horace was sitting at Scullion's end of the table."

"So why would Scullion invite Horace to dinner? I think it's reasonable to assume that Horace did Scullion a favor while he was working at Seamless."

"A favor? What kind of favor?"

"A very big favor. Something that got Horace fired. I think Shelly Urban knew about it, but it was so bad, such a serious breach of the rules, that she refused to tell us."

"Maybe Horace gave Scullion an unauthorized search on somebody?"

I nodded. "That's my guess. They don't allow just anyone to search for anybody. The person has to owe money on a debt, sign an application for a loan or some other legal matter."

"Right."

"We know the Deacon received threats. Claudia told us that."

Uncle Mike pulled out a stogie and tucked it into the corner of his mouth. "Go on."

"Due to those threats, the Deacon got in touch with Arlene and then the Deacon asked Burrascano to urge us to take Arlene's case about Porter's disappearance."

"Keep going. I'm liking this."

I stepped over to the table and my notes. "The Deacon didn't give a shit about Arlene's scrapbook. Arlene would never do anything to put the Deacon in jeopardy. She's just a heartsick lady who will love Porter despite all his faults until the day she dies."

Uncle Mike chewed on the unlit cigar. "Yeah, that's true."

"What if Scullion used Horace to skip trace the Deacon?"

"Now hold on—"

"I know, I know. I might as well try to skip trace the Lone Ranger."

"Right." Uncle Mike grabbed his stogie and pointed it down at the scrapbook. "The Deacon is a myth. You need an identifier to skip trace someone—a name, a social, or an address."

"I believe there are people who know the real name of the Deacon. Old timers. Guys in the mob from years ago that might be willing to take a quiet bribe. Old guys who don't exactly have social security."

"I guess."

"What about Arlene, for example? You heard the way she reacted when we told her what the Deacon said,

'Rosario and Roberta at the Flamingo.' She knew exactly what the Deacon's code words were about. I think it traces back to the Deacon's real name."

"But Arlene would never—"

"That's just an example. Now, let's take a look at Eliot Scullion. He said at one point that he had moved back to New Jersey. Then, at last night's poker match, he said he should've never moved to New Jersey; somebody should've told him what it was like."

"Fine. Scullion was lying about New Jersey."

"This morning Scullion talked about his childhood in Florida." I took a breath and rifled through my notes. "According to Scullion's bio on his business website, he went to high school in Florida. Information I pulled on Scullion's father showed he was an accountant. If his family moved from New Jersey to Florida, the question is why?"

"They like the sunshine?"

"No. I had O'Rourke do a skip trace on Scullion. I called Irv too. There are no records of the Scullion family back in New Jersey. Scullion's father didn't start work as an accountant in Florida until he was forty. In fact, he didn't exist until he turned forty. No marriage certificate for Scullion's folks, no birth certificate for Eliot Scullion and no record of Scullion's name change."

"Yeah. Irv mentioned that Scullion changed his name. Where did he find that?"

"Irv said that sometimes their databases pick stuff up from interviews or articles. Maybe Scullion slipped up at some point and talked about a name change."

"Mysterious. What do you think, Sherlock?"

"In the scrapbook, I have FBI reports about Porter and the Deacon being seen going to New Jersey from New York. Shortly thereafter, they showed up in a small town in Florida. I also have an article about an accountant who embezzled from the New Jersey mob and went into witness protection around this same time period."

"What was the name of the accountant? When he was in New Jersey, before he went to Florida."

"His name was Franklin Cullen."

"Let me see that article."

40

LATER THAT EVENING, I STOOD WITH WIT IN BOBBY'S ROOM at the Bellagio. Hans Becker stood to Wit's right. Uncle Mike stood to my left. The heads-up match had been going on for some time. Scullion had drawn even with Nicole.

Hans had a goofy "cat that ate the golden goose" smile.

Nicole faced Scullion as before, the same professional blond dealer in the middle. Nicole wore the exact same clothes as yesterday, the WagerEasy Sports Betting Insider sweatshirt and green visor. Scullion wore the fancy gray suit and silk gray tie that he'd worn when he'd given his keynote address.

Outside the windows, a crowd of pros huddled together. I had talked to some of them earlier. They were nervous, but optimistic. They had faith in Nicole.

Nicole studied her hole cards. She had the first option as the dealer with the small blind. In her customary rhythm, Nicole waited for what seemed to be a prescribed amount of time.

Her hand moved slowly to her chip stack, grabbed chips and then shuffled them over and over. The click-clacking of the chips was the only sound in the room. Nicole didn't look at Scullion but at the blank felt in the middle, soon to be the repository of the flop, the turn, and the river cards.

Nicole seemed to be envisioning the cards that would end up in the middle. Maybe Scullion had begun to think about the reasons behind Nicole's deliberate moves, trying to guess what she had. If so, he'd be thrown off his game.

"Twenty thousand," Nicole said, tossing in the chips.

It caught us by surprise, as if we'd become mesmerized by the rhythm of her fingering of the chips.

Scullion let out a breath and his hand shot toward his chip stack. "Let's see a flop." He called.

Nicole had tested Scullion's patience. His impulsive moves were on display.

The cards were a king of hearts, nine of diamonds, and a three of spades—a rainbow. If the player was working on a flush, they could eliminate that possibility.

It was Scullion's turn to bet under heads-up rules. He threw in the same bet as before, twenty thousand.

Nicole went through her practiced series of actions. The long gaze into the middle, the stare at Scullion, then back again to the middle, until her hand traced its familiar arc toward the chip stack, the fingers extended as her fingertips and long polished fingernails delicately caressed a portion of the stack, then clasped the chips, and transferred the cargo around and down toward the felt, where the rhythmic shuffling chorus would begin again.

Scullion sat on the edge of his seat, tense, his hands in his lap. From the way his arms and shoulders moved, I could tell his hands and fingers must be twisting and churning beneath the table. I would bet that he had a king in his hand. A pair of kings was a good hand in heads-up. He didn't raise Nicole on the opening bet, so maybe he wanted to trap her.

To trap a player, you'd want them to be as heavily invested in the pot as possible or pot-committed. That would make it difficult for a player to walk away or fold. What distinguished a pro was their willingness to give up on their investment. The pro would then digest what they'd learned, and move on to the next hand without second thoughts.

Scullion cleared his throat. I wondered if he was about to start in on his toxic table talk. If so, he probably felt good about his hand.

"Today's conference was quite interesting," he said, scratching the back of his head.

Nicole kept up the click-clack of the chips.

"My attorneys tell me my investment in 2ndBetOnDebt has decreased significantly in value. Yesterday, I could look forward to a huge profit based on a quick sale of the company to a private equity group I'm involved with, and today, I am the proud holder of shares in a private company controlled by Mr. Tony Zino. I hold a minority interest with no decision-making power. I'm the big loser."

Nicole called. I was surprised she didn't fold, but then I never could get a good read on the cards she held.

The turn was an ace of diamonds.

Scullion stared at the ace. By his facial impressions, Scullion hated the card. Nicole was impassive.

Scullion bet the same, twenty thousand. He wanted to entice Nicole to stay in the hand.

Nicole went through her routine.

"My lawyers tell me the new owner can do what he wants with the company. Zino has a certain responsibility to the shareholders, but he has a broad range of powers. It wouldn't be worth it for me to proceed with legal action. It's just one of the risks I take, I tell myself."

I was getting a look inside Scullion's head through his stream-of-consciousness table talk. Scullion had taken a hit with Zino's takeover of Second Bet.

"I have plenty of other investments, plenty of other wins. I unloaded a large chunk of stock in WagerEasy yesterday. It has gone down steadily ever since. I'm not sure what the problem might be. The stock of every other sports betting operator is going through the roof. I'm glad I bought options to short the stock."

"Raise," Nicole said, pushing in chips.

"That ace must have helped you." Scullion bent down and studied his hole cards. "Interesting." He grabbed chips. "Raise."

The pot was growing. The pros outside the windows craned their necks to see. I hated being an observer. I hated knowing only part of the story. Those damn hole cards.

Hans was smiling again.

Beside me, Uncle Mike shifted his weight to relieve the pressure on his bad leg. I should've found him a chair.

Nicole waited and waited.

I studied Scullion. If my series of deductions was correct and he was the killer, what had it been like for him the day of the drive-by shooting at the valet stand when he bent down over the Deacon? Scullion must've relished that moment; the long years of tracking it had taken for him to avenge his family were finally about to pay off.

The split-second timing required to bend down over the underworld's legend and shoot the Deacon at point blank range was masterful. The pent-up emotion that must've been released would make anyone think they could do anything. They might even think they could beat a pro at heads-up.

How had Scullion felt when he had shot Horace in that small, sterile meeting room? The shooting was probably nothing more than house cleaning, sweeping up loose ends.

Nicole was shuffling the chips, staring at the king of hearts, nine of diamonds, three of spades, and now an ace of diamonds. If she had two diamonds, the flush was back in play. If she had ace-king, she'd have two pair—a great hand in heads-up. But what if Scullion had two kings as his hole cards giving him three of a kind or a set? No, he hadn't raised her on the opening round of betting. Scullion didn't have the discipline to stop himself from raising her at that stage. Or did he? Maybe, as I first thought, he was trying to trap Nicole. No, he had only one king in his hole cards. Now he had to deal with that ace in the middle.

Were these the scenarios spinning through Nicole's head? She couldn't fold now. Or could she?

"Some players take risks," Nicole said. "Some put on a show. They're really not risking anything at all."

These were the first words Nicole had spoken throughout the heads-up match. She had remained mute through yesterday's play.

Wit glanced at me with a worried look. Uncle Mike took the toothpick, a cigar substitute, out of his mouth.

Scullion appeared shocked. His little game had been hijacked.

Nicole stared at Scullion; not once did she glance toward the crowd. These two were in their own world now, the chips secondary.

"Raise," Nicole said, adding more chips to the pot.

Scullion sat back and took a deep breath and rubbed his eyes with his hands. He was now the player who was heavily invested. Had he trapped himself?

"Remember, you were at the pre-Super Bowl party given by WagerEasy? WagerEasy was the sponsor of The Sports Betting Insiders. You were there." Nicole's words flowed like an indictment read out in open court.

Scullion's smirk was absent. His mouth hung open and his shoulders sagged.

Scullion reached for chips as if it was a lifeline. "Call."

The dealer burned a card and then dealt the river card. It was an ace of spades.

Scullion hated this ace even more than the last ace. I could almost hear him thinking out loud, "*if Nicole had an ace in the hole, her three aces would beat my two pair of kings and aces. If Nicole didn't have an ace, then she must be mad. No, she was a pro. She must have an ace."*

"Check," Scullion said.

"You bet a million on the 49ers. Then you talked Tanner into betting a million on the 49ers, remember? You made the wagers on your WagerEasy account by calling someone you had standing by back in New Jersey. You made a big deal about it. You called Franzen over, the WagerEasy rep."

Nicole stared at Scullion. "Forty thousand."

Scullion looked toward Hans. You didn't need to be a poker pro to see Scullion's Adam's apple bobbing up and down. "What are you getting at?"

He glanced at the pot. His hand reached unsteadily for chips and knocked over a portion of the stack. He snatched them up and fingered the chips. "Raise twenty thousand."

"You know the laws," Nicole continued. "You set up WagerEasy. Every gambling operator has GPS software to ensure bets aren't placed outside the state. You ratted to the state of New Jersey about the proxy bet you made. The state has frozen your WagerEasy account, but you'll get all your money back. Your lawyers will make sure of that."

The crowd gasped.

Scullion looked around at the faces in the room. Hans was staring down at his shoes. Others looked like they wanted to find a rope and hang Scullion. We were all gamblers. When we bet and lost, we accepted it. We didn't look for ways to welch.

Somebody inside the room must've switched on their cell because the crowd outside Bobby's Room clearly must have heard every word between Nicole and Scullion. The outrage outside could be heard even inside the glass-enclosed room. "Scullion" had suddenly become synonymous with "motherfucker."

"You ratted on WagerEasy and all of those people lost their jobs, including me. Then you made money on WagerEasy in the stock market."

Scullion laughed, a weak, high-pitched laugh. He glanced toward the crowd outside.

"Your lawyers have filed a motion to release all your funds, including the amounts you wagered. They claim you're an innocent victim."

Scullion bit his fingernail.

"You mentioned my father yesterday," Nicole said. "Let's talk about your father. Your family's move from New Jersey to Florida."

Scullion was visibly shaken. His hand trembled as he reached to loosen his tie. "My father?" he mumbled.

"Yes, your father." Nicole shouted, her face red.

Scullion stared out at each one of us. Maybe he was looking for a friendly face. He thought he'd be able to graduate to the big leagues by beating Nicole and be accepted by the poker world.

"Keep my father out of it," Scullion said.

"You started this." Her anger had spread through the crowd. "I'm all-in."

Scullion peeked again at his hole cards. "You must have an ace," Scullion muttered. "Fold."

The crowd outside roared. Even those of us in the room who were expected to remain silent couldn't help but react to the quick "fold."

"What the fuck?" Hans said.

"Caved like a rookie," Wit chuckled.

"Damn," I said.

Nicole stood up and threw her hole cards face-up in the middle of the table.

"Jeesus," Uncle Mike said.

It was a jack and a seven, a bluff. She had nothing.

41

ABOUT TWO HOURS LATER, THEY TOOK AN EVENING BREAK in the poker match.

The game had gone downhill for Scullion since the big win by Nicole. Scullion had tried to bounce back with more chatter and some big bets, but his heart didn't seem to be in it.

"Are you going to talk with your guy?" Wit asked Hans at the break.

It was noble of Wit to even suggest a stoppage, because as one of Nicole's backers, he had everything to gain. Nicole was trouncing Scullion. She must be "up" almost three million. If I was in Han's shoes, I'd do everything I could to convince Scullion to call it quits.

"Yes. We might decide to throw in the towel," Hans said.

"Probably the thing to do," Wit said. "Let me know."

Hans walked off and met up with Scullion.

Wit turned to me and clapped me on the back. "You were right about Nicole all along, Eddie."

I thanked him, but I didn't tell him how relieved I felt.

"Where did she come up with all that stuff about WagerEasy? Everybody here in Vegas was wondering why they shut down." Wit scratched his chin and a slight smile flickered across his face. I'd seen that look before in late-night poker games when he held the winning hand.

"I wouldn't know," I said with a grin.

"Well, wherever she got the news, I'm glad she got it. I wouldn't have gone "all-in" on that hand. But I always say, 'if you're going to bluff, bluff big.' I just don't listen to my own advice."

I asked Wit to keep me updated on the status of the match and went into the casino with Uncle Mike. DiNatale was at the Horseshoe Bar. He nodded slightly in our direction.

We stood near him, but we didn't shake hands. We didn't want to telegraph our relationship with the mobster to others, especially to Jake, who nodded in my direction as he wiped a glass.

We'd assigned DiNatale the task of keeping track of our other two major suspects—Tanner and Jalbert. Although I felt we had a strong case against Scullion, Uncle Mike insisted we follow the usual routine.

"Keep all the suspects in the stable until we're absolutely one hundred percent certain," Uncle Mike had said.

DiNatale got up off his bar stool and acted as if he was reading the electronic odds board on the wall inside the sports book. "Tanner is in the third row. His buddy has been making a few bets on the horses for him. Losing as usual. How's the match going?"

"Nicole is up big," I said without looking the mobster's way. "They might call it."

DiNatale snickered.

"How about Jalbert?" I asked.

"I've got a guy on him. He's at the bar in Caesars. Blade will be tailing Scullion."

I had gotten to know DiNatale's guys by now. We'd been on several field trips, including the collection call on Karmazin at The Kremlin. Blade was in the crowd outside Bobby's Room.

"You've got the bases covered. Thanks."

"Let's have a chat with Mr. Tanner, Eddie," Uncle Mike said. "I've got a few follow-up questions. Thanks for the help, Vic."

"You got it," DiNatale said.

We walked into the sports book. Tanner sat at the end of the row in the middle section. I felt like a vulture swooping in to pick at the last bits of meat on the carcass.

Uncle Mike stopped at the end of Tanner's row. "Mr. Tanner, good to see you."

Tanner looked up. "I suppose you guys came for the keys to the place?"

"No, I wanted to ask you a couple of questions," Uncle Mike said.

"Why would I tell you assholes anything?"

"Remember, we're just messengers," I said.

"It's about Scullion," Uncle Mike said.

"I don't care what or who you want to—"

"Did you know Scullion has filed an objection with the state of New Jersey on his Super Bowl bets?" I asked. "Since he made a proxy bet on his WagerEasy account, Scullion will get his money back."

"A proxy what?" Tanner shrieked.

I went through the whole thing again. How Scullion had placed the bet with a buddy located in New Jersey using Scullion's WagerEasy account. I felt like I knew Scullion's scheme better than his lawyers did.

Tanner was inebriated, but by the time I explained it a second time, he started to understand.

"I get it. Scullion had me sign a promissory note for my million-dollar bet on the 49ers. And he talked me into making the wager. Son of a bitch. I bet he never planned to tell me." Tanner stood up. "What do you guys want to know?"

"You were at The Kremlin on Sunday night," Uncle Mike said. "Were you betting over at The Kremlin? We heard you could get good odds on the 49ers and good odds on prop bets."

Tanner's beating had been a reminder to bet only with the illegal bookmakers. I thought it best if we didn't mention it.

"Yeah. Me and Scullion were over at The Kremlin during the game," Tanner said, picking up his drink. "He knew the owner, a guy named Karmazin. We had dinner with the Russian."

"What kind of bets was Scullion making?" Uncle Mike asked.

"You name it. We were betting prop bets, you know. Keep the action going," Tanner said.

"Drink some vodka?" I asked.

"Yeah. We were shit-faced for sure," Tanner said, slurring the word shit-faced with a stupid grin because he was again getting very close to shit-faced status. "Wait. There was something weird that happened. What was it?" Tanner stared up at the rows of flat screens above the ticket sellers televising sports and horse races from around the country on a Wednesday evening. "I know. Scullion had lost a bet for a lot of money, or maybe he had lost the money in the casino. I can't remember, we were throwing a lot of money around. Scullion asked Karmazin, 'want to go double or nothing on what I owe you?' Karmazin said 'yes.'"

"Why did that seem weird?" Uncle Mike asked.

"We were betting at the sports book, not with the Russian," Tanner laughed. "Who bets money with a Russian? You might never get paid. If you bet at his casino, you'll get paid or the guy loses his casino license. You get a certain comfort level at a casino sports book, you know?"

"I know. Yes, that is weird," Uncle Mike said.

Uncle Mike glanced my way. We had hard evidence linking Scullion with Karmazin, the guy who we suspected of bringing in the Russian shooters. Now we could confront Scullion.

"But other than that," Tanner said. "It was another wild night. Hey, you guys don't need somebody to consult for you, do you?"

Uncle Mike clapped me on the back. "Let's have a long chat with Scullion. We'll bring DiNatale along."

As we walked back to the bar, I got a call from Nicole. "Eddie, they called the game. Wit told me. It's over."

I could feel the relief in her voice, together with a note of both disbelief and bitter resentment. She wanted to tuck the win away and, at the same time, take down Scullion for every dollar possible.

"Congratulations. We have to celebrate," I said. "You did great."

"A group of us will be meeting at the bar, but I have to go home first, shower, and change and decompress."

"Sure. Let me know when you get back," I said.

"Okay. Bye. Love you."

"Love you, too."

We hadn't broadcasted it yet—but it was official. We were back together again.

Uncle Mike was close enough to hear the four-letter word. "It's about damn time for you two. C'mon, let's get DiNatale."

We caught up with DiNatale in the bar and told him we needed to see Scullion.

"You think he's our guy?" DiNatale got out his cell. "Blade told me he followed Scullion up to his room." He held the cell to his ear. "Damn it. The fucker's not answering."

"What floor is Scullion on?"

"The top floor."

42

DiNatale used a keycard so we could access the elevator to the top floor of the Bellagio, the floor of Scullion's penthouse room.

"What room number?" I asked.

"I don't know," DiNatale said.

"How did you get that keycard?" I asked him.

"I've got privileges," DiNatale said. "It's my town when I'm here."

We reached the penthouse floor and got out.

"I don't see Blade," DiNatale said, pulling out his cell and calling again.

Uncle Mike and I walked around the corner, where a sign pointed to one group of rooms to the left and another group to the right. I went to the right and Uncle Mike turned left. We had our guns in hand.

I walked down the hall, checking for any door that might be slightly ajar. Since Blade hadn't answered his cell, I didn't know what I'd find.

When I reached the end of the hall with an exit sign for the stairwell, I heard the faint buzz of a cell phone. There were bloodstains on the carpet. I stepped to one side, my gun in my right hand, and shoved the exit door with my left side. The door didn't budge.

I planted my feet and put my right shoulder into it. Blade was slumped against the door in a pool of blood. I rolled him over and saw the bullet hole in his forehead. Damn.

———

Scullion was loose. He must've propped the body against the door and then headed down the stairs. He could exit the stairway on the floor below and then take the elevator to the second or third floor, where he'd gain easy access to the parking garage.

In the lobby, Uncle Mike, DiNatale, and I discussed our next move.

"He's got to be running to Karmazin," DiNatale said. "He's probably looking for protection."

It was a good conclusion.

"Scullion might consider Karmazin a loose end," Uncle Mike said.

"Scullion has my permission to take care of the Russian," I said.

"If Karmazin supplied the shooters, we'll find out," DiNatale said.

I didn't think DiNatale would kill Karmazin. At the moment, he had the best insurance money could buy. He owed money to the mob, and he was current on his payments.

"We better take precautions," Uncle Mike said.

DiNatale grunted approval. "We better not all drive up to The Kremlin at the same time."

"Good point, Vic. Uncle Mike and I will take a cab," I said.

"I'll get some of my guys and we'll go through the entrance outside the parking garage." DiNatale got on his cell and we went through the double glass doors. I was shocked to see night had fallen. That's life in the casino—you lose track of time.

I asked the valet for a cab and pulled out my cell.

"Who are you calling?" Uncle Mike asked.

"Nicole."

"Why? Isn't she inside?"

"No, she went home to change and decompress. The match was called. Scullion quit."

"Good for Nicole."

"Maybe we're making a mistake. Nicole isn't answering." I did my best to put myself in the shoes of an egotistical billionaire murderer who had just been taken down several notches at a poker table by a woman. "Scullion's motto is 'even when I lose, I win.'"

"He refused to lose that Super Bowl bet he made with WagerEasy," Uncle Mike said.

"Scullion worked for years to find the Deacon. Would he let Nicole walk away with his money?"

"You're right, Eddie. Vengeance is Scullion's thing. Damnit. You know where Nicole lives, right?"

"Yeah." My cell buzzed again. "Wait a minute. I got a text from Nicole. She says, 'Eddie, come quick. Somebody is outside.' Damnit, no way she'd text me instead of calling me back."

"Scullion probably forced her to text you. That way he can get you, too. I'll call DiNatale and let him know not to expect us at The Kremlin."

———

We had the driver stop a couple of blocks from Nicole's house.

"Nicole's house is perched on a rocky outcropping," I said. "It gives her a great view, but I shouldn't have any trouble climbing up from the ravine to the back of the house."

Uncle Mike grabbed my shoulder. "Be careful. Scullion might have help. The Russian shooter that got away might be with him."

"Don't worry."

"I'll go up the street and wait near the front. Send me a text."

"Okay. Take advantage of cover."

It wasn't the greatest plan, but we couldn't call in the police. I assumed Scullion was already in the house holding Nicole hostage. She'd be the first one Scullion killed. He wouldn't have much more to lose at that point, and losing wasn't in his vocabulary.

Would he have killed Nicole already? Maybe. But it was my bet Scullion wanted me to witness Nicole's murder before he dealt with me—additional payback for my role in today's takedown of Second Bet.

I walked down into the ravine that ran behind Nicole's house. It was deep enough to be cloaked in darkness. The desert wind had begun to howl, and I was thankful. It would cover up the sound of the gravel crunching beneath my feet. Due to the ongoing construction on the lots up and down Nicole's street, I wouldn't have to worry about neighbors.

I was able to cut a path across the steep slope, but the loose rock forced me to take it slow. If a larger rock became dislodged and tumbled down, it could draw attention.

Behind me, I caught sight of a reflection. It could be a hunk of glass or metal, but the streetlights above weren't able to penetrate the darkness.

I hunkered down by a boulder. The reflection flickered again, this time from another location. Was it the glint from the eyes of a coyote or other animal? The shadowy figure moved soundlessly across the ravine, advancing toward me quickly. I pulled my gun.

Every minute counted. Uncle Mike was approaching the front of the house. Nicole's life hung in the balance. Precious seconds ticked away.

The shadow took on human form—a woman. The reflection was a penlight, and she signaled me from the deeper part of the ravine, then climbed up.

I recognized her and holstered my gun. "We meet again," I whispered. It was Claudia. She wasn't breathing hard. She'd scaled the severe slope like a spider. Her tight-fitting, all-black suit accentuated her muscular physique.

She examined the deck of Nicole's house above. "I've been in touch with Vic," she whispered. "If he's got her, one of us has to go in there. Scullion will expect you. He'll be glad to see you." She seemed to know we had little time.

"Then what?"

"The one outside—me, breaks in shooting while the one inside—you, protects her.

"You read this in a book?"

"There's no time to waste arguing. It's our only chance to ensure her safety."

She was right. A moment ago, I wanted to break in through the back of the house and throttle Scullion with my bare hands. What if the Russian shooter was there? I couldn't strangle two guys at once.

Could I trust Claudia? She'd been the Deacon's right hand, the one he depended upon for the cloak and dagger stuff. She'd followed me into the parking garage of The Kremlin Casino the night of the Super Bowl. She'd been following Uncle Mike and me around the casino, and I never spotted her once. She was good, and she had lots of reasons to make this work. She wanted the guy who murdered her boss.

"Okay."

"They'll frisk you."

I nodded and took a deep breath. Claudia wanted me to think things through. This was an "operation," and we needed a plan. "When do you come in?"

"We need to wait a while. The first few minutes, they'll expect someone and be on alert. We need to be patient."

Being patient wouldn't be easy. Nicole would expect me to take action. "Right."

"Get him talking. Get them comfortable. Look like you're trapped."

"Then what?"

"Improvise."

"Mike is coming toward the front of the house."

"I'll text him."

"You want his number?"

She smiled, at ease with the situation. It wasn't so easy for me. Adrenaline spiked every time I thought of Nicole in danger.

"I've got his number."

Claudia had texted Uncle Mike as the Deacon last night. "Right."

"Go in the front. We don't want them to worry about the back of the house."

"See you inside." I wished I had a better feeling about the hastily formed plan.

43

I STOOD AT THE FRONT DOOR. THE CURTAINS WERE DRAWN tight. No sign of any activity or anything out of the ordinary. Maybe I was wrong. Maybe Nicole was just jumpy and thought she heard somebody outside.

I rang the doorbell. Footsteps approached the door and then stopped. I stood in front of the peephole.

A few seconds later, Nicole opened the door. She was still wearing the WagerEasy sweatshirt, her hair a tangled mess and a bruise welling up on her cheek.

"Come in," she said in a shaky voice.

I walked right in without commenting on the bruise. I reminded myself of the mission—I would give myself up in hopes of saving Nicole. The thought kept my anger from running amok and getting us both killed.

One step inside and I had a gun in the small of my back.

"I'm sorry, Eddie," Nicole said.

"Steady," the man said in a thick Russian accent. "Hands in the air."

"You watch the gun and I'll be steady-Eddie," I said.

"Make with the jokes. You killed my brother."

"Next time, tell him to shop for his handbag somewhere else."

"Get in there." He herded Nicole and me into the living room—kitchen area. The blinds were drawn tight here as well.

Scullion stood near the kitchen counter. He had ditched the coat and tie. His shirtsleeves were rolled up to his elbows and his shirttail hung out. "Welcome. I knew you'd run to the rescue." He turned toward Nicole, waving his forefinger as if disciplining an unruly child. "And you told me he wouldn't come."

The urge to throttle Scullion rifled through me. The Rusky still had his gun on me. I took a deep breath.

Scullion turned to me. "Where's the old man? You two are always together."

I put my arm around Nicole. "Some things we don't do together."

"Ah, a rendezvous. How sweet." He waved his gun at me. "Keep your arms up. Did you frisk him, Ilya?"

I stood for the frisk and Ilya found my gun. They might be suspicious if I'd left the gun with Claudia.

Ilya placed the gun on the counter. "What are we waiting for?"

"Easy," Scullion said. "We're going to have a little chat first. I have a feeling the old man will come along any minute. These two always work as a pair. You wanted both of them, right?"

"Yeah." The Russian gave me a hard stare and poured himself a shot of vodka from the bottle on the counter.

Scullion motioned with the gun. "Take a seat on the couch, Eddie. You too, Nicole."

We sat on the couch along the wall only a few yards from the kitchen counter. Usually, the couch came with a view through the sliding glass doors to the deck and beyond.

I wanted to congratulate Ilya on his speed and endurance, leaving his comrade to face DiNatale's gunmen alone in the mall. Then I recalled the mission—stay patient. Let them get comfortable.

"They broke into my house," Nicole said.

"And as you can see, Nicole offered us drinks. I'm having a scotch." Scullion raised his glass. "A toast to the winner."

"Eliot was telling me about his background," Nicole said. "He prefers that subject to the heads-up match. I called him a fish—a gutted fish."

She seemed to understand the need to buy time. She and Scullion had just tried to "kill" each other in the heads-up match and now the match had mutated to another level.

"And Nicole decided to be a good listener," Scullion said.

"Yeah," the Russian said, taking another shot of vodka.

"You don't have to convince me," I said, crossing my legs and getting comfortable on the couch. "I'm sorry I missed some of your speech, Eliot. I have lots of catching up to do."

Scullion waved his gun around as if to clear the air. "The information won't do you much good, but I'll continue."

The Russian grunted. It sounded like a disgusted grunt.

"I was telling Nicole about my father. I wanted to be sure she had the full story." Scullion's sarcasm wasn't lost on me. I had been the one who'd prompted Nicole to mention Scullion's father.

"You see, my father was driven mad." Scullion took a sip from his scotch as if to memorialize the statement. "It started one day when we were driving back from the store. We were only a few blocks from home when it happened. Someone rear-ended us. My father cussed a blue streak as you would expect. We pulled over to the curb. I was worried about what he might do, so I got out of the car with him.

"The other driver and his friend had gotten out of their car and met us. The two men seemed very friendly. They asked my father if he wanted to call the police. It seemed funny to me the way they asked the question. As if they didn't expect that my father would want to call the police. I kicked at the back bumper and it was loose and bent in the middle. There was other damage, too. I pointed it out. My father told me to be quiet and get in the car.

"I didn't get in the car. The men seemed nice, almost too nice. They asked my father if he didn't want to take the 'little guy' home and they could sit down and talk things over—make things right? To my surprise, my father agreed."

Scullion stopped and sipped his scotch. His story flowed, but there was an edge to the words as if he'd lived this scene from his childhood over and over again, and he'd never come to terms with the troubled memories.

I had an idea what the story was leading to. I wondered how long would be "'long enough'" for Claudia.

Scullion cleared his throat. "After we'd moved from New Jersey to Florida, my father seemed to be settled and happy for the first time in a long time. After the accident, my father changed. He became nervous and anxious. His anger was always at the boiling point and always directed at me. I wasn't sure whether to blame the two men from the accident or not. For a long time, I thought I had done something wrong. It preyed on my mind. I couldn't do enough to please him or change him back."

Scullion chuckled. "Of course, what I just told you was revealed to me only through years of therapy—one of the advantages of the wealthy. My father was a hard-working accountant. He was always trying to borrow money. Whenever we drove anywhere, he'd be looking in the rearview. He was haunted and angry."

"Why are you putting us through this, Eliot?" Nicole pleaded, on the edge of the couch. "You mentioned my father first."

Scullion raised his gun toward Nicole. "Shut up. Just shut up."

"You don't have enough poker experience, but you want to play a pro," Nicole said. "You should expect to get stomped."

The Russian took a step toward me, brandishing his gun, a wild grin on his face.

I braced for a showdown. What would be my first move? I had two guns aimed at me. I had to wait it out.

Scullion set his drink down, his eyes wild. "Shut up or I'll—"

"I'd like to hear it, Eliot," I said in my calmest voice. "Go ahead."

Nicole dropped back onto the sofa, folding her arms and cussing under her breath.

Scullion picked up his scotch and sipped. The Russian stepped back to the counter. He poured another shot of vodka, never taking his eyes off me.

"My father left us a couple of years later when I was fourteen," Scullion said. "A critical time, my psychiatrist told me. Much later, I learned the full story. The two men who rear-ended us that day were contract killers hired by the mob in New Jersey. Supposedly, my father had embezzled from the mob and had testified against them. Our family went into witness protection in Florida."

He didn't look at us as he told this chapter of the story. His eyes were focused above us, into a dark past. Perhaps Scullion's parents had told their young son a lie about the reasons for the move. I pictured a boy torn from his neighborhood and friends, trying to find ways to cope with a new school and make new friends.

"The two men were Porter "the Pastor" Pearson, and a man they called the Deacon. They demanded every penny my father had. They even forced my father to embezzle from his new clients in Florida, some of whom were quite wealthy. When they'd finished, my father disappeared from the face of the earth."

"I hope there's a happy ending," I said. I couldn't help myself.

Scullion laughed. It wasn't the kind of laugh that made you want to laugh along with him. It was a shrill, piercing laugh that made you want to run for the exits.

"Yes, yes, my good friends. Now comes the good part." Scullion was like a kid talking about his awesome reptile collection.

Leave it to me to open Pandora's box. At the same time, I was fascinated by Scullion's story. The main characters in Arlene's scrapbook had come to life.

"It took time and money to find out the full story. The Feds had gotten testimony from my father. At this later time when the contract killers appeared, the Feds refused protection. They had some excuse for dropping my father— he hadn't followed their rules or something. It was bullshit. But with enough money and enough retired agents, you can get copies of files if you dig hard enough and long enough. That's how I came up with Porter's name."

Scullion sipped from his scotch. His eyes bugged out; a crooked grin played on his lips. Years of bitterness had rotted his insides. "I found Porter quite easily. He lived in Chicago. We took him out on a rowboat and dropped him into a small lake."

"Where?" I wanted details for Arlene.

"That's a strange question to ask." Scullion stopped and stared at his watch. "An odd detail to ask someone describing murder, I must admit." He scratched the back of his head and then stretched his neck as if trying to regain some lost thought. Maybe his corporate fat cat persona was attempting to instill some logic. "Ilya, why don't you take a look out front?"

Nicole grabbed my arm.

The Russian wasn't happy to leave me or the vodka for even a brief period of time. Then he seemed to weigh things and decided Scullion's order made sense. He headed toward the front door.

"Don't be long," I said. I could only hope Uncle Mike was ready for him.

Before my eyes, Scullion transformed back into the storyteller—the maniacal eyes, the gruesome grin and hunched shoulders—the tormented little boy alive in the past.

"I swore I'd get the two men who'd preyed on my father. Before Porter died, and after much persuasion by my well-paid partners, he gave me the name of the mysterious Deacon."

I waited, anxious to hear the Deacon's true identity. The front door opened.

"Yes, you wanted details about the lake. Of course, Porter had passed away, mercifully I might add, by the time we dragged him onto the small boat. We tied heavy concrete blocks to his legs. My companions had brought a long rope and steel cable. They knew their business.

"It took me years to discover the man who had called himself the Deacon had not died. That was the story I first heard from reliable sources—that he was dead. But he hadn't died. He had spun one clever story after another to cover up his disappearance. It took lots of work and money to unravel."

"With Horace's help," I said.

"Yes, poor Horace. You are well informed. Imagine my surprise to find out the man who called himself the Deacon had adopted the alias of Tony Zino."

"What about his real name?" Again, I couldn't help myself.

Scullion nodded as if he was getting there. Just remain patient. "The Deacon had taken great pains to mask his identity. I had to go to great lengths not only to find him, but to catch a man like that off balance. I had to get to know the habits of Zino and his friends. I had to find a reasonable way into the business in which he worked. And then I had to develop a plan."

"Eddie," Nicole said. "I don't know how much more of this—"

"Wait." I hadn't heard the front door close. Ilya hadn't come back. I didn't want Scullion to notice, and I wanted the name.

Scullion nodded his appreciation. "A man like that is on watch every minute. He had a network of bodyguards. I had to find the right time and place. His stepbrother was near the very top of the Chicago mob."

It all came together for me. "Burrascano?"

Scullion smiled and nodded. "You surprise me again."

An explosion of shattered glass broke the spell. It was the window over the sink. Scullion turned and fired. I grabbed Nicole and we dove to the carpet, my body over hers.

The sliding door flew open. Claudia fired. Scullion got hit in the left upper body and fell to one knee behind the counter. More shots missed the mark.

Scullion pointed his gun at me. I dove toward Scullion's gun hand. Scullion's gun went off beside my ear.

A moment later, I realized I wasn't hit. I looked up. Scullion's legs were splayed on the floor. I glanced around.

Claudia was standing up slowly, her hands still holding a gun in two hands, in firing position. But Scullion had dropped behind the counter when Claudia first shot him. She wouldn't have a clear shot.

I turned toward the hall.

Behind me, Uncle Mike stood at the entrance to the room, breathing hard. He also held his gun with two hands in firing position. He had the perfect angle. He must've gotten off the shot that killed Scullion.

Uncle Mike's face and jacket were covered in blood.

"What the hell?" I asked.

Claudia checked to be sure Scullion was dead, then turned to Uncle Mike. "Are you wounded?"

"No, it's the Russian shooter outside. I couldn't risk the noise of a gunshot. I had to cut his throat," Uncle Mike said.

"Damn." I was shocked. Then I recalled all the training Uncle Mike had received on the force.

"Eddie, thank God you all showed up," Nicole said.

"I suggest you all leave," Claudia said. "I'll get people to clean this up. No way the cops will believe a story about the Deacon."

I couldn't argue with her.

"Wait a minute. This is my house," Nicole said, taking a step toward Claudia. "Who the hell are you?"

"She's working with us, Nicole. It will be fine." Nicole was clearly in shock.

"Mike, leave the jacket," Claudia said.

"I'll stay," Uncle Mike said. "Eddie, it would be best if you and Nicole leave. Don't go out the front door."

"Okay. I'll be in touch." I put my arm around Nicole and escorted her through the house to the attached garage.

44

A WEEK LATER, NICOLE AND I WERE AT A FAMILIAR crossroads. I was about to leave Las Vegas—again. My decision had been made. I'd tried to conquer Vegas once, and I knew better than to try a second time.

I sat on the back deck of her house, the desert sun rising, the glass windows of the hotels and casinos in the valley below, glittering with the promise of a new day. I knew how to leave Las Vegas, but Nicole did not.

Nicole was at the pinnacle of her poker career. Her big bluff of Scullion in the heads-up match had taken on mythic proportions. There was talk of endorsements, a reserved spot on the poker tour, invites from Europe, all the juicy goodies a poker career could offer.

The new crowd of zombie-geeks, fresh from a million hours playing poker on home computer terminals, mentioned

Nicole's name in hushed tones as if she'd become the Tiger Woods of poker.

Nicole came out and sat down beneath the umbrella beside me, coffee cup in hand.

"I love this time of day," she said. "I rarely get to see the morning light, but when I do, I love it." She was used to breakfasting in the afternoon.

Our chance to confront Scullion and convince him to surrender to the police had never materialized. But justice for the Deacon had been delivered. Burrascano was happy the killer of his stepbrother had been found.

Arlene had been given just enough details by Burrascano to let her know Porter had been killed and that Porter's murderer had been found and "taken for a ride." Arlene was old school and knew these were all the details she could expect, and she was happy with the result. Her nightly dreams of Porter had ended. Chalk one up for Eddie O'Connell's PI business.

I had managed not to fall back into my old Vegas habits. From the moment Nicole's house had been cleaned up, and Burrascano's men had taken the bodies of Ilya and Scullion to some place no one would ever find, I'd made my plans to leave.

Uncle Mike had already left town. The Deacon wasn't my hero anymore. I saw how vengeance had sent Scullion over the edge and I wasn't going to take one more step down that path. I had to let go and give up on those dark thoughts—the condition I referred to as "Childress on the brain."

It didn't mean I'd shun thoughts of my mom. If anything, the investigation had brought the past a little closer for me.

We promised Hadlow we'd meet up again at the next conference, but we knew that would never happen. Uncle Mike would tell her about Zino as soon as Burrascano could get all the Deacon's accounts in order. Money on the street had to be accounted for.

"When is your flight tomorrow?" Nicole asked.

I wasn't going to try to persuade her to leave with me. Maybe she wanted what the poker life had to offer, and if she did, I wouldn't stand in her way. Maybe another sports betting show would come along in Vegas. Hell, maybe the virus everyone was talking about would make "decision time" academic. I didn't know.

Then there was her beautiful house on the man-made hillside overlooking her house of cards empire. How could I even think of pulling her away to go with me?

"Eddie," she whispered, "my agent says she has a line on a sports betting show." She paused for dramatic effect. "It's in Chicago."

I sat up and nearly knocked my coffee cup off the armrest. "What?"

"I guess Illinois has finally gotten its act together."

I tried to measure my response. "That's fantastic." I guess it wasn't that measured.

"I've given it a lot of thought. Maybe I'm on top right now. My game has never been better. But we both know it won't last." She turned to look at me. "I've been trying to prove myself for a long time. First, I wanted to prove to my dad I could make it on my own. Second, to prove I could make it as a pro, and third, to prove I could make it as a sports betting prognosticator. I'm officially done with proving myself. The drive to compete has to come to an end at some point, doesn't it?"

"For some people, it never ends." For Scullion, the drive to compete mutated into a "win at all costs" mentality that ended with his death.

"I'm not one of those people."

This was when I could be stupid and why I hadn't been able to find someone and settle down. "I've just got a start-up PI business. The rest of the time, I manage Uncle Mike's bar."

"And you have a two-bedroom apartment," she said, laughing. "I know."

"I just don't want there to be any—"

"How many nights have we spent in a poker game or at a craps table? We've been down that road together and now it's time for us to take a new road. You can show me how you do it."

"What?"

"How you manage without nonstop action."

"It's a deal," I said. I wasn't about to say I was an expert on the subject, but I muddled through day to day without action.

"But there's one more thing. We both know it's my father. It will start up again."

Her father was old-fashioned when it came to his kids. His unreasonable demands caused one fight after the next. Nothing Nicole could do seemed to please him, leaving her no option but to start over in Vegas. Since she'd left, maybe he'd gotten into fixed races.

I reached out and stroked her hair. "Why don't we talk to him together?"

"You think he'll listen?"

"You've been gone a while. Maybe he's changed."

"Let's hope so." She looked back inside. "I'll miss this house. It was supposed to be my hideaway. What a joke that was. The house was a trophy of sorts, tangible proof of my poker winnings. Well, I don't need anything to prove myself." She paused. "I called my realtor today."

"You did?"

"I hope there's room in that two bedroom."

"Absolutely. I'll even sleep on the couch."

"You don't have to sleep on the couch." She laughed, and we held hands like school kids. "You know what I can't wait to do? Someday, I want to come back here to Vegas, to the Strip, and walk in like a tourist."

"You got it."

ACKNOWLEDGMENTS

I really appreciate the support I've received from so many. I'd like to thank my critique partners who see the pages before the second or third draft. These brave readers include the Tuesday Night Mystery Critique Group and my Thursday night critique group. I would also like to thank my fellow writers at Rocky Mountain Fiction Writers, Pikes Peak Writers, International Thriller Writers, Inc. and Rocky Mountain Mystery Writers of America for the meetings and conferences they've presented over the years that have provided me with insights into the craft of writing.

To my fellow handicappers, best of luck. Stay in control and seek help, if needed.

To my editors, developmental editor Steve Parolini and copy editor Susan Brooks, thank you. To my design team, book cover by Steven Novak and Interior by Ali Cross, thanks for your hard work.

Lastly, to my family. My wife, Kathi, and sons, Greg and Mark. You make it all worthwhile.

ALSO BY
TOM FARRELL

THE WAGER SERIES
WagerTough
WagerEasy

ABOUT THE AUTHOR

Tom Farrell has worked as a golf course starter, a chemist and clerked at City Hall in Chicago while attending law school. He is the author of The Wager Series, including *Wager Tough* and *WagerEasy*. *Wager Tough* was selected by Kirkus Reviews as one of the Best Indie Books of 2021 and one of the Best Indie Mystery Thrillers of 2021. He has served as Vice President of Rocky Mountain Fiction Writers, a nonprofit corporation, and was a 2021 finalist for RMFW's Independent Writer of the Year. His articles have appeared in Mystery & Suspense Magazine. Now retired from practicing law, when he's not handicapping he can be found on the golf course or at a local jazz club.

Visit him at www.tomfarrellbooks.com.

9 781736 593257